THE
PIERCED
HEART

THE

PIERCED
HEART

A Novel

Lynn Shepherd

DELACORTE PRESS

NEW YORK

Copyright © 2014 by Lynn Shepherd

Published in the United States by Delacorte Press, an imprint of Random House, a division of Random House LLC, a Penguin Random House Company, New York.

Delacorte Press and the House colophon are registered trademarks of Random House LLC.

Library of Congress Cataloging-in-Publication Data

Shepherd, Lynn
The pierced heart: a novel/Lynn Shepherd.
pages   cm
ISBN 978-0-345-54543-5
eBook ISBN 978-0-345-54544-2
1. Private investigators—Fiction. 2. Serial murder investigation—Fiction. I. Title.
PR6119.H465P54 2014
823'.92—dc23
2014010836

Printed in the United States of America on acid-free paper

www.bantamdell.com

2 4 6 8 9 7 5 3 1

First Edition

Book design by Caroline Cunningham

For Elizabeth

I thought it was some trick of the moonlight,

some weird effect of shadow, but I kept looking,

and it could be no delusion . . .

—Bram Stoker, *Dracula*

THE
PIERCED
HEART

CHAPTER ONE

THE AUSTRIAN EMPIRE, MARCH 1851

THE TRAIN LEFT PRAGUE at 8:35 PM on 15 March, arriving at
Vienna before noon. It is the fifth day since Charles Maddox left
London under grey skies and a louring rain, and he could have done
the whole journey in little more than two, had he been so minded, but
he had reasons of his own for prolonging this first excursion beyond
his native shores. His passage has been paid for, for one thing—and
handsomely, which is why we see him stepping down not from the
back of the train, stinking of pipe smoke and garlic from hours pent up
with squawking chickens, raucous soldiers, and mumbling old nuns,
but from the rarefied atmosphere (in every sense) of the carriage labelled ERSTE KLASSE. On the platform he finds a porter already waiting to take his bag, though that exchange does not take place, it must
be said, without a somewhat condescending lift of the eyebrow when
it becomes clear that one rather battered trunk is all the English Herr
possesses. He has learned, this luggage lackey, that a great deal can be
deduced from the state—and scale—of a gentleman's baggage, but the
lamentably little this particular passenger carries sits rather oddly with
the arrogance in his air and the lift of his chin. And there is, on the

other hand, no question at all that Charles Maddox's clothes are far too unkempt for the company he has kept, hour after hour, in the well-upholstered surroundings of his designated compartment, watching out the window, and being watched in his turn—did he but know it—by each succeeding change of fellow travellers. And what would they have seen, the thoughtful French priest, the two plumply self-satisfied Belgian merchants, the family of pretty and excitable Flemish daughters with pinch-faced governess in vigilant attendance? A grimly beautiful young man, with a head of rowdy dark-bronze curls, and a film of something very like despair that greys his skin and dulls what must otherwise be the most arresting blue stare. Looking at him, you might well deduce—as the priest did, having studied him intermit-tently over the pages of his Aquinas for most of the distance from Liège to Cologne—that this is a young man who keeps his griefs close, for whom pain is a private matter for himself alone. And you would be right. For his part, Charles has studiously avoided contact of any kind with his companions, rather to the annoyance of the eldest Flemish daughter, resplendent in her ribbons, who has been scrutinising him every bit as intently as the Monsignor, though with quite another mo-tive in mind.

Charles's interest, insofar as he had one, has been in the landscape—the miles of lined flat fields that run here and there into whitewashed red-roofed villages, then dissolve again into darkly thick-quilled for-ests, and distant glimpses of domed churches and sun-glinting spires. It is so common for us now, to travel by train, that we cannot imagine what it was like then, to watch a whole new world at such unprece-dented speed—to observe a continent unroll in a rectangle of glass, and see with a cinematic eye, long before that word was even coined. For a man like Charles, blessed with what a later century will call a photographic memory (and for a man of his profession *blessed* is in-deed the word), the rush of images is almost too much, and it is with some relief that he spends a slow day of exploration at a foot's pace, first in Antwerp, and then in Leipzig, though rather more frugally the second time, since his allowance will not otherwise suffice. And now he comes at last to his final destination tired and claustrophobic, and in need of a bath. But there will, it seems, be no time for that. He has barely left the platform of the Eisenbahnhof when he is accosted, with the utmost courtesy, by a small thin man wearing impeccable livery, who addresses him by name and then gives a low bow. The man— it seems—has no English, and Charles no German, so he is uneasy at first, to find his bag seized in a surprisingly vigorous grip, but when he follows the man out into bright sunshine and a row of standing carriages, he is relieved to find that the one he is led to bears the same crest as the letter of invitation he has in his jacket pocket. The battlements and barred helm of the armorial bearings of the Baron Von Reisenberg.

Now what, you might be wondering, could a peer of so proud and ancient a lineage want with the company of a struggling and rather scruffy young private detective? And why, moreover, should he be so earnest to secure it that he is prepared to pay his passage half-way across Europe? Pertinent questions, I agree, though to answer them I will have to take you backwards some three months, to that room on the first floor of the tall elegant house off the Strand which for thirty years served Charles's great-uncle as his office, when he was universally acknowledged to be the foremost thief taker in England. The self-same room where we would have found Charles himself, that cold day at the turn of last year, deep in discussion with a portly balding man in a sombre suit of black of a decidedly clerical appearance, but who was not, as it transpired, the clergyman Charles first took him for, but the official representative of the Bodleian Library in the University of Oxford. It is an institution with a proud and ancient lineage of its own, and unique collections that, as this Mr Turnbull carefully explained, are not only priceless but ever more costly to maintain. So if a foreign gentleman—a nobleman no less—should unexpectedly approach the Curators with the offer of a quite alarmingly large sum towards the upkeep of one of the Bodleian's finest and most famous bequests, it would be a rash custodian indeed who dismissed such an offer out of hand. Just as it would be a most imprudent one who failed to ensure that judicious enquiries were made before such a very conspicuous donation was accepted. Enquiries, Mr Turnbull conceded at once, which the Curators themselves were clearly not in a position to conduct, but which a man like Charles—energetic, discreet, intelligent—was admirably placed to undertake on their behalf. And enquiries, as it turned out, that have been both foreseen and forestalled, since the Baron Von Reisenberg accompanied his offer with an invitation to anyone the Curators might wish to appoint, to visit him at his ancestral home, and verify his credentials to their full satisfaction. As for Charles, he did not hesitate. Even though his great-uncle's health is frail and his mind failing, Charles has leapt at the chance of being weeks away, a thousand miles from London, and his memories, and that house just off the Strand. It may be that you know what has driven him so desperate to be gone, but know or not, it will not be a secret long.

The coachman straps Charles's trunk to the roof of the heavy and rather old-fashioned coach, then opens the door and fusses about with blankets and a flask of brandy, both of which seem to Charles to be irritatingly unnecessary, since even if there is a chill breeze the sun is bright, and inside the carriage the air is warm. As they move slowly away, Charles lowers the glass so that he can see the city, fighting down what he knows is rather an unreasonable exasperation that he wasn't able to snatch a few hours to see it for himself. They cross the slow deep blue of the Wien River, and then skirt the huge fortifications that for a few years yet will circle old Vienna in a many-pointed star. Perhaps the coachman senses his passenger's impatience, because all at once they turn off the main road and take one of the slower and more winding routes across the gardens that ring the ramparts like a stacked under the open barn and mounds of seasoned timber await the cooper's croze. There are chickens picking at the grass between the cobbles, and the air smells of wood-smoke. The rain is now trickling down the back of his neck so he turns and makes his way to the door of the house, where the coachman is waiting to show him down the low vaulted passage to a room with a table laid before a fire, and a metal tureen warming on the hearth. The farmer's wife is withdrawn and wary, and will not meet his eye as she ladles the meat onto his dish, but the food is hot and surprisingly appetising. Some sort of stew, clearly, but flavoured with a dry peppery spice he cannot name. He makes a half-hearted attempt to ask her what it is called—knowing full well she cannot possibly speak English—and is not much the wiser when she mutters something that sounds like *"paprikash,"* before turning to poke the already roaring fire. Charles has by now drained the flagon of rough red wine she had placed by his plate, and gets to his feet to find the privy: If dinner cannot wait for their destination, they must have a good deal more than an hour's road ahead of them. The journey must have tired him more than he realised, because for once in his life he takes a wrong turn on his way back and finds himself on the other side of the yard, where he can see the coachman and an elderly thickset man in a leather apron talking in lowered but earnest voices behind the coach, as two stable-boys back new horses into the shafts. If he had stayed in the kitchen they would have been screened from his view, but from where he is now Charles can see the urgency of the coachman's gestures, and the unease on the farmer's face. Something has clearly unsettled the old man, and Charles sees him cross himself. Intrigued but not unduly alarmed, Charles strides out towards them, intending to thank his host with a handshake and one or two of the kreuzer coins he acquired in Prague, but the man starts at the sight of him and retreats at once to the farm door without a backwards glance. Charles looks to the coachman but he, too, is not meeting his gaze. Charles shrugs, storing the incident away for his first letter home to his uncle Maddox. Then he sets a foot squarely on the carriage step and swings up into his seat.

The sun is already setting and the temperature is dropping fast, and Charles appreciates, now, both the blankets and the brandy he had derided in the warmth of a Viennese afternoon. As they pull away down to the main road the rain begins again, but now it is a thin freezing miasma that speckles the carriage glass and chills the air to ice. It is soon too dark to discern much beyond the faint glow cast by the coachman's lamp, and Charles can only guess at the lay of the land about them by the scattered lights visible on distant hills, clustered like constellations beneath the strange stars. And as the hours drag by and the sound of the hooves clatters monotonously on, Charles is lulled into that hallucinatory half sleep that dries the mouth, and hollows the eyes, and meddles memory with mirage. He will wonder, afterwards, if it was the effect of the wine, or the oddly metallic-tasting brandy he downed too fast, and if he was dreaming or deluded when he glimpsed the flicker of pale blue lights advancing and receding through the trees; whether the howling in his head was merely farm dogs driven mad by foxes, and not the black-pelted wolves he thought he saw ringed about the road, panting and steaming as the horses reared in terror and his own heart battered against his bones. And then as the beasts closed in and he felt their rank breath hot on his skin—as he heard his own voice crying out aloud, did he really see the pack fall suddenly back into the darkness, whimpering and craven before a faceless figure silhouetted against the sky, and a hand of silent power raised against the moon?

"Herr Maddox! Herr Maddox!"

Charles starts up and looks about him wild-eyed. The coachman is staring at him through the window, and Charles reaches over and winds it down, all too aware that his hands are trembling. The man looks at him narrowly, then signals for him to get out of the coach. The sky is clear now, and the moon high above the forest, but of man or wolf or even dog, there is no sign. The coachman is speaking to him again, and from his gestures and pointing fingers Charles eventually realises that they have stopped at the head of a sharp decline, and the man wants him to walk down to help spare the horses. For the next half an hour Charles trudges behind the coach as the horses slither and jerk in the mud, and the rain collected in the wheel-ruts flickers ghastly reflections up onto the overhanging trees. As his ears become attuned to the silence, Charles can hear small animals moving in the dark, and once, he is sure, a deer plunging away into the shadows. Then as the near horse suddenly loses its footing and the harness clatters against the side of the coach, a huge white owl swoops noiselessly down, barely a wing tip away, ghostly with its wraith-enormous eyes.

The lower they descend the colder it becomes, and the damp air thickens with tendrils of mist that hang in the air like flaws in ice. And then they turn a final bend and the trees open to reveal the long black curve of the Danube, glittering in the moonlight. The coachman brings the horses to a halt and opens the door for his tired and shivering passenger. The last stretch of the journey follows the bend of the river along a wide and wooded shoreline until Charles sees a high promontory jutting out into the water, and above it an immense baroque *schloss* standing foursquare, its steep roof soaring to a tiered tower crowned by an onion dome. A few minutes later they are approaching a narrow stone causeway, barely wider than the carriage, which ascends forty feet or more to a vast arch cut directly into the cliff, overlooked on either side by the circular turrets of the gatehouse above. Here and there lamps are burning in the turret windows, but when they emerge on the other side of the archway Charles can see not one single light in all the castle's smooth and closed façade.

The archway opens onto a paved courtyard where the castle overlooks the river, dropping sheer below. The carriage comes to a stop by a huge oak door studded with nails and surmounted by a weathered stone crest. A smaller door has been cut into the wood, which puts Charles suddenly in mind of the college gates he saw in Oxford, and as the coachman unstraps his bag and lifts it down, the inner door opens. Charles is not sure, at first, if he is in the presence of his host, but when the figure in the doorway clears his throat and welcomes him softly in excellent though heavily accented English, he is no longer in any doubt.

With all that we will discover of this man—and all he will be to this story—we will pause, here, a moment and allow Charles's first impressions to have full sway. So what is it he now sees, as the high clouds shred across the moon, and the wind echoes wildly about the high walls? A tall man, taller than Charles in fact, if he were not slightly stooped. A long dark coat of some heavy matte material that reflects no light. An antique lamp swinging from one hand, the wick cut low and the flame guttering. A high forehead and thin silver hair wisped about the ears. Yet these are but details. What draws and holds the gaze, is his face. The extraordinary pale eyes, heavy-lidded and ashen-lashed. The head too small—surely—for a man of such a height, and the bones of the skull painfully visible under skin stretched so white Charles wonders for a moment if the Baron is an albino. And when he holds out his hand the fingers Charles takes briefly in his own are as wan as a corpse an hour old.

Charles bows. "Freiherr Von Reisenberg."

"I am pleased to welcome you to my home, Herr Maddox," the Baron replies, his voice still low, as if he suffers from the night air. "I know you come here on a visit of business, but I hope, nonetheless, that you will lack nothing while you are with us, and that when you come to leave, you will take with you all that you come here to seek."

It is no doubt the result of learning the language in academic fashion and rarely speaking it, but the formality of the Baron's speech has a curiously distancing effect, and as Charles follows him into the lofty stone-paved hall it is as if those few paces across the threshold have borne him centuries back. Here, as outside, no lights are burning, and in the weak glow of the silver lamp Charles wonders again, with a jerk of unease, if his eyes are once more deceiving him, for as the swing of the lantern throws shadows like blackened branches spiking across the walls it seems for all the world as if the great room has been built inside the forest that presses close upon the promontory on every side. And he is sure—*sure* this time—that he can see the glitter of animal eyes, and the shape of figures in the darkness, hunched and hooded—

He checks his pace a moment, but the Baron does not turn or slow, and as he rounds a corner ahead and the dark pours back, Charles makes haste to catch him up. They follow a narrow passage to a flight of steps, then ascend a long spiral stair of worn and pitted stone, and Charles finds himself at last, breathless with the climb and more than a little unnerved, in a small, windowless octagonal room ringed by bookshelves and lit only by the fire in the grate. A door opposite stands open onto a bedroom where a great carved four-poster has been warmed and turned, and a bottle of Tokay wine and a plate of cold cuts and cheese is awaiting him.

"I beg you to excuse me," says the Baron, turning to face him. The flames cast a golden glow about his features, but the effect is oddly artificial—like a black-and-white film wrongly re-coloured.

"I have myself already dined," he continues, "and will not, therefore, join you. I am cognisant, likewise, that you have had a long journey, and would no doubt prefer to sup in privacy, and retire at a time of your own choosing. I anticipate much pleasure in making your acquaintance, but will reserve that gratification for the morrow, when you will be rested. Should there be any comfort I have omitted to provide, do not scruple to ring for one of the servants. They have been

London he fell asleep over the night before, having tried—and failed—to decipher the tiny annotations pencilled thick about an article titled "On the Mutual Relations of the Vital and Physical Forces," by one William B. Carpenter, MD, FRS. He sits up and realises that the fire that should have died by now is bright and well stoked, and the table that bore an empty bottle and the remains of his supper now carries a tray of breakfast and a pot of coffee. Someone has been into the room while he was sleeping, and Charles looks quickly about him—a reflex he immediately recognises to be ridiculous, since there is clearly no-one there now. He disentangles himself from his bedding, slightly pink about the cheeks at what the maid might have seen, and makes his way to the washstand, where he douses his head and neck in water and looks about for a mirror. Which, rather oddly, he cannot find, either there, or anywhere else in the room. He shaves as best he can without one, since it's not an article he ever carries with him, then dresses and pours himself a cup of hot thick black coffee before going over to open the shutters, scratching absent-mindedly all the while at a little raw patch on his neck. The room, he finds, has a view of the river and the wooded bank beyond, and from his elevated eyrie he can see the cormorants on the water wheeling and squawking in the gusting wind, and three storeys down the creeper-covered wall, the paved courtyard before the castle door, where a lad in a red cap is carrying what looks like a plate of offal down towards the gate. There's a small vessel buffeting the river current, but the boat and the boy are the only signs of human habitation visible for miles. Charles turns away and sits down to his breakfast, a little concerned at how much of the day has already gone. Half an hour later he emerges from his room and makes his way downstairs. At the foot of the spiral steps he finds an archway opening onto a gallery that rings three sides of the hall. One part of last night's strangeness, at least, is now explained: The branching shadows Charles saw in the gloom were cast by nothing more uncanny than the antlers and ancient weaponry fixed around the pale walls, and the eyes in the darkness no more than glass reflections from the stuffed heads of huge long-dead dogs, their teeth bared in a permanent vicious snarl. And as for the figures he glimpsed lurking in the shadows, he sees now, with a quick snort at his own idiocy, that they were only suits of armour, assembled for battle about empty air.

And empty air is all the rest of the hall contains, at least at this moment. There is no sign of servants, and certainly no sign of the master of the house. The day outside is bright with sun and loud with a western wind, but inside the castle is both dimmed and silent—a curious muffled silence which seems to suck even the echo from the stone. Charles hesitates a moment, wondering whether to go down, when he hears a door open farther along the gallery—a small low door which must be directly below the tower and dome above. The Baron emerges from it, then carefully locks it behind him with a large iron key, before proceeding slowly and thoughtfully towards where Charles is standing. So thoughtful is he, in fact, that Charles almost has to step into his path to attract his attention.

"Ah!" says the Baron, starting back. He is wearing, Charles notices, exactly the same clothes as he wore the night before.

"I apologise, Freiherr—I did not intend to alarm you."

"No, no," says the Baron, composing his features quickly. "You have merely anticipated me. I was about to send a servant to enquire whether you would care to begin the business of your sojourn at Castle Reisenberg."

He starts to walk on, gesturing Charles to accompany him, and Charles sees him glance back towards the locked door, and finger the key he has placed in the pocket of his long dark coat.

"I infer," the Baron continues, his voice still low and slightly rasping, "that the Curators of Sir Thomas Bodley's Library require two quite distinct categories of reassurance from your visit here?"

Charles averts his eyes. "I am not sure I understand your meaning."

"My dear young man—if I may presume to call you so—if I were a functionary entrusted with a role such as theirs, presented with an offer such as the one I have made, there would be two matters I should wish to ascertain. Firstly, that the benefactor in question was indeed the man he claimed to be; and secondly, that there would be no danger, now or at any future time, of any—"

He pauses a moment, clearly searching for the apposite word.

"—*embarrassment,* shall we say, arising in consequence of accepting such a gift."

Charles reddens, despite himself, and he hears the Baron laugh softly. "There is no need for embarrassment on *your* part, Mr Maddox. You are merely carrying out the task you have been assigned, and the Curators, in their turn, merely fulfilling the duty they owe. I take no offence; indeed as I have already stated, I should undertake exactly the same enquiries, were I in their place."

"I confess I have wondered," begins Charles, as they descend the stairs, "why you chose the Ashmole Bequest as the recipient of your generosity. I was lucky enough to be allowed to view it when I met the Curators in Oxford, and while the illuminated Bestiary is unquestionably charming and no doubt priceless, some of the other items—"

The Baron smiles at Charles, revealing, for the first time, a line of sharp discoloured teeth and pale receding gums. "You are referring, I deduce, to the astrological and alchemical treatises that make up a great part of the collection?"

"Those of Simon Forman in particular. I read only a few pages, but the man was quite obviously a charlatan—all that nonsense about conjuring astral powers and summoning spirits. And claiming he could treat illness by casting horoscopes and letting blood according to the phases of the moon? It's ludicrous, not to mention fraudulent. Small wonder they threw him in gaol."

"And yet he saw more than a thousand patients a year," says the Baron softly.

Charles lets out a snort of derision. "If some of them were healed, it had nothing whatsoever to do with wearing Forman's amulets or reciting his so-called magical incantations. He cured by coincidence, or— at best—*placebo.*"

He stops, aware—and amazed—that his companion does not seem to be agreeing with him. "You do not concur?"

The Baron raises an eyebrow. "I would observe merely that such learning was not condemned as preposterous at the time. I am sure I do not need to remind you that Sir Isaac Newton conducted alchemical experiments of his own. Or that Sir Elias Ashmole was himself an alchemist, as well as a founder of your Royal Society."

"But that was nearly two hundred years ago! There have been so many advancements in scientific knowledge since then—there is no excuse for such absurd superstition—"

"Advancements there have indeed been," interrupts the Baron. "And yet we are no nearer finding the answers to which the alchemists aspired than Ashmole or Forman were, for all the efforts of the scientific establishment. Alchemy, Mr Maddox, was concerned not merely with the transmutation of base metals, but the transfiguration of the human soul, that it might commune with that secret energy which both illuminates and animates the *kosmos*. The energy of the ancients which is now lost to our sceptical, matter-of-fact nineteenth century, the energy that lights the *aurora borealis,* and throbs in the deep places of the earth, and which our forefathers marked with sacred sites of standing stones."

Charles stares at him, open-mouthed, before remembering his manners and his mission here, and inclining his head. "I bow to your far greater knowledge, Freiherr."

By the time they come to a halt before a large wooden door, Charles has already revised all the many unsettling impressions of the last twenty-four hours and come to the conclusion that all can be explained by his host's increasingly obvious eccentricity. The Baron is evidently one of those idle aristocrats whose wealth allows the indulgence of even the most outlandish of whims. But if some of that wealth can go towards preserving the Ashmole Bequest, then it is not—clearly—for Charles to stand in the way.

So there is a rather superior smile on his lips as the Baron opens the door and gestures him to enter—a smile that slips slowly from his face as he takes two, then three steps forward, and stands gazing about him. It is the most beautiful library Charles has ever seen. A wood-and-gilded coffered ceiling, shelves that reach from frieze to floor, and all along the wall before him a line of tall windows shielded by heavy muslin drapes, giving over the river rampart onto the water below. And at the far left, a man with a thick dark beard and deferential dress is laying papers carefully onto a desk.

"In anticipation of your requirements," says the Baron, "I have taken the liberty of requesting the custodian of my own—very much more modest—collection to furnish you with certain documents that may be of assistance in your task."

The two of them proceed at a stately pace past book-stands bearing volumes held open by velvet ribbons, armillary globes mounted on circular frames, and glass cases containing what look to Charles to be original mediaeval manuscripts.

"This is astonishing, sir," he says, as overwhelmed as a child let loose in a toy-shop. "I congratulate you."

The Baron inclines his head. "A library such as this is not the work of one man, or even of one generation. Some of the books you see here have been in the possession of my family for more than five hundred years. Many others have been acquired more recently, either by my father, or by myself. My father spent his life as Court Librarian in the service of the King of Wurttemberg. I still recall being permitted, for the first time, to enter the royal apartments and view my father at work—cataloguing, classifying, restoring. I had a natural curiosity, as a child, and my father took care to nurture it, and to instil at the same time a proper regard for correctness of method, and orderliness of thought. His own passion—as the books you see about you amply attest—was for history, and for literature. He was an avid collector of such works, and endeavoured to imbue my young mind with something of his own enthusiasm. I fear I was a sad disap-

pointment to him, however, for my own interests inclined quite another way."

Charles smiles. "I fear that I, too, disappointed my father by failing
to follow in the course he preferred for me."

"Indeed?" says the Baron, stopping and looking Charles full in the
face for the first time. "And what would he have chosen?"

"Medicine," replies Charles, flushing a little, though whether at the
memory of that disastrous experiment, or at the opinions he was just
asserting, it would be hard to say. "My father is—was—a distinguished
physician, and at his insistence I, too, followed a medical training for
some months. But I had no aptitude for the work, and an insufficient
empathy—or so I was told—for the sufferings of my fellow men. The
surgeon who supervised my studies observed once that I approached
illness as if it were an intellectual puzzle—fascinated by determining
the nature and cause of the complaint, yet all but indifferent to the
consequent task of effecting a useful cure."

He stops, the smile dying on his lips, and fearing he has said too
much, for there is an odd expression, now, in his host's eyes.

"Did he, indeed," says the Baron eventually. "I see. We must talk of
this again. But I am afraid I have to leave you, for the moment, to the
care of the excellent Herr Bremmer, as I have business of my own to
attend to. When you have seen all you require, he will escort you to the
dining parlour, where you will find luncheon awaiting you. Good
morning, Mr Maddox."

And with that he is gone.

Charles turns to the librarian, who bows low, then leads Charles
towards a baize table, where he has unrolled a large scroll and secured
it carefully with small leaden weights. He is wearing white cotton
gloves, and asks, in perfect English, that Herr Maddox please refrain
from touching the parchment. It is, he explains, a representation of the
Baron's family tree, originally crafted more than a century before, and
added to, with great care, with each succeeding heir and alliance. And
it is indeed a beautiful thing—the paper thick and finely textured, the

calligraphy exquisite, and the finely detailed coats of arms as bright as they must have been the day they were first inked. Herr Bremmer is now looking at Charles expectantly, and he realises suddenly that he is being shown this item not as an artefact, but as evidence. He takes his notebook quickly from his pocket and asks his companion if he can assist him in deciphering the German inscriptions. Half an hour later he has six pages of notes covering every conceivable aspect of the Baron's antecedence, as well as the extent of his estates, the history of his *schloss*, and the identity of his successor, should the present Baron Von Reisenberg die—as seems likely—without a son of his own.

As a vetting, it is surely as positive as the Bodleian Curators could possibly expect, and by the end of it Charles is beginning to wonder how he is to fill his time for the rest of his allotted stay. When a silence descends, Charles ventures a half-idle question as to the nature of the "business" that has called the Baron away, but Herr Bremmer affects not to understand him, his eyes fixed on the task of re-rolling the scroll. Charles watches him, aware of a first flicker of premonition— a detective instinct that tells him all may not be what it seems. It's possible—he acknowledges at once—that the man is nothing more than uncomfortable with the prospect of discussing his employer's affairs with a stranger, but the slight flush on his thin cheeks argues for something else, something more. In the meantime Herr Bremmer has placed the scroll carefully in a long paper tube and gone to ring the bell, and by the time the servant appears he is smiling and bowing and putting himself at Charles's disposal if he should require more assistance. It is as if the question had never been asked.

There is a contrariness in Charles—a reluctance to accept no for an answer—that has stood him in good stead in his chosen profession almost as often as it has landed him in trouble, so it will not surprise you to hear that he is now making a mental note to enquire about the

Baron's business when he sees his host at luncheon. But when the servant opens the door to the vast blood-red dining-room Charles sees at once that a table that could easily seat two dozen is set now only for one. Candles are lit, even though it is scarcely past noon, and the heavy brocade curtains are drawn. The servant has already closed the door behind him, and of other servers there is no sign, so Charles helps himself from the rather ostentatious silver-gilt tureen, and then eats in a combination of silence and frustration. When he finally pushes the plate away and gets up, he realises the Baron is standing silently in the doorway behind him. How long he has been there, Charles has no idea.

"You have already eaten, Freiherr Von Reisenberg?" asks Charles, somewhat wrong-footed.

The Baron shakes his head. "I rarely dine during the day, Mr Maddox, and confine my diet always to a strict vegetable regimen."

Which might explain, thinks Charles, both the pallor of his skin and that slight tremor he notices now in the Baron's hands.

"It occurred to me," continues Von Reisenberg, "from your remarks earlier this morning, that you might be interested to visit my collection."

"I thought I had already done so—"

The Baron is already waving his hand. "I do not speak of the library—it is a bauble, an affectation—"

Charles raises his eyebrows—to judge only of the few treasures he glimpsed that morning, the Von Reisenberg archive is worth a King's ransom, and a scholar's rapture.

"Do not mistake me," continues the Baron. "I have a just appreciation of the value of the volumes I am fortunate enough to possess, but that value—to me—is largely *sentimental*. I believe that is your English phrase?"

Charles nods. "Sentimental value, yes, that is the phrase. Because they belonged to your father."

"Quite so. Whereas my own collection is of quite another order, and quite another value. I rarely invite visitors to see it, and never on the strength of so slight an acquaintanceship, but it seems to me that you are of a cast of mind—and an intelligence—as might appreciate its worth."

Charles is well aware that he is being flattered, and part of his mind notes how very skilfully the Baron has both gauged and engaged him. But there is another part of his mind that wonders what exactly this curious man might be hoarding in this extraordinary and seemingly half-empty house, and whether it might have some bearing on the task he has been sent here to achieve.

He casts his napkin down on the table. "I should be honoured, sir."

They proceed from the dining-room up the stairs, and Charles assumes for a moment that their destination is the door he saw the Baron lock so carefully a few hours before, but no—he is led to another larger entrance on the farther side, to a room exactly above the library, and of exactly the same height and grandeur. Only this is not a library. Indeed the only space it resembles, in Charles's experience, is the magnificent North Gallery of the British Museum, where more than a thousand specimens of minerals, crystals, metals, and geological ores are displayed, catalogued from Achmite to Zunder-ertse, and offering the captivated visitor—as Charles well knows—everything from a chunk of meteorite known as the "celebrated Yorkshire Stone, weighing 56lbs, which fell near Wold Cottage, in the parish of Thwing, in the East Riding," to samples of hydrous oxide of iron, "among the most remarkable varieties of which species are a shining brownish-black variety used as hair powder by the Bootchuana natives beyond the Great River in South Africa."

The British Museum boasts four galleries the size of this room, but the Baron's is as crowded and as carefully curated as any one of them. There are tables bearing scientific instruments, some clearly antique and probably of immense value, and others with the stains of recent use, including one microscope that still bears a slide covered with some thick reddish residue. There are cabinets of the Baron's own mineralogical specimens, each one scrupulously labelled in Latin, German, and (in rather smaller lettering, it must be said) English; and one whole case of precious and semi-precious stones which are larger than any Charles has ever seen in Bloomsbury—soapy rose quartz, the square spikes of a deep purple amethyst, and a frost-opaque diamond the size of Charles's fist. And rather more unnervingly, a case of human body parts jarred in ethanol—greyish brains like fossilised coral; two hearts cut carefully in half, one healthy, one diseased; a shrivelled penis and testicles; and a deformed foetus that has Charles turning away and quickening his pace. At one end of the room the wall is hung with framed prints that look from a distance like conventional landscapes— wild sceneries beset by storms, and ruined towers standing against glowering clouds. But as Charles draws closer he realises that the pictures are not landscapes at all but industrial sites—the towers are furnace chimneys, and the clouds the belch of smoke and sooty tar. He glances back at the Baron, a question in his eyes, but his host merely gestures him, by way of explanation, towards another series of tables ranged along the windows. When he approaches the first of them, Charles is at a loss to know what he's looking at—there's a kidney-shaped glass retort, some sort of burner, a few scraps of rust-coloured wood, and a ceramic bowl containing a waxy colourless substance, crumbling white at the rim. Then he notices a diagram propped at the front of the table, but the writing is so small he cannot see to read it in the dim light. He reaches up—without even thinking—to raise the blind, but finds his hand at once stayed by the Baron's dry and surprisingly forceful grasp.

"I would ask you not to let in the light," he says softly. "I find it— distressing."

Looking at him at such close range, at those pale eyes and the red marks on the flaking pallid skin, Charles wonders for the first time if the man has some sort of medical condition—something exacerbated by his monkish diet that renders him sensitive to the sun, and accounts for the rasping hoarseness in his throat. A disease such as *xeroderma pigmentosum* will not, of course, be discovered for the best part of a century, but Charles has seen patients suffering from *lupus* before, and deliberates whether to mention it—after all, what kind of medical care can be on offer here, so many miles from civilisation? But before he can find words of sufficient tact the Baron begins to speak again, and the moment has passed. "This particular display documents a discovery of some note achieved by means of a process termed dry distillation. This involves—in simple terms, you understand—the heating of a solid material to produce a gaseous substance, which is then, in its turn, rendered solid by the action of water, or of alcohol. Hence the items you see here. The diagram before you sets out the various stages of the experiment—the heating, the separation of the various residues, and so on. And, of course, the final result."

Charles looks closer at the ceramic bowl. "It looks a little like paraffin wax—"

"It should do so, for that, indeed, is what it is. From the Latin *parum affinis*, meaning 'lacking affinity,' because this particular wax—"

"—does not react with other substances. Yes, I know," says Charles, a little too quickly. But he is impressed, despite himself: For all his ancestry, the man does seem to have devoted himself to serious study. "So this part of your collection is devoted to the re-creation of scientific discoveries?"

"It is dedicated, Mr Maddox, to the re-creation of *my* scientific discoveries."

"But I thought paraffin was invented by a Scotsman—Christianson, or some such name—"

The Baron's eyes narrow. "Robert *Christison's* work *succeeded* mine. The invention was, without question, *my own*."

Charles stares at him, and then at the line of baize tables and then, once more, at the man before him, all his condescending preconceptions crashing about him. *How did he not know this?* After all, it would hardly have been that difficult to find it out. He curses himself silently—why on earth didn't he research his host in London when he had the chance—why was he so stupidly arrogant as to assume that no aristocrat could ever be renowned for anything other than his lineage?

"Am I to understand," he says slowly, "that *all* of these displays relate to your own inventions?"

"Most of them concern my experiments with coal tar, and the useful substances that may be obtained therefrom. I am sure that you will come upon some of them, even in England. Creosote, perhaps, or pittacal?"

"Pittacal?" says Charles, his head still spinning.

The Baron smiles. "I see you are no linguist, Mr Maddox. The name derives from the Greek for 'tar' and 'beautiful.' It is, I confess, a rather charming tale. I had succeeded in creating creosote some time before, and one of my farmsteads having at that time a persistent problem with stray dogs, it occurred to me that its strong odour might be efficacious in deterring them, if painted onto the wooden gates. I was not, as it happens, correct in this assumption, but by happy accident I discovered that the reaction of the dogs' urine with the creosote produced a stain of the most remarkable dark blue."

"Serendipity," says Charles, who is indeed no linguist but is, all the same, rather well read in his native tongue. "A 'happy accident.'"

The Baron bows. "Quite so. And thus—after various refinements to the process—I invented pittacal. The first dye made by man to be produced for widespread sale. It has, indeed, financed much of my subsequent work. As you will see."

For the next hour the Baron conducts Charles on a tour of his accomplishments, from the antiseptic, to the perfume base, to the bright red dye, pointing out the little triumphs of each discovery, the specific challenges of each process. The pictures, Charles realises now, are of the factories and ironworks the Baron has established across large tracts of the Austrian Empire: The man is clearly not merely an eminent scientist, but a hugely successful industrialist, and Charles can scarcely imagine the wealth that industry must be earning. It occurs to him that the over-elaborate dinner service he had dismissed as silver-gilt—and therefore rather vulgar—may well, in fact, be solid gold.

By the time their perambulations are concluded the setting sun is flaming the Danube into a glitter of molten topaz. Charles is just starting to wonder when dinner might be served when the door opens and a man in small wire-rimmed spectacles and a long dark coat makes his way briskly towards the Baron. It's the first time Charles has seen anyone in this house move at such a pace, and he is intrigued to see what can have provoked such urgency. The man bows stiffly, then takes the Baron aside. Charles affects to be engrossed in the method for producing a particularly evil-smelling oil the use of which he has still not fully grasped, but he takes care to stand where he can observe the faces of the two men. They speak in German, but that's hardly a surprise, and in any case Charles doesn't catch any more than a stray word or two—something that sounds like *Leiden,* which Charles guesses may be a reference to the town—but there is no mistaking the anxiety in the bespectacled man's eyes. After a few moments' earnest discussion the Baron returns to Charles's side and begs leave to absent himself for a few moments.

"An unexpected visitor requires my presence."

"A Dutchman, I gather."

The Baron frowns; then his face clears and he smiles briefly. "A 'person from Pörtschach,' in fact. But I hope his intervention will be of significantly less import than that famously endured by Mr Coleridge. Should you prefer, I can have a servant escort you down to dinner directly."

"No," says Charles at once, suddenly not at all interested in food, and very interested indeed in the identity of the bespectacled man, and the fact that he has not heard the huge castle door open, or caught any sounds of arrival downstairs.

"I will continue my examination of your gallery, Freiherr Von Reisenberg. There is so much I have not yet had a chance to look at. One rarely has the opportunity to view so impressive and unique a collection."

The Baron bows, clearly flattered even if his expression remains studiously impassive. "In that case I shall return as soon as I am able. And I know that in *your* case, Mr Maddox, there is no need to ask you not to tamper with any of the items I have displayed here."

Left to himself, Charles takes a further, slightly brisker turn about the room, and writes a few lines in his pocket-book, to remind himself of any facts he should verify on his return to London.

He finds himself, finally, before a carved wooden door at the far end of the room, and looks about him quickly before trying the handle, though he has little hope of finding it unlocked. But he is wrong. The door swings open, and for the second time that day, Charles stands astounded at what he sees. But this time it is not wonder that assails him, but a horrified disbelief.

The room is dark, and the woman is sleeping. One arm flung out above her on her pillow in touching abandon, her bosom rising and falling with her gentle slumbering breath. There is a half smile on her face, as if her dreams delight, and her thin lace nightgown has slipped slightly to reveal a beautiful white breast, its nipple slightly hardened in the cool air. It is a tender scene, its intimacy all the more moving for its very mundanity. Were it not for one thing. The bed she is lying on is inside a glass box, and the woman is not a woman at all.

She is wax.

Charles circles slowly around the case, noting the flawless detail—the pale blue veins that seem to run beneath her skin, and the eyelashes inserted, surely, one by exquisite one. He can only acclaim such craftsmanship, but the more he stares the more uncomfortable he becomes with the nature of that stare—the voyeur this model makes of him, and the motivation of the man who keeps it hidden here. He wonders suddenly—before ruthlessly crushing the thought as he feels himself harden in response—how real the body is beneath the bedclothes.

And then, as the dying sun drops beneath the roll of clouds a last arc of light floods red through the darkened room and Charles sees that there are at least a dozen other waxen figures ringed about the walls, and all of them female. Women stretched languorously on silken couches, their eyes closed, offering their naked bodies to the spectator's gaze; women in openly erotic postures, golden-haired and blue-eyed, their legs spread and their genitalia monstrous and unnaturally distended, either hairless or covered with what looks like animal fur; young girls smiling serenely with their bellies hollowed out to show the foetus in the womb, or their breasts peeled back to expose the organs beneath. Some mere torsos, others headless, and one, knees bent and open, whose heart has been emptied from her bones and laid, glistening, on her own belly.

However impressed he had become, these last few hours, with his host's achievements, there is nothing that can justify what Charles has discovered here—no scientific objective, however high-minded, that can make this chamber of horror anything but pornographic and obscene. Charles is no *ingénue,* he's been present when living women were cut open to free an unborn child, or the dead dissected in the interests of instruction, but it has never occurred to him that someone would want to mimic such things for the sake of a private and perverted gratification. For that is surely what this is. Because he notices now as he did not at first that the glass case surrounding the sleeping girl has a door with a little silver lock. And since she cannot get out, there is only one other purpose it can possibly fulfil.

"I see that I was wrong. Your curiosity, Mr Maddox, has out-run your courtesy."

Charles spins round to see his host standing at the door, his antique lamp once again in his hand.

"I did not give you permission to enter this room."

"The door was unlocked—I thought, that is to say, I assumed—"

He stops, his face red. There is no word for what he is doing that does not give him away. And the Baron might well counter that even if he has been invited here to verify, he has certainly not been licensed to spy.

The Baron watches him a moment, then pulls his coat about him as if he feels the cold. And it is indeed chill in this high unheated room. Then he walks slowly towards the waxwork of the sleeping girl. "One of the glories of my collection," he whispers, placing his hand briefly on the glass, where it leaves no mark. "Her name is Minette. One of the great *chef d'oeuvres* of the master ceroplast Philippe Curtius. Crafted in France in 1766, and fashioned—so they say—in the likeness of a mistress of Louis the Fifteenth. There is another—not so fine—in the exhibition of Madame Tussaud, in London, which employs, likewise, a hidden clockwork heart. I had assumed a man such as yourself would have seen it."

"I have no taste for the grotesque," replies Charles, a little sharply.

"No more have I," says the Baron in an even tone, watching Charles all the while. "I can assure you I have not acquired and displayed these things for that reason, but for what they illustrate—what they ape."

"I do not understand you." Charles's voice is cold now, his revulsion near the surface.

And something of this the Baron clearly senses, but when he speaks again it is in tones not of self-justification, but of self-possession. "You may have noticed, earlier, that the sequence of my chemical discoveries ceased some fifteen years ago. It was then that I turned my attention to other fields of science. And most especially, to the science of the human mind."

Charles remembers the journals upstairs. But he says only, "It is not a subject I have studied."

"Have you not?" replies the Baron. "I should have thought that, in our age, there is no higher and more compelling field for any man who wishes to be considered a *true* scientist."

If he intended it as condescension, it has its effect, for there are two spots of colour now, in Charles's cheeks. Yet the Baron makes no move to apologise, but turns and walks slowly up the room.

"In the time that has passed since then I have devoted myself to the examination of Mesmerism, which can induce both the stupor of cat-alepsy and the ferment of hysteria, and of Galvanism, which can seem-ingly re-animate the dead. And I have returned, again and again, to those mental phenomena that science *cannot* explain—those states of consciousness that hover between death and life, just as these figures I have collected here mimic the living, but are not so, and disquiet us with the very semblance of breath."

He stops now before a case hung—unlike all the rest—with long velvet curtains.

"Somnambulism," continues the Baron, "catatonia, lunacy, and the horrors that murder sleep, these, Mr Maddox, have been my study. The twilit region of the dreaming mind that superstition only can explain, and where science has not yet dared venture. That," he says, as he sweeps the curtain aside, "has been the darkness I have sought to illu-minate."

Charles recognises it at once—the white-figured woman thrown back over the bed, the grinning monkey-fiend astride her body, and the white-eyed horse leering through the womb-red drapes. Fuseli's

Nightmare—perhaps the most infamous image of the Gothic imagination. Only this is not the painting, or even a print of the painting. It is a copy in wax, sized to the life. As the light from the lamp wavers in the sudden draught Charles has a momentary wild conviction that this girl is actually alive—that her breast is heaving with unfeigned fear. But no. She is animated, only as Minette is animated, by an invisible mechanical heart, as unreal as the demon that bears forever down upon her exposed breast, with wizened fingers that twitch and paw.

CHAPTER TWO

THAT NIGHT THE NIGHTMARES return, and brutally. Charles wakes before dawn to the sound of his own voice crying, and bed-sheets sodden with sweat. He lurches up, wiping the tears from his face, and sits a moment breathing heavily. Then he kicks the bed-clothes away and goes to the window. The room is cold but he is suffocating—desperate for the feel of clean air on his skin. He throws the shutters open and leans out. The sky is overcast and the river dull, and somewhere close by he can hear the sound of barking. He leans farther out and looks down towards the gate and the causeway. There are lights in some of the windows, as there were when he first arrived, and Charles wonders who is wakeful at this hour. Restless suddenly, and curious, he dresses quickly then slips downstairs to the front door, which he manages to open without difficulty, though it occurs to him that getting back in again may prove more problematic.

He wanders first to the edge of the river wall, and looks down at the sheer drop beneath, then turns to face the castle façade. No lights there, apart from his own, high above him. He turns his collar up against the chill, and heads for the gate. The barking is louder now, and Charles realises why he saw the stable-boy carrying a dish of meat: The Baron must keep a dog. And a large one, if the noise is anything to go by. A few minutes later he's making his way down through the arch-way, a little gingerly, since the cobbles are slippery. He stops at the head of the stone causeway and surveys the view. Horizontal washes of grey and black; water, shore, forest, sky. And closer, a building he didn't notice when he arrived, just where the causeway meets the river. A graveyard, and a small chapel with a candle burning in an arched win-dow. There is the barest line of pewter in the east now and Charles starts to walk down towards the road, aware at once how steep the causeway is, and how much skill it must take to get a heavy carriage up here in the snow.

Charles thinks best when he's walking, and as his stride lengthens and his heartbeat rises to meet it, his thoughts begin to fall into some order and his mind lifts itself clear of the strange and stifling atmosphere within the castle walls. The Baron is—at least as regards his name and pedigree—everything he claimed to be, and indeed in many other re-spects far more eminent a benefactor than the Curators can possibly have realised. But every instinct he possesses is telling Charles that the celebrated scientist is not the sum of the man, and he has not yet seen all the castle conceals.

By the time the sun is up Charles has covered the best part of five miles through the forest and he's just wondering if he should turn back, or hope to come upon an inn, when he sees a wisp of smoke ris-ing above the trees. It's not an inn, as it turns out, but a farmhouse, though Charles doesn't anticipate much difficulty in obtaining break-fast in exchange for a few kreuzer. But the old woman who comes to the door is at once wary, and turns to call within the house. She has a small fair-haired child on her hip who must be her grand-daughter, and Charles is struck at once by her resemblance to Betsy, Nancy's little daughter. Nancy who was until very recently a prostitute, but who's helped him now on two of his cases, and looks likely to take Molly's place in his uncle's kitchen. Though not—and he is absolutely intent on this—in Charles's bed. If he cares for Nancy it is not that kind of care, and in any case he is terrified of ever enduring such an experience again—of ever opening himself up to such shame and bitter self-disgust. If the pretty Flemish daughter in the train had only known what revulsion he felt even looking at her, she would have—

"You are staying at the castle?"

Charles starts. There is a man before him now, a man far too young to be the woman's husband. And in any case, he is no peasant; his English is impeccable.

"Yes," says Charles, eyeing the man's starched shirt and dark coat, both of them far better pressed than Charles's own. "I am indeed staying at the castle. I am a guest of the Baron Von Reisenberg."

If he expected that name to open doors—or at least this door—he discovers his mistake at once. The old woman gasps and begins to mutter and cross herself. But the man turns to her and speaks a few words gently in German, and eventually she hoists the child a little higher on her hip and disappears into the house, all without once looking directly at Charles.

"Please," says the man, standing back to make way. "Come in."

Charles is shown into the farm kitchen, where herbs are hanging drying from the eaves and a large dog is lying asleep before the fire. The woman is at the stove, her back to the room, and of the little girl there is now no sign. The man shows Charles to the table and pours him coffee from a painted china pot. An empty plate smeared with fat suggests that he himself has already breakfasted. "My name is Sewerin," says the man, "Dr Jonas Sewerin. I am the medical practitioner for this area. I was called here last night to attend a patient."

"Charles Maddox," replies Charles, rising quickly and extending his hand. "I am on a visit of business to the Baron."

But the man is already nodding. "I am aware of your name, and of your visit, even if I do not know its exact import."

The old woman comes to the table and slams down a metal plate of eggs and meat, and a heel of dark sinewy bread speckled with thin black seeds. Again, she will not meet his eye or speak, and Charles is surprised that the Baron's tenants—for that is surely what this woman must be—show so little courtesy to one of his guests. But seeing his face, Sewerin forestalls him.

"You must remember, Herr Maddox, that this is an isolated and unsophisticated part of the country, where the people have little to do but gossip, and the unknown gives rise not to curiosity, but fear."

Charles picks up his knife. "Are strangers such as myself really so rare?"

Then suddenly, without warning, there is a horrific scream from somewhere upstairs—a girl's voice but half animal, terror-stricken. The old woman turns to Sewerin, her eyes wide in panic, and the doctor is on his feet at once.

"You must excuse me—"

But before Charles can reply, he is gone.

The screams go on and on, muffled one moment, piercing the next, and eventually Charles gets up from the table, feeling that at the very least he should offer Sewerin some assistance. The dog lifts its head and growls as he passes, but makes no move to stop him, and Charles encounters no-one else as he makes his way up the narrow wooden stairs. There is a door half-ajar at the back of the house, and he can see Sewerin bent over a female figure writhing on the bed, and the old woman on her knees at his side. Tears run down her face, and her lips move in silent and desperate imprecation. And when Charles pushes open wide the door he sees that the young woman's eyes are rolled back white in her head and there are flecks of blooded foam about her mouth and neck. Sewerin is attempting to administer some sort of sedative, but the girl's body racks and bucks like a wild animal betrayed, and there is already an ugly scratch across the doctor's cheek.

"Can I help?" says Charles, moving quickly to the bedside. "I have had some medical training—"

But as he takes hold of the girl's flailing hand the old woman leaps to her feet and seizes his arm, tearing at his clothes, shrieking and babbling as wildly as her daughter.

"Do not touch her!" barks Sewerin. "If you wish to assist me, leave this room *at once.*"

Charles gapes at him a moment, but then loosens his hold on the girl's hand and departs.

It is more than half an hour later when the doctor returns to the kitchen, his face pale and beaded with sweat. He leans against the door-post for a moment, then sits down heavily at Charles's side, and takes out his handkerchief to wipe his forehead.

"I owe you an apology, Herr Maddox."

Charles looks at him coolly. "You have every right to treat your patient as you see fit. It is no concern of mine."

"But that does not excuse my discourtesy. Please allow me to explain. As you have seen, Frau Hirte's daughter suffers from a severe disturbance of the mind—"

"That much was obvious," says Charles dryly.

But Sewerin persists. "She has been subject to fits of this nature since she was a small child, but they have grown much worse since the birth of her own daughter. Indeed these episodes have deteriorated so far that she now spends most of her wretched life either curled up like

a beast in pain, or subjecting those about her to an unjustifiable violence."

Charles shakes his head. "I do not believe that anyone suffering
from such a condition can be held responsible for their behaviour, and
therefore the question of blame, or indeed 'justification,' does not
arise."

Sewerin nods slowly. "You are indeed enlightened. The folk hereabouts are pressing for Agnes to be committed to an asylum. They say
she brings the evil eye, and will blight their crops and make their animals barren. The Hirtes can no longer risk allowing her to wander
freely—they have had no choice but to lock her in that room."

Charles thinks of his own uncle, condemned to a life suspended between the light and the dark, reason and madness. His health had been
better in the weeks before Charles left England, and the old man more
like the mentor Charles has loved and emulated since he was a boy, but
who knows if Charles will return to London to find him—as he did
once before—screaming obscenities and soaking in his own urine.
And even further back, even further hidden, is that last memory of his
mother as they carried her weeping away, clawing at the walls, tearing
at her own hair, and crying piteously for Elizabeth, the daughter she
had lost—that little three-year-old sister Charles should have been
watching that day in the crowded Windsor street, but whose hand he
dropped, and whose tears he ignored, turning a moment of boyish
carelessness into a lifetime of self-reproach. Because she is lost and
will never return, and he can never be forgiven for it.

"Such superstition is nothing but a savage and benighted barbarism,"
he says curtly now, turning to his food and tearing brutally at the
hunk of bread—a gesture that does not escape the doctor's appraising
eye.

"I can only agree," replies Sewerin, "but these people have not the education necessary to drive that night away. And when they see Agnes Hirte's condition worsen with each full moon, you cannot wonder that they submit wretches such as she to the barbaric rituals of exorcism, or shun them as lunatics—"

Charles sits back and casts his knife clattering on the plate. "But surely you can disprove such nonsense—show them that the phases of the damn moon have nothing whatsoever to do with her illness—"

"If I could do it, I would, believe me. When I first came here I had the same thought as you. I had all the exuberance of a young man newly qualified. I will edify them, I thought, I will single-handedly banish the evil of centuries of ignorance. And so, for those first months, I kept a diary each time I was called here, chronicling Agnes's condition, but the longer I made my notes the clearer it became: There is no question about it. The fits are indeed worse when the moon is approaching the full. That is why I was called here yesterday, and why I will return this evening, and for the next two nights, until this month's menace is past, and Agnes returns once again to that silent, whimpering creature who is a danger to no-one."

They sit, not speaking, until there are sounds overhead and the doctor is shaken from his reverie.

"I have given you my apology, but not my explanation."

"Please, Dr Sewerin, you need trouble yourself no further. The morning is growing late and I must return to the castle."

"But that is exactly why I must explain," says Sewerin, with surprising vehemence. "When I instructed you so impolitely to leave the room, it was not through any lack of appreciation for the help you were offering—God knows, for my own part, I should have welcomed it. No, it was because I knew what effect your arrival—your very presence in that room—would have on old Frau Hirte, who is herself in fragile health. You must have seen it, surely?"

"I took it merely for a quite understandable fear of strangers— a wish to keep her daughter's condition private—"

"And that is indeed part of it. But *you* represent a far greater fear—a far greater dread. You are an educated man," continues Sewerin, pouring more coffee, "and therefore, no doubt, well able to understand the many scientific advances the Baron has made. But you must also appreciate that such things are beyond the comprehension of the people hereabouts. And the way the Baron behaves—it is inevitable that it should arouse suspicion."

"I'm sorry, I do not understand."

"He is seen often walking by moonlight, and more than once in the graveyard just beyond the castle walls. Some say they have glimpsed him there in the company of young women—some of whom have later disappeared, or sickened to a pale and inexplicable death. It is whispered that he is a necromancer and *nosferatu,* one of the accursed cohort of the Undead, and that he preys upon these young women, bringing their immortal souls to the same forsaken condition as his own."

Charles stares at him. "But surely, she cannot possibly have believed that *I*—"

"She saw the mark upon your neck. She thought you, too, were an Undead."

Charles's hand is at his throat at once. "But it's just a scratch—I don't even know how I got it."

Sewerin shrugs. "I did not say it was rational. Only that it is what these people believe."

Charles gets to his feet and walks to the window, hardly knowing what he does. So much makes sense now. No wonder the old woman started back from him as if from a fiend; no wonder those people at the farmstead crossed themselves when they heard the Baron's name.

"Only last month," continues Sewerin, "another young woman disappeared when she and her brother were on a visit here from Holland. One morning the young man discovered the window open and his sister's bed empty. She was found some hours later at the foot of the castle battlements, her body broken and the marks of teeth about the neck. The work, no doubt, of some wild animal, but you can imagine the terror that spread like wildfire hereabouts. And her body was scarce cold in the ground when the corpse of a local child was discovered horribly mutilated only a few yards from the grave. Within a few days the tomb had been opened and the corpse desecrated in the most horrible manner."

There is a pause.

"Where did they come from?" says Charles eventually.

"I do not take your meaning."

"The Dutch girl and her brother."

Sewerin looks puzzled. "From Delft. But why should that—"

"When I was with the Baron last night he received an urgent message calling him away. The man who brought it was not a servant, and was clearly agitated. I heard him mention '*Leiden*'—"

Sewerin opens his mouth to reply but is drowned out by the sound of hammering on the door, and when it bangs open a moment later Charles recognises the coachman from the castle. He stands there, stamping his feet and clapping his gloved hands together, even though the day is not cold and the sun has risen.

Charles turns in apology to Sewerin. "It seems my presence is required."

Sewerin bows. "I am glad to have made your acquaintance. I hope our paths will cross once more before you return to London."

Charles moves towards the doctor and offers his hand, and as Sewerin takes it he draws close for a moment and drops his voice. "I advise caution, Herr Maddox, and care. I believe that what you overheard was not what you assumed. The word *leiden,* in German, means 'affliction.' Or 'suffering.'"

Charles looks him in the eye for a moment, then nods briefly. He follows the coachman out into the morning air.

Charles sits at the carriage window as they make their way back to the castle at a canter, equally puzzled at why the Baron should be so eager to retrieve him, and how he can have known where to search. The idea that he may have been watched, or even followed, is initially ludicrous, but by the time the coach slows down at the foot of the causeway, Charles is not so sure: If what Sewerin told him is true, he can well imagine why the Baron would not want Charles—or the Curators—to discover it. The horses are already straining up the slope when Charles remembers the story about the graveyard and slides down the glass to look. Up above, on the roof, something catches the sun and flashes in the light, but the graveyard is buried deep in the shadow of the castle, and the lamp is still burning in the little chapel window. And Charles can see now, even at this distance, that there is one grave far more recent than the rest, its watchful stone angels unweathered by age, its old earth newly turned and untouched by green, and a scatter of white flowers that are only now fading to brown decay.

When Charles gets down from the carriage at the castle door there is no-one to meet him, and after lingering for a few minutes in the hall he returns to his room to find lunch has been left, and the fire is burning. And on the table, by his wine, a note in a thin and cramped hand.

> *I must be absent for some hours.*
> *Do not wait for me.*
>   *R*

Charles takes off his coat and sits down on the bed. Then he leans back against the pillows and puts his arm behind his head. An echo in flesh, if he did but realise it, of the waxen woman lying sleeping and unsleeping far below.

When he wakes the room is in shadow and the fire low. He scrambles to his feet, aware immediately of an ache in his neck and a stiffness in his back. He can't believe he's slept into evening, but the sky is dark, and he can hear, far off, the grind of thunder. He's hungry now, even if he wasn't earlier, and gulps the food on the table like a man famished, before going to the window and throwing open the shutters. Unfallen rain hangs heavy in the clouds, and the air crackles with sulphur, even though the storm is still miles away. Charles is rather idly wondering why that should be—some strange atmospheric phenomenon? The direction of the wind?—when there is a distant flare of blue lightning. And then there is another flash and a heavy roof-tile hurtles spinning down and smashes into splinters on the courtyard below, only this time the light is directly above him, somewhere to his right. Charles leans out as far as he can, and thinks he catches a movement on the parapet. He looks down at the windowsill and realises that it's wider than he thought—hardly a balcony but wide enough, just, for him to get a footing. But he'd be mad to try it without some sort of anchorage. He looks back into the room and lights on the tasselled cord holding back the curtains. He ties one end quickly to the bedpost and the other round his waist, then ventures out—with some trepidation—onto the ledge. The stone isn't just narrow but slippery, and Charles slithers twice as he turns slowly round to face up towards the roof. The rain is plunging down now and sheeting headlong into his eyes and mouth, but as the lightning flares again Charles sees the scene above him with the acuity of fever or a diseased dream. On the edge of the parapet, a few yards from the tower, the Baron is outlined against the sky, a dark shape against the greater dark, his long coat whipping and cracking about him like the wings of some vast crow, his silver hair plastered black against his skull. Charles tries to call to him—tell him he is recklessly risking his life—but his words are lost in a detonation of thunder and a bolt of lightning that explodes in a boom of white electric glare. And when the darkness descends once more, the Baron has gone.

Charles edges back down into his room, and then turns to scan the courtyard below. But as he suspected, there is no body, no corpse. Then on some impulse he cannot explain, he opens the door and goes down to the gallery. But as always, it seems, the hall is deserted and only one small lamp burning below. Charles is just about to start down the stairs when he notices that one thing, at least, is not as it was when he last passed here. The little door he noticed before—the door he saw the Baron appear from and then carefully lock—is now standing open. Charles looks around, then moves as swiftly and silently as he can towards it. It's the entrance to a staircase, and Charles realises that it must give access to the tower rooms. He hesitates, then pushes the wooden door a little wider and starts up the steps, only to stop a moment later. He can hear voices. One, the Baron's. The other, a girl's. Light, young, and almost—hard as this is for Charles to absorb— *joyous*. They speak in German, but it seems more formal than a casual conversation—in fact, the only comparison in Charles's experience is the question and answer of the catechism classes he attended for a little while as a boy. But that was before Elizabeth was taken; before his mother lost interest in everything, even her own son, in the abyss of her grief. He listens awhile longer, and concludes it must indeed be some form of interrogation, though what the subject can possibly be, Charles has no idea. Sometimes the girl replies with confidence, and receives affirmation in return; at others, her voice is less sure. No more than ten minutes have passed since the Baron was clinging to the roof in the rain, and yet his voice drones on now, soft, and hoarse, and low. Charles is starting to wonder if the man was ever on the roof at all, or whether the strange atmosphere in this strange house is starting to play tricks with his mind, but at that moment the voices cease, and there is the sound of footsteps coming towards him. Charles considers for a split second standing his ground and confronting the Baron, but some instinct tells him not yet, not yet. So he turns and retreats the way he came, and there is no trace of him remaining when Von Reisenberg emerges and, once again, locks the door watchfully behind him.

It is not till near two that the storm abates, and a good while after that before Charles slips into a fitful and fretful sleep. He dreams again of

Molly, but she is not, now, in the kitchen in his uncle's house, but a cold mimicry of life among the Baron's female figurines. He reaches to touch her face, but it is as if his hand is pushing through thick water—as if he, too, is imprisoned in immobility—but then he is recoiling in horror as the eyes in the fake face brim suddenly with living tears. And when he looks down at her body he sees that she, too, has been flayed to lay bare the unborn child, but these painted wounds gape with real blood-sodden flesh, and the baby—his baby—throbs in her open womb, dying, as she is dying—wax, as she is wax—

He sits up with a strangled cry. The sweat rolls down his back, and his hair is wet against the back of his neck. He takes great gasps of air, willing his heart to slow, his breathing to abate. He has no idea how long it is before he notices there is a line of light slanting across the floor and realises that the door to his room is open, though he's sure he bolted it before he went to bed. Then the light is gone and the room is drowned in dark. A dark he has never seen so deep before. Dark so absolute that he can see nothing, not the outlines of the furniture, not even the tiny sliver of moonlight between the shutter and the sill. He sits, motionless, alert now to every tiny sound in the room, and his senses start to distrust themselves as the fizzing silence mingles with the sound of—what? Bare feet on the thick carpet? A hand drawing back a damask drape? And then he shudders as if stung. An icy finger is running, slowly, teasingly up his bare arm, so lightly it scarcely feathers his skin, but so piercingly it's as if a needle of fire is threading his veins. He puts his hands out wildly, blindly, but encounters nothing, touches no-one. Then he hears the sound of laughter—playful, mischievous laughter—that seems to echo all about the room. He makes to get up but finds himself constrained. Something is binding his wrists, holding him down. He tries to wrench his hands free, but feels a cord dig against his skin. And now his arms are being drawn back behind him—he struggles but the grasp is too strong, and his wrists are forced hard against the wood of the bedstead and he hears the rustle of satin being tied. And now he is in no doubt. A woman is climbing onto his lap and tearing open his shirt with frozen fingers. He can smell her scent, feel the caress of silken ringlets and the tip of a hot wet tongue slipping across his chest and down, down, down. And then there are lips at his throat that sharpen into teeth, and a cold hand that stifles his breathing, and the low murmur of a man's voice, speaking words he cannot understand.

When he wakes the next morning there's a tell-tale stain on the sheets that leaves him red with shame. But there is nothing to say he did not dream it entirely—no marks about his wrists, no tear to his shirt, and when he goes to the door it is locked, and from the inside.

But later, when he strips off his night-shirt to wash, he finds two tiny spots of blood at the neck, which were not there before.

CHAPTER THREE

"WHO IS SHE?"

Charles is standing at the door of the Baron's library. It is eight o'clock, and the storm has cleared, leaving a sky blanched to pallid washy blue and the Danube running high and turbid brown. Charles has not yet breakfasted, but his host must have so done already, or else has no more appetite at this hour than he does after dark. The Baron is sitting, his back to the blinded window, with his pen in his hand and a pair of small wire spectacles on the end of his nose. He does not raise his head when Charles enters, nor when he speaks. It is several long slow moments, indeed, before he places the spectacles on the desk and raises his head.

"To whom do you refer?"

"The young woman I overheard talking with you last night."

The Baron looks at him steadily. "I have no idea what—or whom—you mean. There is no young woman in this castle."

"I am afraid I do not believe you. I distinctly heard a woman speaking with you—a young woman—"

"I say again," interrupts the Baron, "there is no young woman here.

Are you sure you did not dream the episode, Herr Maddox? A large dinner, and several glasses of both wine and *slivovitz* such as I am told is your habit, can produce the most vivid and disturbing dreams. Dreams that take on all the appearance of reality, and deceive the senses, even on waking." He eyes Charles narrowly. "I am sure I do not need to elaborate any further. You have indeed had such an experience, have you not?"

Charles flushes under his intense pale stare. When he replies he has, all unconsciously, brought his hand to his neck.

"This was not a dream, Freiherr. It was observation, not hallucination."

"Ah." The Baron smiles dryly. "I had indeed heard that you place great store by—what was the phrase—*logic and observation*? And indeed, I concur, in some measure, with the principles espoused by your celebrated great-uncle. But were he a scientist, as I am, rather than a mere thief taker, he would know that observation can deceive, and logic cannot always be trusted."

Charles is badly wrong-footed now—unsure whether he's more offended at the casual disparagement of the man Maddox once was, or the fact that his own professional life has clearly been so comprehensively investigated, and without (and this really does concern him) his being in the slightest aware of it. The detective has become the detected, and in the most unsettling manner.

"Even were that true," he says, his eyes cold and his cheeks hot, "I have no reason, on this occasion, to distrust the evidence of my own senses. I had seen you, on the parapet only minutes before, taking what appeared to me to be the most gratuitous and unnecessary risk given the ferocity of the storm, and I came out onto the gallery with the sole purpose of raising the alarm *on your behalf*. I can assure you that by that time I was both wide awake and wet through, from watching at the window."

"If you are so concerned for your health, or for your wardrobe, you would perhaps be better advised to remain within your quarters, unless your presence elsewhere is explicitly requested."

It is barely courteous—barely less than an outright rebuke—and they stare at each other, aware that one of them must retreat, or the encounter break open into absolute animosity. Charles is never averse to a fight, and he's perfectly prepared to press hard for answers, but he's also mindful that all he is likely to achieve is a permanent and uncomfortable rupture that will be almost impossible to explain to his clients in Oxford. He's trying to think of a retort that doesn't constitute a complete capitulation when the Baron—rather surprisingly—blinks first.

"I had intended, yesterday, to talk to you of my work, but I was, as you will recall, most unfortunately called away. That is why I was on the roof last night. To climb to such an exposed place in the middle of a storm might appear *to the uneducated* to be mere folly—which no doubt accounts for many of the impertinent rumours promulgated about me hereabouts—but I would have hoped a man with *your* pretensions to intelligence would have realised at once that a phenomenon such as lightning can, perforce, be studied only in a storm. I have written a number of monographs on this subject, which I should be most happy to show you. I have, for example, offered a theory of my own concerning the variant known as ball lightning, which has hitherto never been explained, and which country people believe to be the sign of the devil's hand. But forked lightning such as we witnessed last night is, I am afraid, only too commonplace and mundane—"

"Then why should you put yourself at such risk to study it?"

Is there now the faintest of flushes across the Baron's hollow cheeks? He picks up his spectacles once more and takes his pen.

"There were some minor observations I wished to make. I believe breakfast awaits you, Herr Maddox."

There is no question of the flush now, and Charles elects merely to bow and depart. But now he has food for thought as well as body.

When he returns to his room, he goes immediately to the shelves of books and looks among them for any written by the Baron himself.

There are several, as it turns out; most on his chemical discoveries, but one in German—*Ueber Blitz ohne Donner*—that judging by the diagrams might well be on the subject of lightning. It's not the first time Charles has wished he had a better facility for languages. But as he flips through pages densely printed with words that seem to go on forever and have nothing like enough vowels, he remembers with a smile something Maddox said to him when he was a boy—Maddox, who devoted so many years to the study of classical tongues but had rather less time for the modern variety. And what was it his uncle had said? *"Life is short, my boy. Far too short for German irregular verbs."* He's still smiling as he puts the book back and scans the rest of the bookshelf to find, rather to his surprise, a copy of *Blackwood's Edinburgh Magazine* from four years before. The journal falls open at a piece titled "Letters on the Truths Contained in Popular Superstitions," and several pages in Charles finds a brief reference to the Baron's name. He's just making a brief note in his pocket-book when there's a sudden loud knocking at the door, and he marks the page with a slip of paper and puts the journal hastily back. It's Herr Bremmer, come to enquire whether he would like to resume his researches in the library. Uneasily aware that he appears to be neglecting the task for which he has been hired, Charles gathers his notebook quickly and follows the librarian out of the room.

He is more than two hours in the library, desperate all the while to return to his room and finish the article. Even at noon he is thwarted when, for the first time, he is accompanied by a silent black-suited servant to the dining-parlour, and thence back to the library once more. When night falls at last, Herr Bremmer accompanies him, as unnecessarily as before, to the door of his room, informs him dinner has been laid there for him, then bows low. Charles closes the door and stands behind it, listening, but it is only when he thrusts the bolt noisily across that he hears the librarian's leather slippers creak softly away. Then he goes quickly to the shelf and pulls out the journal, turning to the page he marked. There's not much, only a few paragraphs. But it's enough. Enough to make him wonder whether there is an answer hidden here that explains everything he has found so unnerving about this place. An answer that might even account for the presence of the girl, and what it is the Baron really wants with her. He shoves the journal carelessly back on the shelf, not caring that it's now protruding at least an inch from the rest, then carefully slides the bolt back and opens the door. Then he makes his way silently to the door beneath the tower, unaware, in his haste and his eagerness, that in the far shadows of the gallery, the librarian is watching.

It is no more than a minute before he hears it. Faint at first, and strangely muffled, but unmistakeable all the same. The sound of a woman's voice. Breaking, gasping. Wailing and rising now in—what? Pain? Fear? He tries the handle of the door, but is not at all surprised to find it locked. He tries the door again, aggressively this time, calling out and demanding to be let in. But there is no answer. The woman's voice stops—suddenly cut off, as if smothered by a clamping hand. And then nothing.

Charles kicks against the door in frustration, but achieves nothing save more scuffs on an already shabby boot. He's defeated, and he knows it. He waits a few moments more, then turns and walks back to his room, where he flings open the window and takes a deep breath of night air. The moon has risen full and whey-faced over the Danube, which runs sluggish and oily in the flooding light, but there must be some trick, some strange reflection off the water that makes the sky above glow brighter than the evening star. He's still trying to puzzle this out when he hears sounds above his head—the sounds of foot-steps. He flings the shutter open as wide as it will go and ventures out again onto the ledge. The parapet is only ten feet or so above his head, but the ground is more than thirty feet below. Thankfully he has always had a head for heights, even if not for languages. He reaches out and seizes a dry gnarled branch of the ancient creeper in one hand, and then another, more confidently, as he feels the bough sigh but stay. The wind is beginning to rise, and the leaves silvering the creeper flutter and whisper as he ascends, slowly, hand over clutching hand, his boots scraping blindly against the slabs for a foothold, and he is soon sweating under his coat, despite the cold. But five minutes later he has reached the crumbling stone balustrade and is grasping the edge and starting to haul himself up and over and seeing, in a staggered disbelief, exactly what it is the Baron has concealed here. And now all is clear—not just the references in the journal, not just the girl, but the Baron's own words, even the specimens downstairs. It is all connected, all is part of the same great and overwhelming secret. And then there is such a sudden blinding glare of light that he closes his eyes a moment, and his fingers slip—slip first and are then crushed by some vicious grinding weight and he is losing his grip and when he opens his eyes again it's to a hail of dust and dead leaves that blinds him until he feels something touch his hair and skin, something dry and leathery but *alive,* and he realises that there is an enormous bat trapped in the branches above his head. He tries to cling on, tries to shield his face against the wall, but as the bat flails closer and closer he cannot stop himself pulling away, and as the shift of his weight wrenches a section of creeper from the wall he is plunging down, falling, clawing, feeling death rush up to meet him on the remorseless stone-paved ground.

But it is not, it seems, his time. Scarce ten feet from the foot of the wall he comes to a gasping slithering stop in the thick tangle of the creeper trunk. His hands are scored and bleeding, but he is not dead yet. He clings there a moment, breathing so hard he can scarcely get oxygen into his lungs, before starting to clamber slowly, shaking, to the ground. The rain is coming down hard now, which is no doubt why Charles does not hear—does not even suspect until he has both feet on solid earth and turns in an illusion of relief to see—

An enormous black-pelted hound. More wolf than dog, its neck ringed with a spiked iron collar, and hackles rigid all along its spine. It starts towards him, teeth bared, growling now, and Charles edges backwards, glancing about desperately for something he can use to fend the creature off—some stick or spade or a brick he could throw—but the dog merely presses closer, the whites of its eyes flaring. There is a frozen second of stillness and then the dog is upon him, leaping at his face, dragging him to the ground. Pure instinct takes over and he kicks and thrashes, but the beast's too strong for him and he feels its hot mouth close about his leg, and knife teeth puncture cloth and skin and bite into bone—

It lasts—what?—a minute? Maybe not even that. And then the vise about his leg is loosed and Charles is lying there, face-down in the dirt, retching, the rain running down his face and neck. He turns over slowly to see a mass of bloody mangled flesh running from his foot to his knee. He stares at it a moment, then doubles up in a rictus of pain, spewing acid vomit across the dark wet ground. But what he does not see, cannot see, is the man standing high above him on the roof, fingering something in the pocket of the long coat that billows about him in the wind. A man who watches quietly for the next half hour, seemingly unperturbed by the downpour, as Charles tries again and again to get up, but can put no weight on his bleeding leg. Watches, indeed, until Charles gives up altogether and crawls with pitiful slowness into the lee of the castle wall, and hunches up against the slashing rain. Whereupon the man above him turns and steps down out of our sight. But not before we glimpse what he has been holding in his hand all this time. It is of ivory, perhaps four inches long, and carved minutely and beautifully with the figure of Actaeon, in the very act of being torn to pieces by his own hounds. And its purpose? It is a hunting whistle. For the summoning of dogs.

✦ ✦

There is a knock on the door and Herr Bremmer shows in a man carrying a small leather bag. It is Jonas Sewerin. He bows as slightly as civility will allow.

"Have you examined the patient?" asks the Baron from his seat behind the desk.

"I have, and I must tell you I am most apprehensive. Herr Maddox is suffering from a dangerous fever of the brain. He seems to have no notion where he is and raved so wildly at the sight of me that I have instructed your servants to strap him to the bed to prevent him from harming himself."

He stares at the Baron, holding his cold gaze. "It is most regrettable that there was such an unaccountable delay in cleaning and treating the wound. I have done all I can but it may still be too late to prevent a putrid infection. And as to how Herr Maddox came to receive such an injury. His flesh has been ripped by what I can only deduce to be the teeth of some wild beast—"

"Herr Maddox was warned," interrupts the Baron, "on the day of his arrival, that I keep a mastiff for the protection of both my property and my privacy—a mastiff permitted to roam freely about the castle precincts at night. If he insists on taking his walks alone, and in the dark hours, then he must accept the consequences."

"I do not believe he was merely walking—"

Sewerin stops, wary that he might have said too much. Because his patient was not quite as incoherent as he has led the Baron to believe: one or two words at least, he was well able to decipher. Words that have left the doctor deeply alarmed.

"Indeed," says the Baron, who has been watching him all this while. "And what leads you to such an improbable conclusion?"

"It was my assumption merely," says Sewerin eventually. "Based on the fact that no sane person would have willingly gone out in that storm."

The Baron raises an eyebrow. "I can only concur."

Then he picks up the pen from the desk in front of him and returns to the document he has been writing.

"Thank you, Herr Sewerin. You may send your bill to my steward."

"But—"

"That will be all," he replies firmly, still intent on his papers. "If my guest requires further attention from a physician I will undertake to provide it. In the manner, and at the time, that I see fit. Good day to you."

When the door has closed the Baron addresses himself to Bremmer. "On reflection, I consider my duty to our rash young guest would be best discharged by placing him in the care of professional attendants. Have a carriage made ready for an immediate departure to Melk."

The librarian bows and turns to go, but his master's voice calls him calmly back. "I have had a message from the coachman enquiring as to my own intentions. Pray tell him my own plans are unchanged. I will depart for England, as arranged, at first light tomorrow."

Bremmer bows low. "I will inform him so, *Freiherr*. And request that a carriage be made available to transport Herr Maddox to the hospital at Melk."

"Not the hospital," says the Baron quietly, without looking up. "The asylum."

❧ ❦

...I have never seen so forbidding an entrance, nor one so deserving of that terrifying inscription Dante places at the gates of Hell, "Abandon all hope, ye who enter here." Above me the blank walls towered, pierced only by windows too narrow for a human hand. As I was drawn towards the crumbling doorway I saw surmounting it the stony figure of Death, bending to place a skeleton's kiss on a swooning maiden's dewy brow. And when the huge door swung closed behind us, I heard the key rasp in the lock, and then nothing but the sound of slow dripping, and the wind in the desolate turrets above. After what seemed many moments, the man ahead of me lit a candle and I was told to follow. A long dark passage opened in the guttering flame, and as our faltering steps progressed, I began to hear the cries of the imprisoned, the pitiful howlings of the mad, and the desperate lamentations of those kept always from the light. And then, as my heart misgave me and I turned, frantic to be gone, I felt myself impelled forwards and a second door opened before us, as if by its own volition, and we descended, down, and down, and down again, to a crypt rank with the stench of death, and lit only by the sickly blue glow of a single lamp.

There was the sound of thunder now, and I could see the ranks of mouldering graves, and the walls lined with the dried and mummified remains of the dead of that horrific place, their heads bowed, bound to stand upright for all eternity in the ghastly windings of the tomb, denied even that rest the Lord allows the wicked and the lost. And then the lamp was extinguished and we were plunged into darkness. A strange and eerie music began now, one moment seeming close, the next high above my head, yearning like the very anguish of the soul. I seemed to feel the soft flutter of something against my cheek, and there was a rush of air so cold as to chill the very blood. As mist began to seep through the icy vault, a woman's spectral voice began to intone in some ancient tongue, and I saw hovering above me in a sudden blaze of light the ghostly figure of a nun, clad from head to foot in robes of glowing white. She came floating slowly forwards, her hooded head bowed, until she was scarce a yard away, whereupon she lifted her face and I saw the blood streaming in torrents from her empty black-socketed eyes. I cried out, and heard others about me do the same, holding up their hands as if to fend the wraith away, and then the nun was gone as swiftly as she had come, her place taken by a hornèd laughing devil, its teeth glinting, and a horde of demons feeding on the flesh of the living damned, who rolled their eyes and tore their hair, and pointed their cadaverous fingers at the hapless audience huddled in terror below. Vision succeeded vision, each more terrifying than the last, and then there was an image I had seen before—that painting so notorious and reviled, of the woman flung on her virgin bed in the throes of *cauchemar*. Only this was no painted canvas—she writhed and moaned before our horrified gaze, as the monsters of her dreams loomed in the darkness above her, and the kneeling demon pressed his scaly hands to her breast, grinning in a hideous mockery of delight. I saw women faint at this, and men reduced to sobbing wretches, begging for relief.

And then there was the clap of a thunderbolt and a man appeared in a column of glowing smoke, clad in a billowing cloak, with a mask of gold concealing his face.

"Citizens of Vienna," he cried. "For centuries, man has yearned to fathom the mystery of death, and plumb the secrets of that undiscovered country from whose bourne no traveller returns. Many have been the imposters who have claimed to communicate with the dead, but I stand before you now to make good that claim. Not by the wiles of necromancy will I achieve it, nor by the *legerdemain* of the magician, but by the genius of the scientist. I have created a machine which, for the first time in the history of mankind, may harness the hidden energy of the universe and breach the impermeable barrier of death."

He raised his arms then, as lightning suddenly illuminated the dank walls of the cavern. "Those of this company who desire to see again the faces of the departed, and hear the voices of those who were once dear, prepare yourselves, and hold fast to your courage, for you will see marvels to wring your hearts!"

The room was plunged once more in darkness, and then, in a sudden ray of moonlight, we could see a young girl, clad—as I deduced—all in black, such that only her face was visible to us, afloat in a sea of utter dark. Before her there was mounted a brass apparatus of enormous complexity above which a glass ball appeared to be suspended in the air. The room fell silent then, as she lifted hands as white as her face and placed them, one by one, on either side of the ball, whereupon the globe began to spin and a ghastly greenish light to glow at its heart.

"Behold!" cried the man in a booming cadence, "as my daughter raises the secret flame, and summons the souls of the long-departed!"

I do not believe there was one of us, then, in all that thronged and silent assembly but held their breath, as the girl lifted her face and closed her eyes, and we saw sparks kindled on the surface of the glass. Then there came, softly at first, the sound of a young woman's voice, rising and falling as if in lamentation, and the whimpering of a little child. And then the light of the globe seemed to gather in strength, twisting into a plume above the girl's head, and we all of us present gasped in terror and wonder as a woman's face became visible in the emerald fire.

An old fellow with grey hair rose tremblingly to his feet in the midst of the assemblage and cried in the quavering accents of age, "It is she, it is my Katharina. It is thirty years and more since she was lost to me."

Then he cast his face in his hands, openly weeping.

And as the globe spun, the rising flame formed the contours of ghostly yearning faces, sighing and whispering from beyond the grave, and those about me cried out, one by one, starting from their seats in recognition, as they called the names of those they had once loved, and held out their hands in an ecstasy of grief.

In short it was, as I hope to have conveyed, the most accomplished *phantasmagoria* I have ever yet beheld, and I commend it to readers of this newspaper who have not thus far had the opportunity to witness it for themselves. Professor de Caus is indeed a worthy successor to his late lamented mentor Monsieur Étienne-Gaspard Robertson, and more than justifies his claim to be *"Maker of Marvels, Worker of Wonders, and Conjuror of the Spirit Fire."* Moreover, the wild rumours that have been circulating about Vienna as to the ex-

traordinary talents of his beautiful daughter will be amply vindi-
cated by the sublimity of dread and wonder you will experience in
her presence.

But I counsel the utmost haste. The Professor will offer only a few
last performances before returning, for a time, to his native England.
We must hope his sojourn there will prove but short-lived.

—Frederick Jager, "A Night at the Phantasmagoria,"

Wiener Zeitung, 5 January 1851

CHAPTER FOUR

Lucy's journal

We are going home.

I sit back and look at what I have just written, and I wonder if I really know what "home" means. It is so long since we have been there, so long that we have been away, all those years in Paris and now here, that I can scarce remember that little house my father tells me is our home. On a starkly beautiful northern shore, Father says, with a view across the bay to the town and the ruined abbey standing high above it. I have a picture in my mind when he describes all this to me, a picture of louring skies, and huge crows thrown against the wind, and a girl in white seated alone, but I do not know if this is memory, or whether I have heard him talk of it so often that I have made his recollections my own. When I told him this his face darkened for a moment, and he would not say why, but I saw his eyes stray to the locket I wear always about my neck, the locket that holds a portrait of my mother, and I had a sudden conviction that the last time we returned it was to bury her.

But this I did not say.

He touched my cheek then, and said I was pale, and no doubt exhausted by the exertions of last night, and I must rest before we begin the task of packing for our journey. I smiled at him because I wished to reassure him, and because there was, after all, some truth in what he said. And what remained unspoken, I can scarcely understand myself, far less explain. When he was gone I went to my casement and looked down upon the street. The sun was sinking, and though the roofs and attics were aglow with gold, the pavements were sunk in shadow, and an old woman in a wool shawl and a threadbare bonnet was shuffling painfully along with her empty basket over one arm. Empty because she is going to the market, where there will be remnants now on sale at half the price of their morning freshness— I know, because when I was a little child I would accompany my mother through the streets at the same hour of the evening, and with the same aim in view. Though when I remember that part of my past now it is not in pictures but in perfumes—the wooden tables with their crates of bitter oranges, their coils of stinking sausage, and their slabs of oozy yellow cheese, mingled with the stale sweat of the tired and short-tempered stallholders. It is strange how strong these impressions are for me, how powerfully an aroma caught randomly in the air can draw me down and backwards, to that one scent I still yearn to recapture, which my mother always had about her, which I cannot ever convey in words, and have never encountered since.

A few moments later, as I idled still at the window, I saw a playbill come slithering in the wind towards where the old woman had paused for a moment with a neighbour. It was splashed with mud and torn at the edges, but that did not matter. I could see the strip of paper pasted to its face, and I knew that it was one of ours. And then, as I watched, the sheet of paper lifted and folded itself for a moment about the old woman's walking-stick, and when she shook it loose and saw what it was, I saw them both gasp and cross themselves, and I heard one whisper harshly, *"Der Teufel tut sein Werk durch den Wahnsinn dieser Verrückten."* The devil does his work through the delusions of this lunatic.

And then I turned and reached blindly for my chair, my breath coming hard at that word I fear so much, knowing that I will wake again tonight, in the midst of the dark, cold and shaking at the moonlit window with no recollection of how I got there, just as I awoke, once, barefoot in the street, being led into the shadows by a man I did not know.

It was my father who saved me. My father who found me and beat the man away, and then carried me, trembling in his gentle arms, back to my bed. My father who has, every night all these years since, locked the door to my bedroom and taken away the key. But now, it is different. Now, when I catch him looking at me in the glass, there is something in his face I have not seen before.

Fear.

It is a paradox, and, perhaps, a punishment. For fear has been our lives, and our calling. We have fathomed it, we have fashioned it, and we have sold it. How often have I heard my father boast that he is satisfied only when our spectators are rendered prostrate in their seats, moaning and shivering in delicious horror. Delicious, Father says, because fear is the very neighbour of ecstasy, even if it is rarely acknowledged to be so. And I had only to look at the women in our audiences to believe him, their bosoms heaving, their lips parted, and perspiration beading their brows. We have laboured, he and I, with the sole intent of intensifying that sensation, of finding new ways to chill the blood, and freeze the heart, and the fame we have gained, and the money we have earned, have stemmed in large part from that joint endeavour. I will not claim the credit is all my own— that would be an exaggeration, and unfair—but there are those in our profession who whisper that when he worked alone my father was nothing but a sorry imitation of the man who once apprenticed him, little more than the travelling showman he had been before he met my mother, with a crate of pretty puppetry, and a repertoire of tricks and mirrors and sleight of hand. But *I* know the truth of it—*I* know he had always dreamed of being a scientist and bitterly regretted that his family was not rich enough to permit him to pursue such a study; *I* know that Monsieur Robertson saw that desire in him, when he opened his door one morning and found my father slumped asleep on his step, having walked all the way to Paris to see the world's most famous *phantasmagoria,* and beg its proprietor for a position, however lowly. It was Monsieur Roberston, in the years that followed, who taught my father all the intricate deceptions of our trade—the use of a gauze curtain dipped in wax, the mounting of the magic lantern on wheels, and the edging of the lantern slides in black, that our spectres might glimmer wraith-like as they loom and recede, and hover weightlessly in the empty air. It was Monsieur Robertson who first brought us to Vienna, and Monsieur Robertson, when he was a very old man, and I still a very young child, who saw me, one wet afternoon, playing with the apparatus, and trying to figure to myself how it worked. When my mother came in and saw what I was doing, she upbraided me sternly for touching the lantern slides, knowing how fragile they were and how long each took to paint, but he interrupted her hastily, saying that I might have an aptitude for the craft, and should be encouraged, and he smiled, saying that I had been christened well, for my name meant "light," and I might bring illumination to the darkness, as he himself had always striven to do. And so it was that I became apprentice as my father had once been, learning not merely the science of our deceptions, but that far greater and more laudable science of optics. It was my father who taught me the use of the solar microscope, and the mathematics of Archimedes, and all the secrets of the patented fantoscope, which Monsieur Robertson had entrusted to no other but him.

I know my mother disapproved of this, lamenting my sad lack of a proper education, and telling me, privately, when my father was not there, that such subjects were not suitable for young girls. And there came a time when I blamed myself for saddening her so, and not noticing that she was growing thinner, and her skin paler, and the shadows were darkening under her eyes, until it was too late, and in my twelfth year she was taken from me. I remember so little of that time now, only scraps and fragments of memory that do not fit with what I have since been told. But I tell myself the explanation is simple—that I loved my mother so much that the pain of her loss was too much for me to bear—that my mind has sought to bury that pain, and it is no wonder therefore if my recollections are confused. I do know that for weeks I never left my chamber, and my father cancelled his performances and remained at my side. Perhaps it was all that time motionless and bed-ridden, perhaps it was because I woke one morning with the white sheets wringing in blood and I had no-one but my father to explain to me what it meant; all I know is that when I was finally well enough to be carried to sit in a chair by the window, I had lost some part of myself that I have never since been able to retrieve. All my happy lightness of heart had gone, all my spirit, and audacity, and careless childish courage. And in their place, the sleep-walking, and the nightmare.

But of the latter, I have never spoken. Not to my father, and not, absolutely, to the string of doctors he has brought these last days to see me, who have looked into my eyes, and taken my pulse, and questioned my father as to my symptoms, and then looked smugly wise and diagnosed hysteria, or nervous debility, or *chlorosis*. There was one—a wheezing fat man with a face all noduled with warts—who even went so far as to suggest that it is my playing of the glass armonica, which is to blame. He had seen, he said, many such cases where the use of this instrument has induced not merely melancholy but madness, by reason of the intolerable tingling vibrations that seem to penetrate the skin, and unbalance the tranquillity of the quietest mind. I tried to tell him, then, that he was wrong—that no-one knows more of melancholy than I, and this new misery is not of that order. But my father silenced me—he clung to the man's words, desperate to believe that my symptoms might have so simple an origin. And to placate him I have not touched the armonica since, vital though it is to the effect of our enactments. But it has made no difference. There has been no respite, frantic as my father is to see one. For it is not my playing that is the cause. I tell him, again and again, that I am not mad—not *mad* but *sick*. But all he does is smile sadly upon me, and caress my hair, saying that all will be well. That I must trust him, and all will be well.

29 JANUARY, MIDNIGHT

And now the last performance has been given.

There were so many people who wished to congratulate my father, so many pressing about us and begging, some in tears, for a private consultation before we departed, and holding out towards me the belongings of the dead, as if those forlorn possessions had the power to entice those who once owned them to return. The toys of lost children, the robes of babies taken before their churching, the wedding ring a young wife must once have worn. The grief—and worse, the hope—washed towards me like a wave, and I found myself drawing back as if they sought to suffocate me, as if it were their sadness that takes unseen form and sucks my breath like an incubus in the night. I saw my father's look of alarm, then, as the crowd of faces and voices closed about me and I felt his hand suddenly upon my shoulder, cleaving through the people and drawing me free.

"My daughter is unwell," he said loudly, as some muttered and pointed. "She is exhausted and must return home now to rest. Please, make way."

And so it is that I have been sitting here now alone these two hours, among the boxes and trunks that are to go with us tomorrow, hearing the bells chime the quarters, and remembering, remembering.

It is still all so clear to me, that September morning, when he came rushing to my bedroom, clutching a page of newspaper a friend had posted to him from New York. I have found it, he said, smoothing the page out on the bed and pointing—It is exactly what we have been seeking. A new attraction for our spectacle, a new wonder that will create a clamour of excited gossip among the public, and command respect even from the learned and aloof. And when I took up the paper and started to read I knew at once what he meant. The article was from the *New-York Tribune,* dated some three weeks before, and it related how three young sisters claimed to converse with the dead by means of rapping on walls, or tapping on wooden floors. The spirits seemed quite amenable to this method of communication, submitting most accommodatingly to different numbers of raps for Yes and No, and for the letters of the alphabet. And yet it seemed that many hundreds of citizens of that great city were more than ready to give credence to it.

> Mrs Fox and her three daughters left our city yesterday, after a stay of some weeks, during which they have freely subjected the mysterious influence by which they seem to be accompanied, to every reasonable test. And to the keen and critical scrutiny of the hundreds who have chosen to visit them. The ladies say they are informed that this is but the beginning of a new era, in which spirits clothed in flesh are to be put more closely and palpably connected with those who have put on immortality; that the manifestations have already appeared in many other families and are destined to be diffused and rendered clearer, until all who will may communicate freely and beneficially with their friends who have "shuffled off this mortal coil."

I looked up at my father and smiled. "It is easy to see how one might counterfeit such a phenomenon. The wonder is that anyone else should believe it."

He gripped my hand, his eyes bright with eagerness. "But they do, Lucy, *they do.* These sisters are attracting the most immense audiences. My friend's letter tells me there have since been dozens of these public *séances,* attended by people who will pay well to see them. And yet the only spectacle those people see is this bodiless 'rapping,' nothing more. There is no unearthly light, no phantasms, no ghostly voices. All those *feu d'artifice* effects *we* might produce—that we *already* produce."

And of course he was right, at least in this. We had long employed the tricks of ventriloquism to give our apparitions speech, and the illusion of the magic lantern might as easily clothe in flesh the faces of the departed as it did the spectres and sorcerors that were our stock in trade. But I was, all the same, uneasy.

I looked again at the cutting, and then up at my father's face. "And you would be content to create such a delusion—content that we should proclaim to the world that we can commune with the dead, in the full knowledge that it is nothing but a lie?"

"What harm could it do? Why should we not trumpet this 'new era,' as these American girls do?"

"It is one thing to conjure images any rational person knows to be harmless illusion; quite another, surely, to claim that we bring back the loved ones they have lost. It would be such a deception—"

"Everything we do is a deception. Of one kind or another."

He gripped my hand once more, avid for my assent.

"And how would you feel," I began tentatively, "if someone were to deceive *you* in such a way? Trick you into believing you could speak to my mother—hear her voice again? Would you not feel it a terrible betrayal—the most terrible betrayal of them all?"

"No," he replied softly, wiping away the tear that had stolen down my cheek. "Not if I never discovered I had been deceived. I think I would be comforted, and overjoyed to see her one last time."

And as he stroked my hand, and I smiled at him through my tears, I found that I agreed.

We spent many days, after that, exploring how we might harness all the guile of our art to this new end. The magic of the lantern might easily command the dead to appear, and we knew, from long years, that the wish to believe is the strongest power an illusionist may exercise; that we had only to show a ghostly face for someone to claim it as wife, or sister, or mother long years dead. But we had need of some mechanism, some imposing device, that would convince those who saw it that it was by the advancement of science, not the profane practices of superstition, that this new wonder had been achieved.

Hour upon hour my father shut himself up alone, going through his journals and his learned books, until he came to me one evening, when I was eating my dinner, and sat down on the chair next to mine.

"Look," he said, opening a journal to where he had marked the place with a slip of paper, and placing it on the table by my plate. It was a drawing of a wooden table, and above it, a large glass ball, suspended between two metal prongs.

"What is it?"

"It is called an Influence Machine," Father said. "And the name seems strangely fortuitous, given the use to which it might be put. I saw one demonstrated, many years ago, and I cannot understand why I have not thought of it before. You see the handle at the side of the table? It connects to a mechanism in the prongs which causes the globe to revolve. The glass itself has been evacuated of air, and a very small amount of mercury inserted, such that when the glass is set to spin it gives off a strange green radiance if touched. It does indeed have the most uncanny appearance."

He must have seen my look of alarm. "The science of it is easily explained, and in any case it is not the science that need concern us. I lighted upon it just now because of this note," he said, pointing, "which seems appended almost as an afterthought. It says the creator of the machine called the light it emits 'the glow of life.' As if it were some hidden and secret energy, which the action of the machine makes visible to man."

"Do you believe it, Papa?" I asked, as I ran my eyes down the paragraph he had marked.

"I confess I find it unlikely, as a hypothesis. But for our purposes, it might do very well."

I could see now, where his thought was tending. "You believe we might harness this secret energy," I said slowly, "to render the spirits of the dead perceptible to the living?"

He smiled. "Clearly we would only *appear* to do so. But we can make that *'appear'* seem only too real to those who witness it."

And that was how it came about. My father procured the apparatus required from a scientist in Ingolstadt, and then spent some weeks adapting it to our purpose, until he announced, with some excitement, that he believed it ready for our first essay. I cannot describe the sensation when first I touched the pillars that suspend the globe, and put my fingers to the hissing glass. The rush of heat across my skin, and the sudden agonising spasm that sent me staggering from the apparatus, my hand at my side. I reached half-blind for the nearest chair as my father came running towards me. "Was it too strong? Are you hurt?"

I shook my head, feeling suddenly, and for the first time by daylight, that same strange claustrophobia I know only too well, when I wake from sleepwalking to the taste of metal in my mouth and a low insistent humming in my ears.

But I told my father none of this, wishing to spare him any self-reproach, and asking only that he adjust the machine a little before we attempted it again. And when I tried it a second time, the effect was indeed lessened, though I could still feel a sharp tingling in the nerves of my hands. But I told myself I could bear it, and I did not wish my father to waste the work of so much time. And yet each month that passes it has worsened, and now I feel myself diseased, as if the mere touch of my hand will taint, and my blood runs not red and full but brackish, like filthy water clogged with soil.

I am not mad—I have told myself again and again, I am *not mad,* but I do so in desperation, and with a rising panic that clutches at my heart. For if it is madness to distrust one's own senses, to see what others cannot perceive, then in truth perhaps I *am* mad. For now, when the room darkens and I place my hands on the machine and the globe begins to spin, I see other colours, brighter and far more beautiful than the sick greenish glow of the glass—spirals of iridescent light lifting coldly into the air, red and blue-white plumes that curl and entwine like water, and waver sometimes like flame in the wind. The night when first it happened I looked across at my father, wondering if this was some new trick—some new effect he had devised to surprise and delight me—but his face was impassive beneath its mask. And when I told him, afterwards, what I had seen, he said, a little sternly, that I must be mistaken. But it was the morning after, I am sure, that he first he talked of England, and of home.

CHAPTER FIVE

THE CITY HAS NEVER been so crowded, so excited, so proud, so dangerous. It has taken nine months, a million square feet of glass, and eighteen acres of Hyde Park, and London now boasts a modern wonder to rival all seven of the ancient world. "Vast, strange, new and impossible to describe," it is a stately pleasure dome decreed by no less a personage than the Prince Consort himself. A temple to technology tall enough to top living trees, furnished with more than one hundred thousand "Works of Industry of all Nations," and designed (in both senses of the word) to fanfare to those self-same nations that Great Britain is not only the world's workshop, but its pre-eminent imperial power. The visitors pouring through the doors of this Great Exhibition each day can see printing presses and folding pianos, silk tapestries and Sèvres porcelain, American pistols and Canadian fire-engines, statuary and stained glass, microscopes and mill machinery, looms and locomotives, a steam hammer that can bend metal and yet scarcely crack the shell of an egg, and the Koh-i-Noor diamond (uncut at present, so rather a drab disappointment to most), as well as a stuffed elephant to display the Queen's *howdah*, and a tab-

leau of stuffed kittens done up in dresses in the German gallery, which
is said to be Her Majesty's personal favourite of the whole display.

Six million will meander this miracle of rare devices before it closes in
October, from families, to foreigners, to factory-owners; thousands on
special Thomas Cook trains from the provinces; and hundreds as exhibitors touting for trade; the fashionable from town, the Sunday-
bested from the suburbs, and today—a designated "shilling day"—flocks
of smocked-clothed agricultural labourers ripe for the ripping. For the
thieves are thick among the gadding crowds, and despite the ranks of
specially recruited constables, some of whom we can see even now
sweating under their tall hats this hot June morning, there's nothing
that pulls in a pickpocket more than a courteous English queue. A
scuffle breaks out briefly, as a rather more seasoned officer spots a
ragged lad with his fingers where they've no right to be, but within
moments calm is restored, and the momentary flutter of anxiety among
the matrons is forgotten as the throng gets its first breathless glimpse
of the splendour in the glass.

Less than three miles away, Buckingham Street is far enough from the
dust and press of the Strand, and close enough to the river, for a breath
of air to lift the summer heat. Down in the basement kitchen Nancy
Dyer is toiling at the tub, her pretty face red with the effort of the
morning's laundry, while her little daughter Betsy sits rolling marbles
for a large black cat which shows precious little inclination to pursue
them, having secured with an unerring feline instinct the only cool
corner of the kitchen floor. In the drawing-room two storeys above,
the master of the house sits at a small table by the open window, one
hand slowly turning pages, and the other holding down the book—
holding it a little stiffly, as we now see, which suggests that the stroke
he suffered some six months ago has not fully left him. In the far corner of the same room Maddox's former henchman, Abel Stornaway, is

helping Billy the servant lad to clear the table of the remains of breakfast, fussing a little, as is his wont, and loading the tray just a little too
heavily for the boy to manage. And up in the attic, Charles Maddox,
too, is at the window, looking down towards the Thames where a barge
loaded with coal is toiling heavily against the tide.

It's a long way from the asylum at Melk, and you may well be wondering how such a distance has been travelled. As well as calculating,
perhaps, after looking back a page or so, that it is nigh on three months
since we last encountered him. Charles is standing at the window now,
so we can deduce that he did not—though it was a close-run thing—
lose his leg to the attack at Castle Reisenberg, but when he turns finally and moves towards his desk we can see that he is limping.
Limping in an impatient furious way, as if he'll be damned to acknowledge it, far less let it hinder him. The document on the desk is a
letter, and as he resumes his pen to complete it, we may perhaps be
able to gather rather more of what has happened to him in those last
few missing weeks.

Buckingham Street, 16 June

Dear Dr Sewerin,
    You asked me, when we parted, to write on my return, con-
cerned about my injury and the consequences of so long a confinement in that accursed place. You will be relieved to hear that
despite the impatience I expressed at the time, I took your advice
and travelled slowly, and so have been in London only two days.
But you may rest assured that the wound that alarmed you so
much is healing—no small thanks to your own timely care, even if
I was too crazed by fever to show my gratitude at the time. The effects of my enforced seclusion will, I fear, be of longer duration.
You know the place, and do not need me to describe its horrors.
Had I not met you, by chance, that morning in the forest, I might
never have escaped them. You alone could guess where they had
taken me, and you alone had the authority to act on that knowledge, and have me, at last, released. I will be forever in your debt,

and it is a debt I would be honoured to redeem, if ever you decide
to visit England.

I have told no-one here of what befell me, and I have not yet
decided what I should tell my paymasters. It is, after all, a tale so—

He stops, pen in mid-air. He has said little—nothing, indeed—of what
he endured all those weeks in the asylum, as if refusing to frame it in
words might help expunge it from his mind. But the images, when
they come, are unrelenting. Waking up in that place and knowing it for
what it was. And then, day after day, night after night, the stench of
urine, the wailing of the demented, and the pitiful shouting of those
imprisoned by mistake, or malice. The chains biting into his wrists and
ankles, and the whimpering of the man shackled likewise to the next
bed, huddled and rocking, hour by endless hour. And worse than any
of these, the silent attendants standing every morning on either side of
his bed, wrenching his jaws open and pouring the bitter gruel between
his teeth, after which he would lie for hours, half-dazed, staring at the
stained and seeping ceiling, trying to force his mother's face from his
mind, telling himself that he is not insane—telling himself that this is
not his family curse—that it is not his punishment for allowing Elizabeth to be lost—

The sound of the doorbell downstairs breaks into his thoughts, and
he listens intently for a moment, before quietly resuming his task. It is
five minutes and more before there is a knock on his attic door and
Billy's pink face appears around it.

"Mr Wheeler to see yer, Mr Charles. *Sergeant* Wheeler, now, should
I say."

Charles sits back; he was not expecting his old colleague today—
indeed any day—and he wonders if it is purely a social call. Half his
heart will be happy to see him, and glad for his promotion, but Sam is
far too sharp not to realise something serious has happened, and
Charles is not sure yet if he has a story that will stand inspection.
"Show him to the office," he says eventually, getting to his feet. "And
ask Nancy to make us some coffee."

Sam hates coffee, Charles knows that well enough, but it serves as a way of dismissing the boy and avoiding his shrewd Cockney stare as Charles shuffles down the stairs like a stiff old man.

By the time he gets to the office Sam is happily ensconced, his feet up on the desk, eating an apple. He gets up smartly when he sees Charles and comes over to shake him by the hand, but he notices Charles's injury at once—just as Charles knew he would.

"How did that 'appen?" he asks, as Charles lowers himself painfully into the hard wooden chair.

"I'm afraid I had a less-than-cordial encounter with one of my host's guard-dogs."

Sam eyes him, chewing. "And there were me finking it were a nice easy number you'd got yerself. All expenses paid and a little 'oliday thrown in besides. So that were why you were away so long? Yer uncle didn't seem to know when I called 'ere last week."

Charles nods, avoiding his gaze. "It took longer to heal than expected. And then I could not travel as quickly as I should have liked."

That's not the half of it, Sam guesses that at once, but this is a friend not a felon, and he knows better than to press him. If he needs to know, Charles will tell him in his own good time. And in any case, this is not, as it turns out, a social call.

"It were the Inspector as asked me to come. Inspector Rowlandson. 'E thought you might be able to 'elp us. 'Cause we're stumped wiv this one, Chas, I don't mind telling yer."

There's no mistaking the bafflement on Sam's round and likeable face as he starts to explain, though at first Charles is hard put to understand why, so ordinary does his story sound.

"Two bodies were found about a month back—both girls, and both wivvin a coupl'a days. First was in the lake in St James's Park, the next in an alley round the back of Shepherd's Market, dead a good few days, the doctor said. And then there was anovver, about a week later, no more 'an a few yards away from where we found the second one. Reckon she'd been there quite a while, judging by the state of 'er. None of 'em much more 'an skin 'n bone, and all of 'em dollymops. You could tell by what they was wearin'. The 'igh-ups are terrified it might get out that there's some sort'a madman loose in London attackin' women. We've put more blokes on patrol but to be 'onest we just don't have the men to spare."

"Well," begins Charles, "I can appreciate their concern, but there are a lot of strangers in town for the Exhibition, and girls like that are easy pickings. Regrettable, but hardly unusual, surely. We must have seen dozens like that in our time—"

Sam finishes his apple and tosses the core into the wastepaper basket. His face is grave. "As far as I recall we never saw none with their 'eads cut off. And not just cut off but nowhere to be found neever."

Charles stares at him, not knowing what to say. Sam puts a hand through his stiff carrot brush of hair and sighs. "And that weren't all. It were weird—like nuffin' I'd ever seen before."

"What do you mean?"

"They all 'ad a great huge cavity, right 'ere, in the chest. It weren't just the 'eads that were gone—the 'earts 'ad been taken out, too. To be frank wiv yer we didn't realise quite what it was wiv the first one—after all she'd been in the drink so we just assumed—"

"Assumed what?"

Sam flushes a little. "Well, that she musta been 'it by somefing in the water. Come on, Chas, we all know what the river can do to bodies. 'Alf-mashed, some of 'em I've seen."

Charles shakes his head. "But that's down to the debris, and the current. Neither of which applies to the lake in St James's Park."

"That's what the quack said, too. And now there's been two more wiv exactly the same. So what do *you* fink it means, 'cause 'e ain't got a bloody clue."

Charles looks at him thoughtfully. "Are the bodies still in the morgue?"

Sam nods. He knows Charles of old, and knows he will want to see the evidence with his own eyes. "The last one's still there. 'Ad to bury the first two—can't keep 'em 'anging around too long in this 'eat. But I asked 'em to keep the last one as long as they could in case you wanted to see 'er."

The door opens then and Nancy edges carefully in with the heavy tray. Sam winks at her and makes as if to pinch her bottom, and as she dodges away the coffee slops from the pot and spills onto the floor.

"Now look what you've made me do!" she cries, but she's not really angry, and Sam knows it. Charles watches a slightly pink-cheeked Nancy put the tray down on the desk and start fussing with a cloth, not meeting his gaze, and he wonders suddenly how many times Sam has been round to the house recently, and whether it was really enquiring about Charles that drew him, or some other motive entirely. He finds himself smiling then—if Sam can overlook Nancy's past, and Nancy can find someone who will care for her and love her daughter, then who is Charles to deny them, especially now Sam has a wage that could support a family.

The Strand is thick with Exhibition crowds, all pouring the same way and most with little "London learning" as to the best way to move efficiently in a mob, so it's heavy going in the heat until they reach the Haymarket and can strike north at their own stride. Here the pace is more sedate, with top-hatted courtiers strolling in ponderous pairs, and the occasional nursemaid with a perambulator and neatly starched small child. All of which is a very far cry from the gloom and the stink that greet them in the Vine Street police-station morgue. Charles has been here before, of course, many times, when he was still a policeman, but it's an aspect of the job he always hated, and never more so than when it was the body of a child he was there to inspect. Or, as in this case, a barely teenage girl with no other choice but sell her body or starve. There's a mortuary assistant swilling a bucket of water over the stone flags, and two more sweeping the floor with brooms thick with sodden human hair, but none of it is doing anything to dispel the reek of putrefaction in the suffocating underground room, screened from the street and snooping by windows painted green and running with moisture (paint, incidentally, so saturated with arsenic that some of the attendants here will not be long in joining those they attend upon). The lamps are lit to dispel the underwaterish murk, and the air is alive with flies. There are half a dozen corpses on the slabs, all in different stages of decomposition, as Charles quickly deduces from those body parts that protrude from the soiled sheets, and the slow drip of fluids onto the floor. Sam goes to find the supervisor, and when the three of them gather about the body they have come to see, and the sheet is lifted from her naked form, the hot stench that rushes to the back of Charles's throat has him retching like a woman or a raw recruit. *Breathe through your mouth,* he scolds himself, his handkerchief clamped to his face, *and concentrate.*

This beheading is no amateur job, he sees that at once. The neck has been expertly sliced in one arcing cut, and the knife, Charles suspects, was bought express for the purpose—no kitchen implement this, for it has scythed through the flesh like a butcher's blade, or a surgeon's saw. But there is one thing Charles did not expect—this corpse should not look like this—not after three weeks, not in this heat. By now she should be bloated, oozing, the skin splitting, the nails falling away. But she lies there, still all but intact, still—almost—human. And there's only one way Charles can explain that.

"Was there a lot of blood, where you found her?"

Sam shakes his head, his voice muffled by his own handkerchief. "Funny you should ask—there weren't no blood there at all. We as-soomed he must'a done 'er somewhere else and dumped the body after."

"And the others—what did they look like—did they look especially pale to you?"

Sam considers. "They *was* very pale, now you come to mention it. But I guess that's not so surprisin', given they'd 'ad their 'eads cut off."

Charles shakes his head. "You don't bleed to death if you die that way. The heart stops within a few moments. This girl has lost far more blood than that. I just can't understand how."

Charles looks again at the girl's body. The pitiful thin legs and the skim of pubic hair. She was scarcely more than a child. He lifts first one hand and then the other, seeing fingernails torn by what was in all likelihood a desperate struggle against death, and marks of bruising about the wrists. She was constrained then, either by hand or tie.

"And you never found the heads?" he says eventually.

Sam shrugs. "To be honest, we weren't really lookin'. If 'e'd killed 'em somewhere else they could be anywhere from 'ere to Whitechapel. But you're sayin' he might 'ave done it there, in the Market? It ain't very likely, surely. I mean, 'ow could someone get away wiv doin' somefing like this out in the open—right in the centre of bloody London?"

"I'm not so sure," says Charles, lifting one of the girl's hands again. "You *could* get away with it, if it was in the middle of the night or the early hours of the morning. And if you were as expert a butcher as this killer appears to be. And in any case look at this—here, under her fingernails. I'm pretty sure that's rat faeces," he says, as Sam first bends to look then backs smartly away. "I think that means this girl died exactly where you found her, in that alley. I think she was on the ground as he attacked her, and at some point she tried desperately to crawl away."

"So where do you fink the 'eads are? Did 'e take 'em? Like some sort o' resurrection man?"

"I don't think so. A whole body would have been far more valuable, so why leave so much behind. And in any case it's a dying trade. There just isn't the demand for cadavers anymore, not since the Anatomy Act."

"So why then? Why does 'e do it?"

Charles takes a ragged breath. "Because I think he takes pleasure in it."

Back out on the street, the strolling crowds are enjoying the sunshine, and the pub opposite the police-station has all its windows open, and paying pundits spilling (in some cases literally) onto the pavements. The air is full of shouts and laughter and the tinny repetition of a barrel-organ somewhere nearby. Charles suggests a quick pint, if only to wash the taste of death from their mouths, but for perhaps the first time ever Sam shakes his head in a quick no, saying he needs to report back to Rowlandson. The two part on a handshake, and as Charles watches Sam go whistling back up the street, he's suddenly aware that he's being observed. At the head of the alley at the side of the pub, where even the midday sun cannot reach, a man is watching. Watching and, it seems, waiting, for it is only when Sam is out of sight and ear-shot that he spits into the gutter, adjusts his collar, and saunters slowly forwards.

"Mr Maddox," he says, in a languid, musical Irish drawl.

He does not offer his hand, and Charles doesn't, either. But the two of them have clearly met, for Charles inclines his head in the briefest of nods. "O'Riordan. What do you want?"

A wink then, and a smile that lifts only one side of his mouth. "Why, information, Mr Maddox. Don't I always?"

"I don't think I should be talking to the press—for a start I'm not official any more, as well you know—"

That smile again, and Charles can smell the stout now, too. "Well, wouldn't that be the very reason I wanted to speak to you. Because you, as we might say, are cognisant without being obeisant, like yon wee Sam there."

Charles bridles. "Wheeler is an excellent policeman."

"I don't doubt it, but the more admirable he is as a copper, the less use he is to me. *He* will feel bound to keep his mouth shut and his nose clean, especially with that nice shiny badge he has so very recently acquired. *You*, on the other hand, are free to apply judgement, and discretion, and—"

"Don't waste your breath flattering me, O'Riordan."

A shrug. "Will I be wasting my money offering you some liquid refreshment in this fine establishment here?"

"Smells like you've had plenty already."

"Well, you took your time, didn't you? Which is hardly surprising. In the circumstances."

"I'm not thirsty," says Charles, turning away, but O'Riordan grabs his arm. "Look," he hisses, and now all that Irish charm is fled, "*I know all about it.* Those whores with their heads cut off and their hearts cut out. First murdered, then mutilated, and their body parts scattered God knows where. Three, is it, now, or four? How many more before Bow Street owns up and admits what's going on? How much longer before this town is gripped by a terror the like of which it has never known before? Because it will all come out, you know. Sooner or later. The tarts are talking, and you and I both know what that means. Better, surely, the police has a chance to present its case—prove what it's doing to catch this fiend before more women die."

"I wouldn't listen to every tale a whore tells you," says Charles quickly, flushing a little despite himself. "It's just some pimp—some street thug—"

O'Riordan smiles. "Nice try, but you're not going to fob me off that easily. I know you've seen those marks on the bodies, and I know *you know what they mean*. I'm sure I don't need to elaborate, not with where you've been spending *your* time of late—"

Charles stares at him for a moment, then looks away. A gesture O'Riordan clearly takes—or mistakes—for acknowledgement.

"Look, Maddox, I'm no fool, and I'm no dupe, either. I know it sounds crazy—like something out of folklore or a bloody freak show— but if there's another rational explanation, well I for one would like to hear it."

Charles is still silent, still staring resolutely into the middle distance; his face is motionless but his brain is in wheels.

O'Riordan nods. "All right, have it your own way. If you change your mind, you know where to find me. But if there's another—if that latest tart isn't the last—"

Charles glances quickly at him.

O'Riordan's eyes narrow. "Let's just say I can't sit on a story like this forever."

And then he spits again and walks away up the street.

Charles turns towards the pub and shoulders half-blindly through the lunchtime crowd to the door, leaving at least one disgruntled customer splashed with drink. Inside, the taproom is loud and rowdy but he scarcely notices either the noise or the slightly stale beer the landlord clatters down in front of him. What the hell did O'Riordan mean? Whoever it was who killed those girls, he was flesh and blood, not some make-believe ogre out of a child's nightmare. And what about that reference to where Charles has been? Was O'Riordan suggesting some madman committed those crimes—some escapee from a lunatic asylum? But how can the man possibly know about that? Charles has told no-one, not even Sam, not even *Maddox*. His heart is beating now, in fear of betrayal, but he tells himself he's jumping to conclusions. There's absolutely no way O'Riordan could have found out what happened to him in Melk. Though what he *might* know, Charles thinks, suddenly alert, is that he's been on the Continent—that he is only just returned from Austria. It's quite possible that news of that trip got round. So is *that* what he meant? And if you add that to the reference to folklore—

Charles tosses two pennies on the counter and pushes the tankard away.

"'Ere," says the landlord, in wounded tones. "That's my best ale, that is."

But Charles has already left.

Back down Haymarket, across Trafalgar Square and towards the Strand, where he calls in at Buckingham Street for a few moments to check on his uncle, and then heads north through Covent Garden where the costers are just heading raucously home, women in twos and threes smoking clay pipes, and the men leading exhausted horses thankful for an empty cart. The noise dips as Charles passes the Bow Street police-station, where the pavements are (unsurprisingly) a little clearer of trodden cabbage and the doorsteps a little emptier of drunks, and once he has skirted the edge of Seven Dials and Tom-All-Alone's the neighbourhood nicens and the passers-by with it, and having safely dodged the cabs and omnibuses on Oxford Street he's very soon turn-

ing into Great Russell Street, and the serene classical colonnades of
the British Museum. Well, perhaps not completely serene, since the
façade will not be finally completed until 1852, and the shouts of
the workmen and the clangs of hammers rise above the babble of the
crowds gathered about the steps for one of the special Exhibition
openings of the King's Library. Charles has been coming to this building for years, and used to live only a few streets away, so he ably evades
the straggling bystanders and makes his way inside. The reading room
is cool and quiet after the heat outside. Double height, book-lined,
with a gallery running round the upper levels, and an ornate coffered
ceiling rather reminiscent of its counterpart at Castle Reisenberg.
Though that particular resemblance Charles crushes before it can gain
any mind.

Most of the desks in the room are unoccupied, the sun having
tempted even the scholars to laziness. There's only one or two portly
stalwarts Charles knows of old, and a much younger man, with dark
red hair and a little pointed beard, who is just taking his seat. Charles
goes to the desk at the far end of the room and asks for the attendant's
assistance in finding a work on the folktales of the countries of the
central European continent. The pasty-faced librarian (who has certainly not been spending any time in the sun) looks thankful to have
something useful to do, and after consulting various catalogues and
running up and down various book-steps, returns to Charles's side
with a small but clearly very aged book. The edges of the pages are
jagged and badly cut, the typeface heavy and Gothic, and the paper
brown with dryness and years. More to the present point, at least, the
title is in German. Charles is about to ask whether the man can help
with translation as well as tracking down, when one of the senior li-
brarians comes a few yards into the room and beckons the young assistant away.

Charles sits down at the nearest desk with a sigh, reduced to the
state of a child with a picture-book. Because there are, he discovers at
once, pictures in this book, even if they are only woodcuts and many of
them very crude. Charles smiles, rather loftily, at page after page of
witches in pantomime pointed hats, some flying on broomsticks, some

feeding their supposed feline familiars (the majority of which look no more menacing than Charles's own cat), and others on their knees, lining up—as far as he can make out—to kiss the devil's protruding arse. But his smile dies when he turns a page to find a young girl lying in an open grave with a stake driven through her heart, and a man taking an axe to her throat, as a huge bat hovers menacingly above him in a darkening sky, and a wolf-like dog-beast grovels in the dirt.

Charles studies the illustration intently for a few minutes, making a note or two in his pocket-book, and glancing up every few moments to see if the librarian shows signs of returning. It's then that he hears a discreet cough from his right, and sees the young man with the red hair is looking in his direction.

"I could not help noticing," the stranger says, in an undertone. "You appear to require some assistance, perhaps with the language of the book you have requested? I am fluent in the German tongue, and would be happy to assist you."

Charles gets to his feet at once, and moves along to the chair next to the young man's desk.

"I would indeed be most grateful. These are the pages that interest me," he says, opening the book at the image of the grave.

The young man scans the text, then glances at Charles, clearly intrigued at his choice of subject-matter.

"I am writing a novel," says Charles quickly. "I thought I might set my tale in some wild and remote region, where such ludicrous beliefs still hold sway. You know how avid the public is for sensation."

The young man nods: Charles's rather grubby hands and ill-matched clothes clearly pass muster for a writer, and especially an unpublished one.

"I see," he says with a smile. "All is thus easily explained!"

Turning to the book again he flicks backwards a few pages, then forwards again. "This section of the volume treats of a species of evil spirit known as *stregoica*. They are the souls of the Undead, condemned to walk the earth forever and know no rest. They are able, if need arise, to run as a wolf, or fly as a bat, or pass through walls like the mist of the air, but preserve in all other outward respects the form and appearance of their human incarnation. They betray themselves only by the fact that they cast no shadow, can abide no mirror, and are never seen to eat the food of the earth."

The young man turns another page. "These spirits may be destroyed only by filling the mouth with the flowers of the garlic plant, and by taking such brutal means as you see depicted here. Those who resort to such methods act only in pity and compassion. To permit the souls of those they love to rest as true dead, and take their place among the angels." He smiles. "Or so such simple people believe."

"And a stake pierced through the heart—that is the only method that may be employed?"

The young man shakes his head. "No, it is equally efficacious to re-move the heart altogether and burn it. These measures—it is believed—will prevent the *stregoica* from leaving the grave wherein they are first laid, and prevent them from commencing their unholy predation upon the bodies of the living."

"And how do they do that—what form does that take?"

The young man raises an eyebrow. "You do not know? I had as-sumed you had already discovered as much. The *stregoica* draw their sustenance by drinking blood, sinking their teeth into the throats of their hapless victims, and rendering them, in their turn, accursed. The Undead may thus be identified by the small puncture wounds which may be observed upon their necks, which do not close, and do not heal. It is the blood of young women the *stregoica* desire most, and that of untouched virgins that savours sweetest of all. They will spare no effort to come by it. Or so it says here."

Charles sits back. If it wasn't clear to him before, it is now. "Vampires," he says softly, shaking his head. *"Vampires."*

So much is his mind working, that it's a moment before he realises the young man is still watching him.

"It is the ideal topic," he says hastily, flushing a little. "Indeed I am surprised it has not been chosen before."

"But did not the Lord Byron commence such a tale? I seem to recall a title of that kind."

Charles says nothing; he happens to have rather an extensive knowledge—of that summer on Lake Geneva when *The Vampyre* was begun, and how both that and another far more famous book came to be written, but it is not a subject he will discuss with strangers. Not now, not ever.

"You are correct," he answers eventually. "Lord Byron's story was completed some time later, by his doctor, John Polidori. But that novel is of a wholly different order. It is—quite literally—bloodless compared with what you have just told me. Compared with what a modern writer might make of it. As I said, the public is avid for sensation—or at least the female component thereof. I cannot believe any rational or educated man would give credence to such absurd and outdated superstition."

The two of them exchange a smile—being, of course, both rational and educated men—and the stranger hands Charles back the book. It's a small volume, and their fingers touch, and there's a moment of clumsiness—a moment when neither draws back, and then both look away. And when Charles does at last glance up and their eyes meet there is—something, some unspoken message that makes him redden and pull back, just as the other man appears to be making a movement, so slight as to be almost imperceptible, towards him. Both are blushing now, and the young man covers his own embarrassment by making a great fuss of extracting his card from the pocket of his coat.

"If I may be of further assistance, please do not hesitate. I will be in London until my own work here is concluded."

Charles looks at it, then tucks the card into the pocket of his coat. "I am afraid I have omitted to bring my own cards with me this morning. But I am indebted to you for your help."

It's a lie—or at least part of it is, since he has those cards in his pocket just now. And even though he is genuinely grateful for the young man's help, he has no desire to see him again, far less tell him where he lives.

Out on the steps he takes a deep breath and tries to collect his thoughts. It's all nonsense—*clearly* it's all nonsense, but he can see exactly what the likes of O'Riordan will make of it, and pure reason is no antidote to that sort of idiocy. No, the only way to confound this ludicrous theory is by finding a better one. The *real* one. And in the meantime he can at least put a question in O'Riordan's mind—make him think twice before he makes a public and permanent fool of himself. Because that's what he'll do, Charles has no doubt of that. But far better for all concerned to end this madness before it ever gets that far—tell O'Riordan there was nothing even remotely resembling bite marks on that corpse in the Vine Street morgue and put a stop to his mischief-making once and for all. But to do that, he'll have to go back and check the body again. And find some good excuse for doing so. Because the one thing he can't afford to do is admit the truth. Even Sam would laugh in his face if he knew what he was looking for. He can hardly believe it himself.

His leg is aching now, and he elects to get an omnibus back across town, forgetful, in his haste, how slow a journey that's likely to be. The 'bus rumbles jerkily, stopping every few yards, down Oxford Street and into Leicester Square. Piccadilly is still in full mercantile mode. The gas-lights are glowing golden in the windows of some of the city's most fashionable and expensive shops, and those stopping to browse are equally so, in their silks, and satins, and scents. But less than half a mile away, as Charles well knows, it's a very different story, in the unlit alleys and passage-ways mazing between the main street and the Market, where two of the girls were found, and one of them, Charles is sure, met her death.

It's gone six when he finally gets to Vine Street, and the attendant does look at him a bit oddly when he asks to be let into the morgue for the second time that day.

"I was just locking up, sir. You can't be too careful."

"I know, Pye, and I'm sorry. But I will only be a few minutes."

"I'm afraid I've extinguished the lamps—"

"Don't worry—if you can find me a bull's-eye lantern, that will more than suffice."

"Very well, sir. I'll be waiting for you in the front office."

And had you been with him, a few minutes later, when he pushed open the door to the darkened morgue, you might have been forgiven for believing—just for a moment—in the possibility of undeath. For as the swing of his lamp sends spectral shadows leering from wall to wall, the corpses under their stained sheets seem to move, and flinch, and yearn for life, and the dull eyes of the dead faces glitter suddenly with an impossible wakefulness. Charles hesitates a moment in the doorway, then swallows hard and makes his way—careful in the dimness on the slime-slopped floor—to where the headless girl's remains still lie.

He stands the lantern on the edge of the slab, and lifts the sheet. Then takes a deep breath and bends over her. It's almost unbearable to breathe so close, but he has to have proof, not just supposition, however rationally founded. He has to look O'Riordan in the face and refute his ridiculous theory with actual observation. And at first, it is exactly as he remembered—so little left of the neck it's unlikely any such marks could remain, even if they had once been there, and the rest so blotched with dirt and putrefaction that he would never have seen them anyway. It's tempting to leave it at that—to get out of this disgusting place as quickly as he can—but he is a scientist, and a purist, and he will do this properly or not at all. He goes across to a table that holds a jug and basin, and dips his handkerchief in the water. Then he carries it, dripping, back to the corpse, and starts to ease the filth from the base of the neck. And as the muck lifts away he finds himself staring—staring in a desperate disbelief—

"What the bloody 'ell are you doin' 'ere?"

The door is open, and standing in its streaming light is Sam. Sam and behind him the attendant and two red-faced young constables, carrying a stretcher.

"I—I—Well—"

But he is saved from further immediate embarrassment, when one of the young constables loses his grip for a moment and the stretcher tilts dangerously.

"Watch what yer doin' there, Madsen," says Sam quickly, with all the sternness of newly acquired rank. "Let's get 'er onto a slab, shall we, before there's a mis'ap."

The two officers manoeuvre the stretcher around the cadavers to one of the few empty spaces, and then retreat smartly to the door. The younger is already looking greenish, and coughing into his handker-chief.

"Found this one in the Market not an hour since," continues Sam, seemingly unaware of his friend's discomfiture, or his unaccustomed silence. "Fort it'd could o' been anovver one for a minute. We've got extra men patrollin' there at the moment, not just 'cause of the killin's but 'cause the knobs want the town to look all clean 'n' tidy for all these bloody tourists. No-one wants to trip over a tart while they're out shoppin' for souvenirs, least of all the old hags that do the Park at night. Sooner the soddin' Exhibition's over and done wiv the better if you ask me. Ain't been nuffin' but more bloody work, and that's a fact. Though when you look at the state those old crones are in I don't know why our killer didn't pick on one of 'em. None of 'em are in any state to put up much of a struggle. It must be young ones he wants, though why he does what 'e does to 'em, Gawd alone knows."

"You said this wasn't another victim, though?" asks Charles, recovering some composure and moving towards the body.

"I were there meself, as it 'appens. We were just movin' on one of the old tarts when anovver of 'em comes staggerin' out of a side alley, screamin' and pointin' back behind her as if all the devils in 'ell were after 'er. By the time I got to 'er she were collapsed on the ground, bab-blin' and sayin' she'd seen some bloke runnin' off towards Piccadilly.

And that's when I saw this one. She were lyin' further along the alley, face-down in the dirt. Can't o' been long 'cause she were still warm."

He takes the sacking from the body. Her dress is poor-quality fabric, and there's a little flower tattoo on her ankle. You wouldn't need to be a detective to deduce this woman's profession. She must have been pretty, living, but her red lips are twisted in pain, and her eyes wide in terror. Her dyed hair is lurid in the glare and her skin is as white as leprosy; *"The Night-mare Life-in-Death was she."*

"The tattoo might 'elp us identify 'er, at least," says Sam. "But there were no blood at the scene, and no signs of injury, not that I could see. And given that this one is most definitely still in possession of 'er 'ead I fink we can safely assume this ain't got nuffin' to do wiv our killer."

But that's not what Charles is staring at. For there, on her neck, are two small round holes. White at the edges. And unhealed.

CHAPTER SIX

Lucy's journal

IT IS MANY days since I have written in this journal, days in which we have travelled across Europe by train and carriage, and seen, once again, the cities that peopled my childhood. Prague, Leipzig, Heidelberg, Paris. I have felt so much better since we left Vienna—felt so much more myself—that I would have lingered far longer in Paris, in the hopes that my recovery might be supported by surroundings I always loved, but my father would not hear of it, saying that we had passages booked for England, and business to be conducted there, though what that business was he did not say, assuring me only that he had arranged no spectacle and planned no performance. It was the following day that we set out once more, north to Ostende, and the ship for England. Three days we were at sea, the water calm and the winds gentle, until the captain came to us one morning as we breakfasted, saying he believed the weather might be set to change, and though he hoped to make landfall before the storm came, we should secure our possessions as well as we might, and make ready to retire belowdecks should need demand it. I found it hard to believe so great a tempest could be coming, seeing the white mares' tails high in the pearly blue sky and the wide sweep of sea barely rippling in the breeze, but the man had some knowledge that I did not possess, for by sunset the clouds had amassed into great heaving battlements of every colour—red, violet, orange, and green, flaming at the west in the dying sun, and darkening behind us as the storm gathered pace. We could see, far ahead in the distance, the lights of the little town my father told me was our destination, and as the wind began to rise the captain rigged the ship as high as he dared, desperate to outrun the storm and make port before nightfall. But there was no time. There was a moment of deathly stillness, when the wind seemed to die in the sails, and then all at once we were struggling to descend the steps to our quarters, as the ship climbed and plummeted in waves twenty feet high, and water bucketed over the gunwales. I could hear sea-birds wailing like lost spirits above our heads, and the deafening *boom boom boom* as the prow thundered repeatedly against the sea. The captain had by then lashed himself to the helm, for fear of being swept overboard, and it must have taken a will of iron to remain there, at his post, as the ship raced madly towards shore. The entrance to the harbour was narrow and perilous, and I clung to my father as the wind threw us, again and again, towards a great flat reef on which so many past ships had foundered.

"There are people on the cliff!" cried my father then, looking from the porthole. "They have seen our plight—some have brought lamps to help signal our way!"

We both watched then, scarcely breathing, as the captain made one last desperate attempt to steer our passage, and suddenly, by what luck or skill I do not know, we were plunging forwards between the two piers of the little harbour and pitching, with a violent jolt and the scrape of wood against stone, as every spar and rope on the ship seemed to spring loose and crash about the deck, against the sea wall.

We were hurled, both of us, against the door of our cabin, and lay on the floor a few moments, scarcely believing we still breathed. And then there were shouts above, and numbers of townspeople started to swarm over the ship, commending the captain for his courage, and helping us up the steps and along a strip of wood that had been laid by way of a makeshift drawbridge between the deck and the wall. The storm was passing fast now, and by the time our boxes were unloaded and a carriage commanded, the wind had dropped and the rain was hardly more than a thin drizzle. I could see little of the town in the gloom, and as the horses pulled away from the quayside my father told me that he had arranged for one of the local women to open up our house and lay in such provisions as we might need.

"I thought you should prefer that," he said, somewhat distractedly, looking back to where a small crowd was still gathered about the man hauling our luggage onto a cart, and pressing close to read the labels, "to spending our first nights in a public inn or lodgings."

I smiled at him, feeling suddenly a rush of hope. It would be a new commencement for us. A new life of peace and tranquillity, where I could be myself, and no longer bear the burden of being *"She who summons souls."*

We crossed a bridge over the water towards the far side of town and turned towards the open sea, climbing all the time along narrow cobbled streets until we drew up outside a cottage with lights in every window and pots of flowers by the door. A bright fire was burning in the hearth as we stood in the vestibule taking off our coats and hats.

"It is but a small house," my father said, and then, more softly, as if to himself, as he looked around, "rather smaller, indeed, than I recall."

"It is perfect, Papa!" I said, but even as I smiled at him I suddenly felt a little faint, and my limbs began to tremble so that I had to put out my hand to steady myself.

"Come," said my father quickly, "it is no wonder if you are tired, after the alarms of our arrival. Go and sit by the fire and I will make some tea. I believe Mrs Croft has left us milk."

And so I sat, looking about me, realising slowly that my father, no doubt from a wish that I should feel at once at home, must have sent some of our possessions ahead of us, for I recognised first one and then another—the little statuette on the mantelpiece, the wax roses under their glass dome, and there, on the low table, the scrapbook I have compiled since I was a child, year after year pasting into it the playbills and the newspaper cuttings and all the little mementos of my father's success. It is a long time since I have added anything to its pages, and I wondered if by leaving it in view my father was encouraging me, in his delicate and discreet way, to take up the scissors once more and thereby find some useful employment to fill my hours. I took it onto my lap and turned back to the very beginning, and the daguerreotype of my mother with my seven-year-old self on her lap. It was a little blurred, where we had not sat quite so still as the artist had bid us, and time had so deepened the contrast of pale and dark that my mother looked a little severe, even forbidding, but it was in every other way so good a portrait, and so very like, that by the time my father returned with the tray, the tears were streaming silently down my face.

"Lucy, Lucy," he said, as he saw what I was looking at. "There is no need to distress yourself so. You must think now of yourself. Of your own health. She would not wish to see you so. She would wish you to be happy."

I smiled then, a little weakly, I own, and took a deep breath, then I sat up straight as my mother always taught me and took the teapot in my hand. "Shall I pour for you, Papa?"

I slept a deep and dreamless sleep that night, and woke to a flood of orange light as rich and strange as anything my father had ever magicked. I did not know where I was for a moment, and started up in my bed, my heart pounding, until I realised it was nothing but the dawn. I had never wakened by the sea before, and when I rose and went to the window the water was running like liquid gold under the huge and slowly rising sun, and the gulls wheeling dark like broken fragments of midnight. And when I looked back towards the town I saw the abandoned abbey standing high on the promontory, its ruined arches black against the flaming sky. I remembered my memory then—how I had imagined that ruin, and the birds circling above it, and some impulse seized me to go outside, in all that glowing light. Not the false light of the *phantasmagoria,* kindled by artifice in the cavernous underground, but the pure bright light of an ordinary new day. I dressed myself quickly, then slipped out of the house as silently as I was able, and turned towards the harbour. The boats were just, at that hour, coming in from sea, and I watched as the fishermen hauled their catch onto the quayside and the fish slithered silver from the nets. The men eyed me curiously though without discourtesy, as I passed, one or two touching their caps, but aside from them, I saw scarce a living soul. It was like a doll's town, all laid out for my own pleasure, and I slowed my pace, determined to be charmed by all I saw—the huddle of brightly painted houses rising above the quay, the neat little boats bobbing on the water, the lobster pots stacked like one vast honeycomb of basketwork, and the horde of hopeful local cats, milling about the landing boats.

It was only when I had crossed the bridge and commenced the long climb to the abbey that I began to doubt my own strength. But I told myself that this, too, would pass. That the sea, and the clean air, and my new life would wash my old troubles away, like flotsam from the white sand. As I drew nearer the abbey I saw that there was a smaller church before it, and a graveyard filled with ancient grey stones, some of them tilted like sails in the wind, as if the wizened mariners buried beneath had the rigging of their own tombs. I was smiling to myself at this idea when I suddenly came to a stop, my hand to my mouth. For there, by the wall where the stones were not so old, and not so lichened, I saw a name I knew.

It was my mother's grave.

I had known; in some part of my mind, I must have known. We had brought her body home, and here, then, she must have been laid. But I did not know which cemetery had received her, and I had no recollection of ever seeing this stone. So moving in its sheer simplicity: BELOVED MOTHER AND WIFE. And the carving of an angel holding a little child. There were tendrils of ivy entwined about the base, and I bent down and removed my gloves so that I could strip the leaves away. I was so absorbed in my task, and in the cleaning of the letters with my handkerchief, that I did not notice there was a little wiry dog at my feet. I did not notice, in fact, until it stood up on its back legs and started to paw my dress, begging in the most insistent and winning fashion.

I looked round and saw that a young lady sat on a wooden bench some yards away, where the cemetery overlooked the town and the sea. A young lady dressed all in white. It came to me then how I had pictured a girl in white here, seated alone, and feared for a moment that my mind had once more betrayed me, and she was no more than an illusion conjured by my imagination, like the colours I had conjured in the *phantasmagoria* flame. But no. This young lady was as real as her dog, which by way of proof had by then left several muddy pawprints on the hem of my gown.

"Jip! Jip!" I heard her cry then, perhaps surmising what had happened. "Come here, you naughty dog! The lady does not wish to be bothered by you!"

I hastened to reassure her that I was, on the contrary, quite charmed by her little companion, and led him back towards where his mistress had remained seated all the while. She was of the same age as me, with a face as pale as my own, but where my hair is thick and lustrous and curls to my waist, hers was dull and brown and cut short about her neck. I remembered how my own hair had been shorn after my mother died, and I was all those months confined to my bed and wondered if she, too, had perhaps been lately ill.

"It is an unusual name for a pet," I remarked, as the dog settled down at his mistress's feet.

She smiled. "It began as a joke. My brother bought me Jip as a gift for my last birthday, and my name being Dora, and the first instalments of Mr Dickens's book having just then appeared, Tom thought it a fine jest to name Jip after Dora Spenlow's little dog. That jest has fallen a little flat since, of course." She sighed, and caressed Jip's rough head. "My pet does indeed resemble his namesake, but I am doing my best not to emulate mine."

I did not know what she meant by this, not having read this book or even heard of it, so I was forced merely to smile and pet the dog, in the hopes of concealing my ignorance.

"I am forgetting my manners," she said, holding out her hand. "My name is Dora—Dora Holman."

I introduced myself, and she perceived then, I think, that my English, though perfect, had the ring here and there of my travels, and she asked if I was visiting the town.

"My father was born here," I told her, "but left many years ago. We have travelled much on the Continent, and now we are returned to make this our home."

"I have lived here all my life," she said, smoothing her dress. "It was once so quiet, this place, but now it draws so many tourists—especially when the weather is bright and they gather in their dozens hoping to see the ghost of the nun who founded the abbey. They say you can see her, wrapped in her shroud, when the sun strikes the highest window at a certain time of day, and there are others who swear she walks here by night, clad all in white. It is all nonsense, of course, nothing more than a trick of the light, or an owl, caught in the corner of the eye, but it draws people from miles about. I confess I do not understand this new compulsion so many have to terrify themselves, whether it be by reading silly novels, or watching even sillier things performed onstage." She sighed sadly. "I fear life brings terrors enough of its own, without one needing to seek them."

I turned away, towards the water, a little ashamed. Nothing in the world would have induced me to tell this girl my past; I wished to leave all that life behind me, on the farther side of the sea.

"That is one reason I come here so early," she continued. "When the weather is good my maid will bring me up here in our donkey-cart, and I can sit here with Jip and watch the sun rise, and see scarcely anyone until she comes again to bring me home. The air is so clear and restorative in the early morning. Or it is usually so."

She coughed then for some moments, and held her handkerchief to her face, and when her hand dropped to her lap I saw there were two spots of blood on the white linen. And then I was sorry, for I knew what that meant, and I saw in her eyes that she, too, knew it, and yet was reconciled to it.

She folded the handkerchief calmly, though her breath was becoming every moment more laboured. "If you will forgive me, I think I should return. It is no doubt the effect of last night's storm. I do not know if you were abroad, but I am told the vessel that came in was all but given up for lost. My father said that one of the old sailors claimed only the devil could have brought that ship home."

She was by then coughing so wretchedly that I feared we could not possibly return to the town without some assistance, and looked about anxiously for someone I might call to. But there being no-one nigh and her maid not expected for more than an hour, I had no choice but to offer her my arm and hope we could descend the steps in time. She leaned heavily against me as we slowly traced the long path back down towards the town, pausing more and more frequently to catch her breath, and it was half an hour more before we reached the tall and handsome house by the harbour that she told me was her home. The maid who answered my ring looked at Miss Holman in alarm, calling out at once for her master, and the last thing I saw before the door closed was a tall handsome man in a formal coat rushing down the passage towards Dora and shouting for the footman to go for the doctor.

My own father was scarcely less distressed when he opened the door of our own cottage.

"Where have you been?" he cried, seizing me by the shoulder. "I have been half-frantic with worry—I thought you had walked again in your sleep and I have been combing the streets for hours, fearing I might turn the next corner and find you as I found you once before—

or the victim of some even worse fate. You are *ill,* Lucy, how could you leave the house without informing me?"

I thought then, too late, that I might have left him a note.

"I am sorry, Papa. I woke at dawn and the sunrise was so beautiful. I have only been walking in the town."

He turned and went back into the sitting-room and sat down heavily on the sopha, and when I followed him I saw that he had his head in his hands. "You owe it to me to be more careful. Remember what I promised your mother on her death-bed. That I would not allow you out of my sight. All these years, I have kept that promise."

I sat down next to him and took his hand. "And all these years I have needed that loving care, but now I am a grown woman. I know my mother feared what might befall me alone in the crowds of Vienna, but what harm could come to me here? Indeed, it seems to be entirely the opposite, for I have found myself a friend."

"A friend?" said my father abruptly, looking up. "But you know no-one here. Who is this *friend*?"

I hastened to reassure him, describing my encounter with Miss Holman, and the house where I had returned with her, and he seemed a little appeased, saying he knew of the family, and her father was a widower and a man of some repute in the neighbourhood. He said at last that he would have a lock affixed at once to my bedroom door, and gave me his permission to call the next day and enquire after Miss Holman's health, and then we changed the subject, by silent consent, and I went to make the breakfast.

7 APRIL

It has been two weeks now, and my Dora and I have met every day. When she has been well enough we have walked a little together and she has shown me the town, the shops selling the pretty ammonites that stud the cliffs hereabouts, and the jewellery of jet that is another of this district's claims to renown. We bought each other gifts that day, matching brooches of intricate carved flowers, and I have mine on the desk before me as I write these words. But she has been too wearied to walk much, and as a consequence we have spent our hours sitting on that bench I now think of as our own. I have laid new flowers every day on my mother's grave, and I have thrown a little ball for Jip, but mostly we have simply sat together in a comfortable silence, looking down at the harbour and the town, and the changing character of the sea, as the wind and the clouds and the water blur and separate into all the colours of the sky.

I do not think I will ever tire of that view, and Dora laughed at me yesterday, saying that I had not even explored the abbey yet, and if I wished, she felt strong enough in the pale new sunshine, to show it to me herself. And so we walked at her slow pace up to the broken salt-bitten cloisters where the monks once prayed, and worked, and sang, and now lie sleeping beneath the thin dry grass. It was a cold day, and there were few visitors wandering the desolate nave, save one or two hardy young men, one of whom tipped his hat to us as we passed, in the most serious fashion. And once or twice I glimpsed the figure of an older, taller man striding ahead of us, followed—or at least so I thought—by a large black dog. I think Jip saw it, too, because he retreated suddenly to his mistress's side, growling and snarling.

"Jip, Jip!" she cried gaily, "I do declare you grow more like Dora Spenlow's bad-tempered pug every day!"

I hastened to excuse her pet, saying I believed Jip was only seeking to protect her, but by then the man and the dog were nowhere to be seen and she teased me, saying I was seeing ghosts. I laughed, then, in my turn, but I could not smile, and I think she guessed I was troubled in some way by her words, for she laid her hand kindly on my arm and said that Alice would be waiting with the cart, and it was time to return for luncheon.

"And you are to eat with us today! Papa has expressly asked me to invite you." And as I opened my mouth in demurral, "Do not worry. We will send a message to your father so he will not be concerned."

There was a little colour in her cheeks as she said this, and it struck me that her breathing had likewise been less strained, despite the exertions of our excursion. I have never had a friend of my own before—never had someone my own age I could talk with, and laugh with—but I am sure that the improvement in my own spirits these last days is in no small measure due to my Dora's companionship, so perhaps it may have been the same for her. I know only that I have dreamed no dream since we came to this town, and neither waked nor walked by night.

And just as I have never had a friend of my own, I have never dined in a house not my home, and I confess I was a little daunted by the prospect of meeting Dora's family. But my fears were groundless. They were so very kind, so very energetic, so very lively, I had no time to feel gauche or in the way, and by the time the roast mutton was being carved by Mr Holman it seemed as if I had known them half my life. Dora has a sister some five years younger than herself, and a brother two years older, who has unruly brown hair, and inky finger-nails, and a ready smile. He is training to be a lawyer, like his father, which I suppose must explain the ink, but he confided in me that if left to his own inclination he would far rather be a poet. He has writ-ten one part of a most ambitious work on the subject of the sack of Rome by the Vandals which he promised to show me, though I no-ticed his sisters seemed not to take his literary ambitions very seri-ously, and ragged him mercilessly upon his lofty choice of subject, saying he had written several hundred lines and yet still not con-cluded even his prolegomena.

Ever since I learned that Dora had no mother, I have kept studiously from that subject, knowing how much it pains me to talk of my own, but there was no such reticence in Bourne House—the late Mrs Holman smiled down benignly upon us from her portrait over the mantelpiece, and was talked of by them all without the slightest awkwardness. It was as if they kept her alive by the simple expedient of treating her as though she were still among them, and it seemed to me that the house was the happier for it. And when they told tales of their many elderly and eccentric relations, it struck me that I knew hardly anything of my own wider family, and resolved to ask my father of them when I returned. After our meal, young Mr Holman offered to escort me back to the cottage, and I found myself blushing in quite the silliest way, and I know I must have looked very stupid as I assured him that I was quite happy to walk the few yards home alone.

I was still preoccupied by this exchange—going through it again in my mind and wishing I had the saying of it over again and more sensibly—when I turned my key in our own lock, and heard the sound of voices. My father's voice and another man's, speaking low, so that I could not hear what it was he said. I closed the door silently behind me and went towards the sitting-room. The door was ajar and I could see my father standing by the fire, and opposite him, on a hard-backed chair, a tall man in a dark coat with thin grey strands of hair and a blotched and haggard face. I took a step back then, hardly knowing what I did, and my father looked up.

"Lucy? Are you there?"

I did not move—could not move.

"Lucy?" my father said again, coming to open the door. "It is unlike you to skulk in the passage like a housemaid. Come and meet our distinguished visitor."

I looked at Father in sudden apprehension—if I was behaving in an uncharacteristic fashion then he, too, was speaking in a way I had never heard before. He took my hand—I might almost say roughly—and drew me after him into the room, and stood me before the man in black.

"This is my daughter, sir. This is Lucy."

I have sat here now, for near half an hour, my pen in my hand, trying to find the words to express the effect that man's presence had upon me. His appearance was unprepossessing, of that there is no doubt, but I am not so easily disquieted by the surfaces of things, knowing from experience how deceptive they can be. There was something repellent about him, but even that repellence had in it a quality of compulsion. I knew at once that this man had the power to compel the gaze—draw it and hold it until he himself chose the moment of dismissal, and I thought, for the first time since we left Vienna, of that spinning glass ball and how it would seize tiny pieces of metal in its invisible grasp, and hold them so hard they could not be torn away.

I stood there, staring at the floor, as my father introduced the man by some grand title that I did not catch, and explained to me, slowly and deliberately, that he had come expressly to see me—that we were fortunate that His Excellency was in England, having disembarked at Grimsby only a few days before. That he was an eminent scientist and had made a study of cases such as mine and might hold the key to my recovery—

"But I am already recovered," I said quickly, looking up at my father. "I am quite well now—I have no need of another doctor—"

"I am not a doctor, Miss Lucy," said the man, in a low rasping voice.

"It was our new spectacle," I continued, still staring at my father, "the ball of glass—that was what ailed me—I have not walked in my sleep once since we left it behind—and now I no longer need perform ever again—"

"I'm afraid you are mistaken," said my father quietly. "I brought you here to convalesce and recoup your spirits, but there will come a time not far hence when we will return to our former life. When we will *have* to return."

"But *why*?" I cried. "I am happy here—I am *well* here."

"Now you are being self-indulgent. And, indeed, selfish. Where do you think the money comes from to pay for this house? For your clothes? The food on the table? We have to earn our bread, Lucy, and the only way we may do that is by the exercise of our craft. You have a duty to yourself, and to *me*, to return in due course to Vienna and play your full part—your full and *usual* part—in the success of our enterprise. I invited our visitor here with that end in mind, and I expect you to give him whatever assistance he needs to effect it."

He had never spoken to me so sternly before. It was as if some monster had taken my darling father's place, some monster with no care for my feelings—no interest in my happiness. As if someone else was giving voice to my father's words, just as we gave sound to our counterfeits of the dead.

"What must I do?" I said at last, my voice small.

"It is not so very daunting, my dear young lady," said the man. "We will start with questions only."

"What questions?" I said, looking for the first time into those strange silver eyes, and feeling my heart begin to beat harder.

"About yourself. About the nature of your indisposition. When it occurs and the form it takes. What seems to exacerbate it. Questions such as these. That is not so very distressing, I believe?"

I looked away. I did not want to talk to this man about myself, knowing by some instinct that he had the strength to prise from me all my secrets—that he could force into words those hidden fears I have striven so hard to suppress, and which, once uttered, I might no longer have the capacity to quell.

"I will try," I said, a little sullenly.

"Good," he replied. "Now we may hope to make some progress."

He told my father, then, that he must absent himself from the room and draw all the curtains close. I saw my father start a little anxiously at this, but the man insisted that these preparations were indispensable to the success of his method, and my father eventually nodded and did as he was bidden.

The man then drew one of the hard-backed chairs to the centre of the room and had me sit upon it. I hesitated a moment and then complied, whereupon he drew a matching chair, set it close before me, and sat down. He said nothing for some moments and I did not raise my head, and then suddenly he reached out and took my fingers in his own. I gasped at the touch of his dry and scaly skin and attempted to draw back, but his grip was strong, and he began to press his thumbs hard into the palms of my hands.

"Look at me," he said softly. "Look at me."

I raised my head at last and looked into those eyes, lit now only by the embers of the dying fire, and so pale there seemed scarcely an iris at all, only the deep black of the pupils, drawing me forwards, as if down a tunnel leading to the dark. And all the while the push, push, push of his thumbs in my palms.

And then he began to question me, and I heard my own voice answer as if it were not my own. A voice distant and slumberous, and as dull in tone as of one deeply drugged. I told him things I had forgotten, or did not even know I knew. I told him of the sleepwalking, and how it afflicts me always at the fullness of the moon, when my bleeds come. I told him, as I had told my father, of the Influencing Machine and the colours that rise from my fingers, so beautiful and cold. But I did not speak of the nightmare, and of that he did not ask.

And when it was over and he released me and let in the light, I sat shivering by the cold hearth, my body burning and my senses so heightened that I could hear my father talking with him in the vestibule, even though they spoke in whispers and the door was pulled shut.

"So what have you concluded? What is it that ails my daughter?"

"It is early to make a definitive diagnosis. But I do not believe her to be afflicted by some mental defect, such as I know you have feared."

"But what other explanation is there for such delusions—those colours she says she saw? Only the mad see things that are not there."

"It is one explanation, certainly, but not, I believe, the correct one in this case. It will be necessary for me to treat your daughter further—to enquire more profoundly into the deeper past. Questions such as the circumstances of the onset of her somnambulism. From what she has just told me it was exactly coincidental with the commencement of her first bleeds—is this true?"

"Both events occurred within weeks of her mother's death. It affected her deeply. Too deeply."

"Indeed. And your observation is apposite. There is something—some profound distress connected with her mother which is more than mere grief, and which I have not yet fathomed. But I do not believe it was the cause of her sleepwalking, or these new colours that she now sees."

"So what *is* the cause? Forgive me, Excellency, but you must appreciate the strain all this has placed upon me. I have even considered placing her in an institution—there were doctors in Vienna who advised it, not only lately but some years ago, when I found her one night in the street, half-dressed and acting like some common whore—"

"You may be assured that I will do my utmost to penetrate to the heart of the mystery. All may soon be elucidated. Good day to you."

14 APRIL

And that has been my life, this last week. I have spent my mornings in the air and the light with Dora, and my afternoons shut away, hour after hour alone in the dark, and with this man. Each time it is the same, the same questions, the same sense of departing from myself, and yet each time I have the sensation that he is drawing me deeper, probing me more intimately, laying me bare. And now when I dream, I dream of him, of those strange eyes, and those dry pressing hands, and the electric energy that seems to flow between us. And three times now, to my shame—I have dreamed so vividly it is more real to me than memory, of his body above me, and his face closing against mine, and that cold mouth sharp upon my neck, and I have woken to the sound of my own voice moaning, and a tingling wetness between my legs that has me twisting into my fevered pillow, with my own hand at my thighs.

I know it is wrong. I know that normal people do not dream such disgusting dreams, or find such pleasure in vileness, and when I walk in the bright breeze with Dora, talking of innocent daylight things, I have to turn my burning face away when the memories come unbidden of what I have done in the dark. And I understand, now, and for the first time, that abhorrent painting we brought to life in our lantern, and the girl who gasps with pleasure at the grinning demon's touch.

MIDNIGHT

Eight o'clock it was when he left me, saying I was almost ready—that the first phase of my treatment was nearly over, and within a few days he might consider me advanced sufficiently for the next to begin. Though he would not, despite my pleading, tell me what that entailed. I closed the door at length behind him and went to the window, watching him away down the street until he disappeared. My father was absent, having explained there were further possessions of ours that had not yet arrived and he wished to make enquiries at the custom-house. With nothing to do but await his return, I lingered there at the window, restless and dissatisfied, as the rising moon made the town into a tessellation of black and slate and grey. And then as I gazed I thought I saw something amid the abbey walls. It was so far away I could not be sure, but I thought I glimpsed a flicker of white, and I wondered at once about the tale they told of the woman who was said to haunt that place. The night was so beautiful, and the moon so near the full, I felt a sudden urge to drench myself in that bathing light, and I took my shawl and left the house as the church clock struck the half hour. There was hardly anybody abroad, and I crossed the bridge and climbed the steps towards the graveyard and the turn in the path where the abbey first lifts into view. I looked up towards it, but there was nothing, just the empty cloisters black against the sky and the clouds running over the moon. I stopped for a moment to catch my breath and caught a movement on the far side of the graveyard. My eyes had not deceived me. There was a woman all in white sitting on the bench, looking out to sea. And bending over her, the figure of a man. A tall man, in a long dark coat.

I hastened forwards as fast as I could, my heart beating against my ribs, and for several minutes the graveyard was hidden from my sight. And when I gained the gate at last and looked across, the moon slipped from behind the last cloud and flooded the graveyard in a sudden dazzling light. The man had gone. The woman was alone, and it was Dora.

I have sworn to tell the truth in these pages, and so I will confess it. All I felt that moment was a terrible overwhelming jealousy. I had thought myself his only charge—his only care—and now I found they had both been deceiving me. Was he treating her, as he was treating me? Why had she not told me that they were acquainted? And what had the two of them been doing here, alone, in the darkness, and without a chaperone? My heart was now pounding so hard I could scarcely breathe, though whether from the effort of the climb or from bitter rage I could not have told. I strode towards her through the gravestones, but as I approached my pace slowed. Her head was thrown back against the bench, and her lips were parted. Her handkerchief was in her lap, and on linen, breast, and skin there was a trail of blood.

"Dora!" I cried, kneeling before her, and taking her in my arms, all my jealousy forgotten in remorse, *"Dora!"*

She stirred then and opened her eyes, looking at me confusedly, saying that she had been dreaming.

"Where is he?" I demanded, grasping her frozen hand, terrified, because she could not walk, and I could not carry her. "He cannot be far away. He must help us."

She frowned at me, as if still half-dazed. "Who are you talking of? There is no-one here. No-one but me and Jip."

But when I looked about me I could not see the little dog anywhere.

"Wait here," I said urgently, taking my shawl from my shoulders and wrapping it tightly about her. "I will find help."

It was ten agonising minutes before I returned with the landlord of the lodging-house at the foot of the steps. I feared that when he opened the door to see my wild face and bloodied hands he must have thought me the victim, or even the perpetrator, of some violent misadventure. But he proved, once reassured, to be both kind and capable and went immediately back into the house to fetch blankets and a small flask of brandy before following me up to the burial-ground. We chafed Dora's cheeks and gave her sips of the liquid, but nothing seemed to warm her, so the man wrapped her in the blankets and carried her down the stairs to the town, saying as he lifted her that she was so light she seemed hardly heavier than his little grand-daughter of eleven. When we reached Bourne House at last we found that Mr Holman had already sent the servants looking for Dora in the streets thereabouts, and had been on the point of going himself to the graveyard, but only in a last desperation, as it was impossible she could have managed that climb alone. But manage it she had, for the Holmans' donkey-cart was in its accustomed place. Nor could anyone account for why Dora should have left the house alone, and in the dark. I thought I might know the answer to that question, but when I hinted I may have seen someone with her, it was clear that none of them recognised the man whom I described. The doctor then arriving, I took the opportunity to slip away, reaching home only a few minutes before my father. I told him I felt unwell and re-tired at once to my own chamber. And tonight, for the first time since we came here, I woke in the dark shivering at my window, and there are scratches on the glass that look like the marks of claws.

15 APRIL, NOON

I have just returned from Bourne House. My Dora slept badly, they tell me, complaining of the noise of some great bird battering at the shutters, though neither her sister nor the nurse heard anything un-toward. They told me I could not see her, but when Mr Holman saw my distress he relented, saying only that she had at last fallen into a fitful slumber and I must promise not to wake her. And so I crept softly to her bedside, and stood watching with her sister Emily, as

Dora shifted and moaned in her sleep, murmuring once or twice, but in no words I could understand. I have never seen her so pale; her lips were almost white and the hand resting on the coverlet hardly darker than the sheet.

"Where is Jip?" I whispered as we left, seeing the little basket empty at the foot of the bed.

"No-one has seen him since yesterday. Tom has gone out to find him—Dora would be distraught to wake and find him missing."

We closed the door quietly and went slowly down the stairs, and as we reached the hall the front door opened and young Mr Holman appeared in the doorway, with a bundle wrapped in sacking in his arms. But when he saw the two of us, his eyes widened in horror.

"No," he said quickly, backing away, "no."

But it was too late. Emily had already seen a small brown paw hanging down and rushed forwards. "But Tom, you have found him!"

And before he could stop her she had lifted the sacking and seen what lay beneath.

"Oh!" she cried, her hand to her mouth. "Who could do such a wicked thing to a defenceless little creature—it is horrible, *horrible!*"

I put my arm about her and turned away. But I had seen—and I still see now—the raw and gaping wound where some beast many times its size had torn open the poor dog's throat, and it had lain unseen and undiscovered until it had bled its life away.

18 APRIL

The morning after they found Jip, Mr Holman came to tell me Dora was dying. That the doctor could not understand why her condition should have worsened so suddenly, but no treatment he had attempted seemed to have made any difference and it was doubtful she would live past nightfall. I wept then, in my father's arms, and begged him to let me go to her. He was reluctant, at first, fearing I had not yet recovered my own strength, but at length he agreed.

I was horrified at the change in so few hours. If she had been pale before, I had no word for how she appeared to me now. Even her hair seemed ashen, and her face so translucent above the ruffled neck of her nightgown that I could see the thin blue veins beneath. Blue, not red, for there seemed no blood left in her, and the spots about the pillow were too vivid to have come from her exhausted frame. I could barely hear her breathing, but as the afternoon drew on and the light faded, her breath came in low heaving gasps, and her breast rose and fell as if in pain. And at the moment she passed from us I saw wings beating against the window, and heard that humming in my ears that has always been a harbinger of woe, and I was overwhelmed and knew no more.

I woke the next morning in my own bed, in the light from the sea, and it was some moments—some moments of blissful ignorance—before I remembered what had happened, and I felt the immensity of my grief engulf me. My father insisted that the doctor be called, and when I heard him say so my heart leapt for a shameful moment, thinking *he* would come, but it was only the portly town practitioner my father had in mind, who could prescribe me nothing more apposite than a tonic cordial and some days' rest.

To this I have submitted with a good grace. Until today, the day of her funeral. I begged my father, with tears in my eyes, to be permitted to attend her to her last resting-place—I would be careful, I said, he could accompany me, we would be there only a short time—but he was adamant, and this time he would not give way.

I have remained here, thinking of her, and watching the sky through the muslin blinds. It has been such a beautiful day, the sun bright and the wind soft, and the white and silent gulls lifting like a benediction in the air. And when it was over, Emily came to me, and sat with me, and told me that they had laid her near that bench she had loved so much, looking out to sea, and how their father had obtained a special permission for little Jip to rest there with her, in a casket at his mistress' feet. We both wept then, and truly I thought my heart would break.

"And she has your gift with her, too," said Emily at last, squeezing my hand. "She was all in white, apart from the black velvet band about her throat, and before they closed the coffin I pinned your little brooch there, as she so loved to wear it. My fingers trembled so I feared the pin had pricked her, but that was silly, was it not," she said, smiling tremblingly through her tears, "for now she feels no pain. And never will, ever more."

※ ※

And now I am awaiting him. He has not been here, not once, since I saw him that night with my darling Dora, but I received word today that he will come tonight, and though I am half-eaten-up with reproach and misgiving, still I have dressed myself in my best gown, and curled my hair, and placed the chairs carefully in readiness. And my hands tremble so, I can scarcely hold the pen.

19 APRIL

It was gone ten when at last he came. I had never seen him so distracted, so agitated. It was as if my own high-wrought state had communicated itself to him—as if we shared some connexion so profound that merely the sight of each other charges the air with silent speech.

"I will not treat you tonight," he said at once, seeing my preparations. "I have decided it is time to proceed to the next step."

He turned towards the window then, and spoke softly, as if for his hearing alone. "Such a night, such a prospect, may not come again."

"Of what does this next step consist?" asked my father, his hand on the back of the chair, and gripping it, I perceived, rather tighter than was necessary. I wondered then, as I have often done these last days, if he has come to regret his decision to summon this man, and it struck me how utterly our positions have exchanged.

"I am ready, sir," I said quickly. "Whatever this next step may be. If you think it will assist me, I am ready."

My father looked at me, and then at our visitor. No words passed between them but I knew the force of that gaze, and a moment later my father nodded, and made no demur when I was told to collect my warmest cloak, for I was going out.

Out into the chill of evening and a full moon now risen dazzling into the sky. There was a little dog-cart waiting at the kerb, and he held out his hand to help me up. We sat so close behind the driver that I could not speak without him hearing every word, and in some small part of my mind I wondered if the conveyance had been chosen precisely to prevent all conversation, so that I could not ask about Dora, or raise questions my companion had no wish to address.

We headed at once out of the town, towards the high lane that leads up towards the abbey precincts, where we came to a halt, and the driver being instructed to wait, we set off towards the ruins. The moon was directly above us, casting shadows sharp as noon, and printing the pale grass black with every curve and arch and line. And yet the abbey was not our destination, and my steps faltered when I realised where, in truth, he was taking me. He turned then, seeing my hesitation, and came so close that I could smell him—smell him as I did in my dreams, when that dry and metallic scent so lingers on my skin.

"There is nothing to fear, Lucy," he said, taking my chin in his hand and looking into my eyes. "I thought you would wish to bid your friend farewell?"

But not like this, I thought. *Not like this.* But how could I say so without giving offence, or receiving rebuke. And so I nodded, and he led me the last yards to the gate, and held it open, gesturing me to go before. I looked at him then in misgiving, wondering why he had led the way thus far but now wished me to precede him, but he merely smiled and lifted his hand towards the bench, and the grave, and the sea.

———

I thought at first that the fog must have rolled in from the shore. I had never yet seen a true sea fog, but the townsfolk have talked of them, and I knew the sailors' fear of ghost ships glimpsed amid the mist, and the muffled voices of the dead luring them to their wreck. But no; tonight the air was clear, and the wide bay glittered silently below us, and I knew that what I saw before me was neither the weather of the world nor the conjuration of man. Where they had laid her, where the earth was still dark with turning, and no stone yet stood, a pale glow rose in feathers of white flame, faint at first but gathering in strength, coiling and recoiling, mingling and separating until it seemed brightness welled from every inch of the grave, now like rain seen from afar, now like God in a pillar of cloud, and now like those eerie lights I saw once as a child, streaming green and white and purple across a frozen northern sky.

I moved slowly forwards, hardly knowing what I did, drawn as to a lodestone, until I could reach my hands into the waterfalling light and watch it run through my fingers, and dip and waver in my breath, and when I lifted my face into the icy flames I felt an energy I had no name for flood my being, as if all my veins ran cold with quicksilver.

I cannot tell how long it lasted, how long it was before I fell backwards, swooning, into his arms and he carried me like a lover to the bench and laid me down, bending over me as he had bent over Dora, his hands at my breast, loosening my clothes. "What did you see?" he said urgently, his face close to mine. "What did you see?"

I tried to explain as I struggled for my breath, that it was what I had seen before, in Vienna. The same, and yet not the same. That this was a light to pierce the heart with beauty and delight, but when I had touched the Influencing Machine it was pain, and the taste of metal in my mouth, and a rush which was not exhilaration but dread. I feared my answer might vex him, but he merely nodded as if my words were merely a confirmation of something he had already surmised long before, and I knew, afterwards, that I had pleased him.

———————

"There is blood on your lip," I said at last.

He stood then and walked away, and I saw him take his handkerchief from his coat.

"You saw nothing, did you?" I whispered, as he stood there, wiping his mouth.

"I have not your gift."

"So why did you bring me here—how did you know what I would see?"

He withdrew a little then, and looked out to sea.

"For centuries tales have been told of emanations of uncanny light at the site of new-dug graves. Some call them corpse candles, others will o' the wisp. In Holland they are the *dwaallicht,* in Sweden *lyktgubbe,* in my own country *irrwisch.* The phenomenon has been attested in every society, and every age, and is attributed, even now, in our enlightened century, to the work of the devil or the presence of ghosts. Many have I examined who have witnessed it, but none has seen it as *you* can see it. It is a rare and precious gift that you possess, and yet there are some, perhaps even here, in this supposedly civilised little English town, who would condemn it as witchcraft, or shun it as the delirium of the insane."

I shivered, remembering what I heard that old woman say, in Vienna, before we departed: *"The devil does his work through the delusions of this lunatic."*

"I would not blame them," I said eventually. "*I* thought I was mad."

He smiled, and I saw his long thin teeth glint in the moonlight. "You are not mad, Lucy. But now it is late, and you are fatigued, and I must return you to your father. We will talk of this more tomorrow."

20 APRIL

I woke this morning to a bright blue sky, and a mind clearer and more contented than I have known for many days. I am *not* mad, I told myself, as I stood at the window looking down at the little pearly waves nibbling at the sand. I am *not mad.* I went down the stairs singing, and out into the sunlit garden to find flowers for the breakfast table. My father had gone, once more, to the custom-house, and so it was that I was alone when the knock came to the door. And as soon as I saw his face I knew something was terribly, terribly wrong.

"What is it?" I implored, as I led him to the sitting-room, my arms full of daffodils. "What is it?"

"Pack your things, Lucy," he said, his voice rasping as if his throat were raw. "We are to leave within the hour."

"But what—" I began, stepping involuntarily towards him. But he made no movement to touch me, and turned away, his face to the window.

"The next phase of your treatment must take place in London. I require the use of certain special apparatus that I cannot obtain in such a remote district as this. I have taken rooms in Piccadilly, and will have a housekeeper in residence, so you will have a chaper-one."

"But why did you not mention this last night? And why should I need a chaperone, when Papa will be with me?"

"Your father has given his permission for you to depart at once. He has business to conclude here, and will join us in due course. I saw him, not half an hour ago, at the custom-house, and it is all agreed. So please, do as I ask, and pack your things."

I had wanted nothing more, all these last days, than to have him to myself, but now the prospect was before me I was suddenly afraid.

"I should prefer to wait for my father to return."

"That is not possible," he answered, turning again to face me, his features blank of all emotion. "I have received a most urgent sum-mons to London that cannot be delayed. I had thought you above such childish and irrational objections. I will await you outside."

And so I did what I was told. I gathered my clothes in my little travel-ling case and placed this journal within my cloak. And before the hour was out he had closed the carriage door behind me and climbed onto the box with the coachman, and the heavy black coach loaded with boxes and trunks was rumbling across the cobbles towards the road.

The last thing I saw, as we passed, was Mr Holman, at the door of Bourne House, and with him the curate of the little church below the graveyard.

I have never seen such terror in the faces of men.

CHAPTER SEVEN

IT TOOK CHARLES A long time to convince Sam that the girl found in the Shepherd's Market alley-way could be the fourth victim of the same murderer. A murderer of the type Charles's great-uncle once called a sequential killer, more than a hundred years before the coinage of a far better-known modern phrase. And Sam's reasoning did hold, up to a point—the girl in the alley was intact, there was no eviscerated heart, not a single drop of blood. In fact, it was only when Charles grasped his friend's arm and forced him to stand in front of the previous victim to show him almost identical wounds on her neck that Sam was reluctantly convinced. And it was only then, of course, that they understood the significance of what the old woman in the alley claimed to have seen, and they realised they might have had their first sighting of the man they had been seeking. But after spending the best part of the night interviewing his drunk and increasingly disorderly witness, Sam is in no very positive frame of mind when he knocks at the door of the Buckingham Street house at just after ten the following day. Though from what Abel Stornaway tells him, he's not the only one in need of sleep, a hot bath, and a decent breakfast.

"I dinnae think Mr Charles has been to bed at all. He's been pacing up and down in the office mostae the night, I reckon."

Sam makes a face, half to himself. It's a poser, this case, and no mistake, but he can't see why his old colleague should be taking it so much to heart. It's Sam's job that's on the line, after all. And a new job at that.

"Can I go up?" he says.

"Of course ye may. Will 'ee be wantin' anythin'?"

Sam shakes his head and starts up the stairs, and when he turns the bend on the first landing he finds little Betsy eyeing him shyly through the bannisters above, and the two of them play a boisterous game of peek-a-boo for a minute or two before Charles hears the commotion and the office door bangs open.

"Nancy!" he shouts down over the landing, and the little girl gapes at him a moment with huge rounded eyes before racing back upstairs and out of sight.

"Looks like you scared 'er," offers Sam, following Charles into the office, but he gets no reply. Charles's sleepless night has clearly done little for his mood.

"What did the doctor at the morgue say?" asks Charles, levering himself back down into his chair.

Sam shrugs. "Said she'd lost a lot 'a blood, but 'e couldn't account for 'ow it might 'ave 'appened. Or what killed 'er. The word 'e used was 'inconclusive.' Which is fancy talk for 'no bleedin' idea' if you ask me. 'E ain't got no more idea 'ow she died than I 'ave."

"And the old woman—did she see anything? What the man looked like—what he was wearing?"

Sam snorts and shakes his head. "She's still soberin' up, but I don't reckon she'll be much use even when she does. Claims she didn't see 'is face, and can't tell us 'ow long the girl'd been there. To be honest, I'm not sure she even knows what bloody day it is. Most of it were a load o' nonsense—just the gin talkin'."

He's fiddling with a button on his coat now, and Charles knows something tricky is coming.

"Look, Chas," he says eventually. "Are you sure about this? 'Cause apart from 'er lookin' so white, I just can't see the connexion wiv this latest one. Those marks you saw—it were just pin-pricks, weren't it? Made by a necklace or such? And given the first two are already rottin' in their graves we can't even say for sure they 'ad the same. It just seems like a wild goose chase to me. An' that ain't like you."

You will have gathered by now that Charles has not told Sam what he was really looking for at the morgue, or shared the conversation he had with O'Riordan that led to it. Because at one level Sam is, of course, completely right. It is, indeed, very unlike Charles to behave in a way that defies logic, logic being one of the two principles Maddox taught him, and which he has always worked by. The very notion that there might be some supernatural force at work here is an utterly insane idea that would have Charles laughed out of any police-station in London if he even raised it as a possibility. But all the same, he cannot completely discount it. For the very simple reason that he has not—even after a sleepless night thinking about it—found another explanation for the marks on those girls' necks. And that's what he needs, because without it there's no way he can close down O'Riordan—or open up to Sam.

"I don't think that's the answer," he says eventually. "There's no necklace I've ever seen that could leave such a scar. Especially only on one side."

They sit in silence a moment, then Sam sighs. "Only time I've ever seen anyfing like that were on me ma's arm after she 'ad our Tilly. After they blooded 'er."

Charles stares at him. *"Say that again."*

Sam flushes. "I know it ain't the same, but when me ma had the fever after 'er confinement, the quack bled 'er. He 'ad some weird little instrument that left a hole a bit like those ones on the girls. But that were on 'er arm, not 'er neck, and it were only one mark not two, an' much bigger."

Charles gets up and goes to the window. "But it might be the answer all the same, Sam. It would explain the state of the bodies—if the girls had been bled, and aggressively, just before they died then they might well have looked that pale."

"But why would 'e want to do that to 'em? And if these marks ain't the same, 'ow does that 'elp us anyways?"

Charles turns towards him. "But that's just it, they *might be*. It's a long time since I let blood, and in my opinion it usually does a lot more harm than good, but I know they've invented some new instruments in the last few years—instruments that might leave marks exactly like that."

"But how are you goin' to find that out? Could take days—weeks even."

"No," says Charles, "it won't. Because I know exactly where to go."

Half an hour later he's in a hansom cab heading along Pall Mall. A hansom cab because impatience has outrun prudence, and the crowds make the 'buses not just slow but sweltering. But even the cab makes heavy weather of such a short journey, and Charles stares out of the window in a simmering and impotent irritation as they travel scarcely faster than a foot's pace up towards Hyde Park, and into the ramshackle village of makeshift booths and stalls that has sprung up about the Great Exhibition entrances. When he steps down from the carriage the air is salty with the smell of the fried fish and sausages which are the Victorian equivalent of fast food and a good deal less refined than the sandwiches and soda water offered by the Refreshment Courts inside. The Exhibition hall catches the full glare of the morning sun, glittering like some exotic Far Eastern pavilion, and although Charles has been rather patronising about this whole endeavour ever since he heard it was planned, even he cannot fail to be struck by the skill of its engineers, and when he reaches the head of the queue and is allowed inside even his breath catches a little at the sight of the vast ironwork nave that opens before him. And *nave* is the right word, for this is truly a cathedral to commerce. At the far end, a living tree stands beneath the arching apse-like glass, and galleries run like clerestories on either side, balconied with red and hung with long pennants of yellow and blue. And as for the exhibits—the sheer range and resplendence on show here staggers the mind. From where he is standing Charles can see a line of huge statues retreating into the distance, horsemen on rearing steeds, enormous bronze urns three men high, reproduction Greek goddesses, and plaster casts of celebrated samples of ecclesiastical architecture. The courts of the exhibiting nations open from the aisle like side-chapels, each bearing its flag like a saint's insignia, and a gold name blazoned above. And everywhere, everywhere, there are people. Moving, milling, pointing, appraising. The noise booms against the glass like a revolution.

If Charles thought this would be a quick dip in and out to pocket the information he's after, then he knows now how wrong he was. Charles—as you may know—is unusually good at finding his way, and his quasi-photographic memory has stood him in good stead (indeed saved his hide) on more than one occasion. But in a place like this, even he needs a map. Happily, however, there are ranks of fresh-faced young men in freshly pressed uniforms handing out neatly folded floor-plans to anyone who wants one, and within a few minutes Charles is making his way up the stairs towards a sign proclaiming PHILOSOPHICAL, MUSICAL, HOROLOGICAL AND SURGICAL INSTRUMENTS. The crowds here are much thinner, but for Charles, this is like Aladdin's cave and a magic toy-shop all rolled into one. He knows at once that he must come back—there is so much here it will take a week's diligence to see it all. So many pioneering discoveries and so many testaments to the human capacity to turn those discoveries to practical use. From envelope-folding machines to oyster-openers, air-

pumps to astronomical clocks. He would have come here for the photographic exhibits alone, and despite the urgency of his task he lingers
longingly over an array of the latest daguerreotype machines, reading
about a recent photographic experiment which claims to prove the
"existence of luminous and actinic rays in the solar beam." Then a man
in Exhibition livery announces that Mr Dawson's talk on "The Principles and Applications of Electro-magnetism" is about to begin, and
Charles is drawn along in the wake of a cluster of sombre-looking
gentlemen towards lines of chairs placed theatre-like for the lecture.
After a few minutes of introduction, Dawson invites his audience to
join him at a case of scientific instruments, so that he can point out
some of the many uses of this marvellous and still mysterious phenomenon, from medical galvanism to a new electrical telegraph already in use in parts of Saxony. And then he turns to the assembly and
asks if they would be so good as to follow him to the adjoining gallery,
where he will demonstrate the creation of electro-static energy. The
apparatus in question is a large glass ball suspended between two metal
pillars and standing on a wooden plinth. It is positioned close by the
balcony, overlooking the teeming hall below, and as Dawson begins to
describe its operation—"a small amount of mercury is injected into a
vacuum, such that the glass globe gives off both light and an electric
charge when set in motion"—Charles's eye is drawn down and across
the crowd to a tall figure in a dark coat and a top hat. And as he
watches the man move away in the direction of the Prussian court a
fist of ice closes about his chest. It cannot be—surely—it *cannot be.* It's
too far away to see his face, and the man has his back towards him, but
the gait is the same, the height is the same—good God, the man is
even holding a small sunscreen to his eyes, to ward away the sunlight
streaming through the glass.

Charles extricates himself from the group and makes his way, his
heart and pace quickening, down the stairs and out into the nave. He
can still see the top-hatted figure, but he's yards away now. He tries to
push through the throng gathered about the hydraulic machinery, but
the press of people is too packed—elderly ladies leaning on sticks, little children dawdling, distracted mothers not looking where they're

going. By the time Charles reaches the Prussian court there is no sign of his quarry. He stands there, out of breath, looking up and down—half the men in the place are wearing the same hats, the same dark coats, but none walks as *he* does, and none carries a sunscreen, even inside. Charles curses under his breath, though not quietly enough, it seems, for a fat and sweaty-faced clergyman gives him a look of rebuke and hurries his dowdy wife and daughters away. And then Charles spots the man again. At the far end now, moving towards the tiered fountain, where refreshments are on offer and food is served. The crowds are thicker than ever here—it's gone noon now—and Charles strains through the queuing hordes like a man drowning, desperate to keep his man in sight. But now the tall figure is no longer moving. He's standing, the face turned away and the back bent, and as Charles draws level and grips his arm, forcing him round, there are murmurs of shocked outrage as the elderly man gasps and nearly loses his footing, and his little padded sunscreen clatters to the ground. And then Charles is backing away, his face red, mumbling an apology, stammering something about mistaken identity. Because this is not who he thought it was, and he has never seen this man's face before.

By the time he has returned to the stairs and the second storey, there is an official standing at the entrance to the scientific galleries, and a coiled red rope barring the way. His Royal Highness is visiting that part of the Exhibition this afternoon, explains the functionary, and the galleries will, in consequence, be closed to the public until six o'clock this evening. Charles starts to say something about it being an urgent matter and police business, then flushes, self-conscious, when the man asks for his name and rank.

"I am here on behalf of Inspector Rowlandson, of Bow Street."

"But you are not, in fact, an officer of the police?"

"No, but—"

"In that case, sir, I will have to ask you to leave. Or else return with some official confirmation of your business here. You can appreciate, I am sure, that when members of the Royal family are in attendance we must exercise the utmost vigilance. We cannot afford to allow vagrants and *hoi polloi* to come wandering in here willy-nilly off the street."

This last is said with a somewhat contemptuous glance at Charles's rather unkempt clothes, and a noticeably firmer grip on the rope.

Charles turns away, as much irritated with himself as with the man. He's wasted all that time—he should never have allowed himself to be side-tracked. He wonders for a moment about finding Sam and coming back together, but by the time he finds him it will probably be nigh on six anyway. He goes back down the stairs, more slowly this time, feeling the ache in his leg at every step, and then stops at the entrance to buy a catalogue. At least he can narrow the search by going through the list of medical exhibitors. And as he makes his way to the exit he sees the Royal party entering by an adjacent door. A line of sober-suited courtiers, and in their centre, the Kubla Khan of this whole affair, resplendent in a short red jacket, blue sash, and tasselled gold braid.

The clock is chiming two as Charles enters the Buckingham Street house. When he opens the drawing-room door his great-uncle is asleep in his chair by the open window. Even now, when he has no clients, and no callers, his clothes are as immaculate as they were when he counted Royalty among his patrons, his stock white, his blue coat new-brushed, and his waistcoat—always a weakness of his—embroidered with silken flowers. On the sill Thunder the cat is stretched motionless to his full length, his whiskers twitching every now and then in the gentle breeze that lifts the muslin curtains. Charles takes a seat and a newspaper, and waits. Perhaps the old thief taker still has some sixth sense and will perceive another presence in the room; the cat certainly does, for he suddenly opens his eyes and rolls languorously onto his back before standing up, splaying his toes, and arching his spine into a perfect parabola. Then he folds his paws neatly invisible beneath him and sits back down into a hen-like (or zen-like) repose.

"You have been out?" says Maddox then, his voice still thick with sleep. His malady has retreated of late, and his mind returned to almost the mastery he once commanded. The old man still tires easily, and becomes irascible as the evening draws, but it is early in the day yet.

"I went to the Exhibition."

Maddox raises an eyebrow. "You have leisure for such a visit? I had thought you were assisting young Mr Wheeler on his case."

"I was—I am. I went in search of a possible lead. A piece of medical equipment that might explain the marks found on the bodies."

"And you did not find it?"

"I was—distracted. I thought I saw someone I knew."

There is a pause, while Maddox watches. Watches and waits.

"I thought I saw the Baron Von Reisenberg," says Charles eventually, avoiding his uncle's eye. "Which is patently ludicrous. The man is half a continent away. It's that damn O'Riordan and his preposterous vampire nonsense."

To which his uncle—who has seen that look on Charles's face before—nods quietly, then waits a minute, then two, before speaking again.

"You have not told me very much of your sojourn in Austria. But I have gathered that all did not go well. Or not, at least, as you expected."

Charles sighs. But it is time, after all, that Maddox should know. It takes some minutes to tell that tale, and when it is finished Maddox does not reply at once, but sits, fingertips joined to fingertips, looking at his great-nephew.

"You did not consider informing the authorities?" he says eventually.

"I didn't think they would believe me. And I wouldn't have blamed them. It was all so bizarre—so implausible—and there was nothing I could offer by way of proof. Even the doctor who assisted me could offer only supposition, nothing more. It was inconceivable, in those circumstances, that my word would be credited against that of a member of their own nobility. I decided that all I would achieve by such a step was a delay to my departure."

"And now?"

"I have finished the report and will send it to Oxford today. But I have told them only what I have ascertained as to the Baron's lineage, and nothing more. Because there is nothing I can prove, and they would only think I had gone insane. Sometimes *I* think I was insane for a while—confined in that infernal place, with the mad, day after day. And then this afternoon—when I thought I saw him—"

He gets up awkwardly and walks to the window. "Even now, I have scarcely any memory of the day before I was incarcerated—images of the attack come to me only fitfully, like the half-glimpsed hallucinations of fever."

But what Charles does not say, even to Maddox, is that despite the acute pain he still suffers, he is terrified to resort to the only medical relief available; for laudanum was what they gave him in the asylum, and laudanum, even in strictly analgesic quantities, brings on bad dreams, and makes malicious mirages of whatever unwholesome fears the mind can feed it.

"All I have," he says at last, "is five characters in my own handwriting, and I have no idea why I wrote them."

He pulls his notebook from his pocket and hands it to Maddox, who takes it and opens it a little clumsily to the last entry. Below a paragraph of rather untidy notes on the Baron's maternal ancestors there is one line:

BEM 47

"The numbers refer to a date?" says Maddox, after a moment.

Charles shrugs. "I don't know. It might mean something. It might mean nothing at all. And yet even now I cannot shake my mind free of the conviction that I had discovered something—or was about to discover something. Something that might explain why the Baron was so intent to remove me—to silence me. And yet even that might be nothing more than the perverted logic of paranoia. In fact there was one officious little bureaucrat in Vienna who suggested that the whole damn episode might have been merely some macabrely laughable error by the Baron's coachman—that he might have taken me to the asylum by mistake, when it was the hospital that was intended all along. He kept saying it was the only *rational* explanation." He laughs, bitterly.

Maddox closes the book and hands it back to him. The pallor of his nephew's cheeks and the shadows under his eyes explain themselves now. Maddox had encouraged the trip to Austria, thinking Charles needed distance and detachment after Molly's death, and that lingering in this house, and this room, and speaking to no-one of what had happened, as Charles had been doing for the best part of two months, was no way to achieve it. And when he returned from Europe bearing, it seemed, an even greater burden, Maddox had considered breaching the young man's silence but postponed the moment of it, and I will not be surprised if you conclude, as a result, that he and his great-nephew resemble each other in more ways than their mere appearance, and share not only an acute intelligence, but that same fearsome privacy of personal feeling that we have seen in Charles already.

Maddox shifts in his seat now, clearly hesitant. "When you spoke of the Baron just now—were you really implying—"

Charles laughs sardonically. "That he is a vampire? Now *you* are probably thinking I have gone insane! No, you need have no fear, dear Uncle. My wits are not so far wasted. But there was no question that the villagers near the castle lived in fear of him. One crossed himself at the mere mention of his name, and an old woman shrank from me in terror simply because she saw a tiny mark on my neck. I had not understood its full significance until yesterday, at the Library."

Maddox studies him. "There is still something there. How odd. After all this time."

Charles's hand is at his throat. "It's just a scratch. It's nothing."

Maddox nods. "And yet, one can understand why an illiterate peasant woman might have drawn the conclusion she did."

"The man has only himself to blame," retorts Charles angrily. "If he did not behave in such an erratic and unaccountable fashion he would not invite such gossip. But however peculiar his conduct, you and I both know it must have some logical or medical cause, and all the rest is nothing but superstitious drivel."

"You believe him to be ill?"

Charles nods. "I wondered more than once about *lupus*. That might account for the lesions on his skin, and his distress in the presence of bright lights."

Maddox considers. "I recall, likewise, many years ago, conducting a case on behalf of a gentleman whose brother suffered from exactly those symptoms. Though in that case the young man was also affected by an extreme blanching and recession of the gums, which gave him the most unfortunate, and indeed lupine, appearance. More relevant, perhaps, in this instance, his condition had also rendered his urine a deep purplish red, such that to the untrained eye, he might well have been thought to express blood. The same curious disorder was said to afflict the third King George in his madness, and my client's brother was also unpredictable and eccentric on occasion. But neither he nor our late monarch—living as they did in a civilised and enlightened society—was ever accused of being an evil spirit of the unquiet dead. Yet in a wild and isolated region of Austria, amid a populace prey to the worst excesses of superstition? If the Baron does indeed suffer from the same unfortunate disease, he will not have been able to conceal it entirely, and one might well imagine the rumour promulgating among the ignorant that a man who excretes blood must, perforce, be ingesting it. For a man of science, such as you describe him to be, the irony is almost exquisitely apposite."

Charles scowls. "I do not take your meaning."

"Because those peasants are only doing—in their own primitive way—what he himself does. What you and I do."

"Which is—?"

"Applying the principles of logic and observation."

"My dear uncle, you can't seriously be suggesting—"

"Oh, I do not say that it is a reasoned or a systematic process of thought they undertake. Merely that, at heart, it is the same: We are all seeking an explanation for what we observe, whether from superstition or from science. Indeed, have not some of our greatest advances stemmed from precisely such a procedure, even—or most especially— when the forces at work are invisible to the eye? We disdain the ignorance of those peasants at Castle Reisenberg, but in past centuries one would have been persecuted, or worse, merely for positing the existence of forces as powerful, and as apparently magical, as magnetism or electricity. And think of the ability we now possess to capture a living likeness on a plate of glass, or dull the senses to such a depth that surgery may be performed without pain. Our forefathers would have deemed such things the stuff of necromancy. And with good cause. And that being the case, could there not be other phenomena that we condemn now as childish superstition, which might one day prove to have no less a basis in science? Even the alchemist's elusive goal might one day prove within our grasp."

Charles has by now turned to look at him, remembering how the Baron had said something almost exactly the same. "But you're not saying you actually *believe* in vampires, and the Undead, and all the rest of it?"

Maddox shakes his head slowly. "Clearly not. No rational man could believe it. I merely observe that for all the discoveries that have been made since I was a boy, it seems to me all we have thus far learned is how much we do *not* yet know. And nowhere do I believe that to be more apposite than in relation to mankind itself, and the powers and terrors of the human mind."

The room is silent then, but for the ticking of the French clock, and the ripple of the curtains in the heavy air. And at last Charles stirs and rouses, as if shaking his mind free from memory.

"And your current case?" asks Maddox. "You mentioned Patrick

O'Riordan. I remember that young man when he first started at the *Daily News.* Charming, loquacious, and altogether unscrupulous. As I am sure you are aware."

"Indeed," replies Charles dryly. "And not above manipulating the facts to manufacture a story. As he is clearly doing in this case."

"I see—so the mutilations on the bodies are not in fact—"

But then there's a knock and Nancy's face appears around the door. She looks pale, despite the heat, and the blond curls slipping from her cap are plastered to her forehead, and there's a beading of sweat above her lip.

"Mr Charles—"

"What is it, Nancy?" he says, a little brusquely. "I am talking with my uncle."

She opens her mouth, then closes it again, looking, for a moment, as hesitant as a child. And she's so tiny one might easily make the mistake of thinking her equally helpless. But not Charles; he knows how resilient she really is—how gutsy her life has made her. Which makes her present unease all the more unusual. "I'm sorry, Mr Charles. It's only that I was up at the market just now for the vegetables and one of the girls I used to know in Granby Street was there. Sal, 'er name is. She's been lookin' for me."

Something in her tone catches Charles's attention, but he misinterprets her nervousness, thinking it's her past—and the pimp she left there—that has come back to trouble her.

"You're safe here, Nancy," he says, more gently this time. "Both you and Betsy."

She swallows. "I know, Mr Charles, and I'm grateful, yer know I am. But it weren't that. Sal knows I work for you now, and she were askin' if I'd 'eard anythin' about that man—that murderin' bastard as is doin' for the girls."

Charles and Maddox exchange a glance, and Charles remembers what O'Riordan said about the whores talking. So the rumours have reached Granby Street now. Time is running out.

"What man, Nancy?" asks Charles, keeping his voice deliberately neutral.

The girl's eyes widen in disbelief. "I can't believe you ain't 'eard—it's all over London! They say he hacks off their 'eads and 'ides 'em no-one knows where—that 'e does fings to the bodies that the police don't want the rest of us knowin' about. Weird fings—like what only some mad person'd do."

Nancy's pretty face is really troubled now. "An' it'll be full moon in a couple o' days. The girls are petrified 'e's gonna do it again."

Charles starts, then swears under his breath, cursing both himself and the police for failing to see something that was patently obvious even to a horde of common prostitutes. Because she's right: It was full moon when the first girls died. And it's nearly full moon now.

Nancy looks from one to the other. "But you musta known that, surely. They wouldn't o' called 'im that name else."

Charles feels his fists clench, because he knows suddenly what she's going to say.

"What name, Nancy?"

"The Vampire, Mr Charles. They're callin' 'im the Vampire."

She looks at him, waiting for him to tell her that she is being absurd—that the very idea is ludicrous. But Charles is not laughing, and neither (we might observe) is Maddox.

"What can I say to 'em, Mr Charles?" she says pleadingly. "They're all bloody terrified—"

She looks across at Maddox and flushes. "Sorry, sir—I don't mean 'ta swear, but Sal says 'alf the girls are too scared to work, and if they don't work, they don't eat." She takes a deep breath. "And it ain't just that. One of the girls Sal shares wiv 'as disappeared. I knew 'er, too—nice kid. Bit too fragile for the trade if you ask me, but the poor cow didn't 'ave no more choice about it 'an I did. A few days ago she went out an' never came back."

Charles tries to sound reassuring, but his words belie his unease.

"Well, perhaps she's just found herself a new admirer and gone off with him to Brighton. Enjoying the sunshine while it lasts—"

"You don't understand," says Nancy, tears gathering in her eyes. "Alice's missin' too. An' she never took Alice wiv 'er when she was workin'. Not ever."

"Alice is her daughter?" asks Maddox.

Nancy nods. "She's six, a bit older'n my Betsy. I used to mind 'er sometimes, before I came 'ere."

There is silence. Charles knows what he has to ask, but he needs to find a way to do it. As kind a way as he can.

"What does this young woman look like?" he says at last.

"She's fair, like me. And she 'as a little flower tattooed on 'er ankle. For 'er name."

"What sort of flower, Nancy?"

She stares at him. "A rose. 'Er name's Rose." And then her voice falters as the truth breaks suddenly and terribly upon her. "But you knew that already, didn't yer. She's dead, ain't she? An' it were that bastard as killed 'er."

Charles takes a step towards her. "We don't *know* that, Nancy—not yet. But if it *is* her, then we stopped him before he could do anything to her." He swallows. "She's in one piece, Nancy. Her body hasn't been touched."

Nancy sits down heavily in a chair and gets out her handkerchief. "She didn't deserve that, Mr Charles—she never did no 'arm to anyone. An' where's Alice? Where's 'er little girl?"

Charles shakes his head. "I don't know. I'm sorry. There was no child with her when they found her. But you can help us, Nancy." He crouches down next to her and takes her hand. "Can you come with me—look at the girl we found and tell us if it really is Rose? We don't know who the other girls were, and that's one reason why we haven't caught this man yet. But if it *is* Rose—then at least we'll have something to go on."

She looks at him for a long moment, the tears spilling over and running slowly down her face. And then she nods.

Charles sends Billy up to Bow Street with a message for Sam, in the hopes he'll be back at the station, and by the time he and Nancy arrive at Vine Street it's to find his old friend waiting agitatedly outside, his face grave. Nancy takes one look at him and falls weeping into his arms, which tells Charles more about the state of play between them than mere words ever could. He leaves the two of them together and goes down into the mortuary to look for the attendant. They find a clean sheet (not an easy task in this place) and do their best to make Rose seem at peace, but there's only so much they can hide. There's no disguising that the girl Nancy once knew died in fear and in pain. Nancy's had her own share of both in her young life, but this is too much, even for her, and she turns her face into Sam's shoulder, her body racked by sobs. Charles, meanwhile, has sought out the police doctor and requested a full *post mortem* examination. Though the man—perhaps understandably—bridles at such an interference from a mere civilian, and informs Charles in somewhat chilly tones that such an expensive (and clearly, in his view, unnecessary) procedure requires a formal requisition from Bow Street, and only when such a notification is received will it be carried out, and not before.

Charles has a good deal to do to contain his impatience, but it can't be helped. He thanks the man for his help with only the faintest hint of sarcasm, then withdraws to wait for Sam and Nancy outside.

London has never seen such a richness of race and nation as it has these last months of the Exhibition, and even on this commonplace street there's a family chattering excitably in French and two Indian gentlemen strolling, hands locked behind their backs, in bright turbans and long white cotton robes which are clearly more comfortable in this heat than the shirt, waistcoat, and heavy black woollen jacket

Charles himself is wearing. When Sam and Nancy finally emerge, the three of them walk down to Piccadilly and Charles hails a hansom and tells the driver Granby Street. The driver raises his eyebrows—it's not often that someone in this privileged part of town gives him that particular address, at least during daylight hours, and he winks knowingly when Charles hands Nancy up into the cab, but the sight of Sam's uniform has him touching his cap quickly and moving the horse along. They travel back past Trafalgar Square and the Strand, and then cross the river at Waterloo Bridge. The walkways are thronged with families taking the air, and enjoying the breeze off the water, but Charles sees Nancy bite her lip and look away at the sight of one young woman strolling with a little girl. A little girl with bright golden curls and a rag doll swinging from her plump hand.

The driver pulls up eventually at a small dingy house, and when Charles goes to the driver to pay he realises that they're barely three doors along from where Nancy used to live. As far as he knows, she hasn't been back here since he found her on the doorstep in Buckingham Street on Christmas Eve, and when she steps down from the cab he sees her look briefly at her old lodgings and then turn her back.

"Don't worry, Nance," says Sam, who has obviously divined—or been told—her apprehension. "That Arnie won't dare come near yer while I'm 'ere."

She nods, the ghost of a smile on her face. "But one look at you an' the girls won't talk neever. Let me go in an' explain, an' then I'll come out an' get yer."

She pulls her shawl up over her hair, then hurries up to the house, where she stands waiting, shifting nervously from one foot to the other, until the door opens and she disappears inside.

Charles and Sam kick their heels—literally, in Sam's case—for a good quarter of an hour, then the door opens again and Nancy beckons them in.

She leads them through a sitting-room scattered with discarded stock-ings and underclothes through to a pokey back kitchen that reeks of damp, even in this warm weather. There are three girls there, a redhead and a blonde perched nervously on rickety wooden chairs, and a third standing with her back to the window. All are in some stage of half dress, with thin peignoirs pulled hastily over corsets and bloomers. There are cups and spoons strewn across the table, and a jug of milk with seaweedy white grease just visible beneath the surface.

"D'yer want tea?" says the fair-haired girl at the table. Charles shakes his head, but Sam has a stronger stomach—or greater diplomacy— and accepts.

"So what yer want wiv us, then?"

It's the girl by the window who speaks. She's clearly a lot older and more street-hardened than the other two, and Charles suspects she's also the one who came looking for Nancy.

"I don't see what soddin' point there is you comin' 'ere. We can't tell yer nuffin'. An' even if we could, we bloody well wouldn't."

Charles sees Nancy glance nervously at her, but he's heard much worse. And besides, there's a quality of nervousness about this girl's bravado that argues for something more than just the whore's habitual contempt for the rozzer.

"We want to find the man who killed Rose," answers Charles evenly. "And we want to find her daughter. I assume you would all want to help us do that."

There are surreptitious glances, then, from the two at the table, and Nancy goes over to the girl at the window and puts her hand on her arm. "They want to 'elp, Sal. Really. You can trust 'em."

Sal looks at her scornfully, but says nothing. And that silence seems to be permission enough for the others, because a moment later the redhead looks up at Charles. "It were Wednesday a week back when we last saw her."

She must be the youngest—probably no more than fourteen—and it's not a London voice either; Wiltshire or Dorset, Charles guesses, and he wonders what choice or necessity has brought her, so young, so far from home, and so far down.

"Do you know where she was going?"

A shake of the head.

"Had she been seeing any clients in particular lately?"

Another negative.

"Or perhaps someone new? Someone who might have been giving her trouble?"

A hesitation now.

"Well," says the third girl, "I did 'ear her mention one bloke—said she'd seen 'im two or three times. Told me 'e were givin' 'er the creeps."

"In what way? What made her say that?"

The girl shrugs. "All I know is she was scared. That 'e did fings to 'er that she didn't like. I don't know what. When I asked, she just clammed up."

Sam puts his cup down. "Was there anyfing else you remember? What 'e looked like per'aps? Or where she picked 'im up?"

She shakes her head. "I never saw 'im. But it were up the West End somewhere."

Charles and Sam exchange a glance.

"Is it possible it was Piccadilly?"

"Could be. She worked that beat a lot."

The red-haired girl leans towards her then, whispering something the men can't catch.

"What did she say?" says Charles, barely breathing now.

"Lou says she thinks 'e were a foreigner."

"And she 'ad the little girl wiv 'er when you last saw 'er?" asks Sam.

There's a silence then, and as it lengthens Charles realises the fair-haired girl has started to cry.

"What is it?" he asks, moving towards the table.

"I said," the girl stammers through her tears, "I said it weren't right to turn 'em out—not when we knew they 'ad nowhere else to go—"

Charles takes a deep breath. "So she didn't leave here of her own accord."

Neither of the younger girls will look at him, so he straightens up and turns to Sal, realising now that her coming looking for Nancy was prompted more by guilt than by real concern. "I assume this was your doing."

The girl's look is defiant, but her cheeks are red. "That brat of 'ers was a bleedin' nightmare. Waking up screamin', week after week. And then if that weren't bad enough she started wanderin' round in the middle of the night—I 'ad two johns up and leave and not bleedin' pay after she came in on us—standin' starin' at 'em at the end of the bed, it completely put 'em off. I told Rose—if she couldn't find someone to look after the kid when she were on the job then that was it, they both 'ad to go."

The merest glance tells Charles that Nancy had been told none of this, and it will do nothing to make Rose's passing easier for her. Because now she will start wondering if none of this might have happened if she'd still been here—if she'd still been around to mind the child—

Something of the same thought must have been in Sam's mind, because he goes to Nancy and takes her by the arm. "Let's go, Nance," he says softly. "We've got all we're gonna get 'ere."

The cab is still waiting outside and Charles watches Sam help Nancy into it. She has her handkerchief to her eyes, and her shoulders are shaking with her sobs.

"You not comin', Chas?" says Sam.

Charles shakes his head. "I'm going back to the Exhibition. They should have re-opened that gallery by now."

"Right you are. I'll take Nancy back then go on to Bow Street. If our man really is a foreigner come for the Exhibition we can get the 'Ome Office to give us a list of arrivals for the last few weeks. And then we can start knockin' on doors, startin' in Piccadilly an' workin' outwards. It'll be a lot'a bloody boot-work, an' a bit like lookin' for a needle in an 'aystack, but at least we know what sort o' needle we're after now."

The Exhibition halls are quieter, and the light softer, now that the sun is dropping and the gas-lamps are lit. Charles negotiates a party of large sturdy ladies armed with notebooks and lorgnettes, and returns up the stairs to the medical and surgical section, catalogue in hand. It's just as well he's prepared, because the exhibits are ordered according to no classification method Charles has ever come across, with cases of lancets and trusses placed next to samples of mineral teeth and dentistry instruments, and something calling itself an *aneuralgicon*, developed and sold by one C. T. Downing, MD, and designed to "apply warm medicated vapour to *tic douloureux* &c." There are stethoscopes and microscopes, anatomical models and artificial limbs, hearing-aids and homeopathic tubes, but Charles is not going to be distracted. Not this time. Because now he knows exactly which exhibit number he's looking for:

> **666. Ross, A.** *Bleeding instruments, as substitutes for leeches*
> *and cupping instruments, adapted to apply to any part of the*
> *body. Invented by Baron Heurteloup; manufactured by*
> *J. Scholl, Berwick-street, Soho.*

The irony of that exhibit number doesn't escape Charles—everything about this wretched case seems to be conspiring to conjure the uncanny. But to judge of appearances there could be nothing more relentlessly pragmatic than the instruments in this velvet-lined box. One is a glass syringe with a scale etched on the side and a key-shaped closure; the other a brass scarificator—a metal knife for opening the vein which will leave (as Charles sees at once) a circular hole of exactly the same dimensions as those found on the bodies of the girls. He looks round for someone to speak to but the gallery is sparse of people, of both the spectating and the selling kind, and it takes a good while to track down a shiny-faced young man with spectacles and very damp palms. He is clearly so far down the chain of command that he's been lumbered with the evening shift, and seems, in fact, to be deputising for at least a dozen different exhibitors. Charles's heart sinks as he watches him plough through a pile of manufacturers' catalogues and ledgers, with apparently very little idea of where to find what Charles needs.

"So you don't actually work for A. Ross and Sons?"

"Er, no, not exactly," says the young man, becoming more flustered by the moment. "Mr Ross asked me to stand in. He's attending a dinner engagement this evening. At the Royal Society."

His spectacles are misting now and he takes them off and rubs the lenses on his handkerchief before carefully putting them back on. There are two sore red patches either side of his nose. "What was it you were after again?"

"A list of people who have purchased the Heurteloup scarificator since the Exhibition opened. It really can't be that difficult, surely."

"More so than you might think, sir," says the young man, pushing his spectacles onto his forehead now. A large drop of sweat falls onto the ledger open before him. "I think you will have to come back tomorrow. I can't make head nor tail of Mr Ross's handwriting."

"How many more times—this is an urgent matter. A *police* matter."

"I'm afraid I can't help that, sir." He closes the ledger, and then picks up a pile of loose papers.

"Ah," he says, a moment later. "This might be more to the purpose."

"What are they?"

"Delivery receipts. I'm afraid there aren't any names on these, just addresses, but they may be of some—really, sir, there's no need for that—"

Because Charles has already seized the papers from his hand and is going through them. Fifteen minutes later he has his answer: one scarificator was sent to Guy's Hospital, four to Harley Street, one to Albemarle Street, two to Jermyn Street, and one to the Albany. And three of those addresses are within half a mile of Piccadilly.

⊰ ⊱

Piccadilly is a glow of beautiful brick and stone frontages in the June-evening light, and none more so than the gloriously proportioned façade of the Albany. Then—as now—this beautiful Georgian building, with its symmetrical wings east and west, offers some of the most exclusive and envied apartments London can afford (though those wishing to appear well informed should be aware that it is fashionable these days to refer to it without the definite article). By 1851 its bachelor lodgings had already housed both the famed and the infamous—Byron and Gladstone both had rooms here, and on this particular summer afternoon those in residence include an eminent historian, several Lords, a clutch of MPs, and a notorious Irish swindler who will in due course give Dickens meat for the character of Merdle. At the Doric-columned porch of the main house a suitably obsequious porter in perfect white cotton gloves conducts him up to the first floor, then knocks on his behalf before bowing and discreetly retiring. He fully expects a similarly deferential manservant to open the door, so he is somewhat taken aback when the door opens. Because this man is clearly nothing of the kind.

"Baron Von Reisenberg?"

"Yes? Who are you?"

"Sergeant Samuel Wheeler of the Metropolitan Police, sir. Detective Branch. Can I come in?"

The nobleman frowns. "What is it you want?"

Sam looks back down the stairs, where two elegantly dressed and coiffed young men are slowly ascending the steps towards them, chatting in a modishly desultory manner. One of them looks up and gives Wheeler a frankly inquisitive stare.

"It's a routine matter, sir," Sam continues, turning back again. "But all the same I 'spect you'd prefer to discuss it in private."

The Baron stares at him with undisguised antagonism. "Very well. But I can spare you only five minutes. I have an appointment that cannot wait."

Sam bows and follows him through the dim vestibule into the sitting-room beyond. The walls are upholstered in red damask and hung with ornate frames, and there are so many pieces of furniture—sophas, Pembrokes, chests of drawers, even a piano—that the thick turkey carpet is barely visible beneath them. The blinds are drawn, and the room almost completely airless.

"Very nice," says Sam, as he begins to wander about. There is a door to what is clearly a bedroom, but that is ajar. "You're 'ere on yer own, are you, sir?"

"Of course I am alone. These apartments are designed only for one."

"You didn't bring yer own servants?"

"I find such attendance ... irksome. My intention in hiring these rooms was to avoid such inconvenience by availing myself of the services of the establishment's own domestics. Not that I consider my household arrangements to be any of *your* business."

There is a pause.

"I repeat," says the Baron heavily, watching Sam glancing at the papers on the tables, and the letters on a small silver tray, "I have only five minutes."

Sam turns to face him. "Are you aware, sir, that four young women 'ave been murdered in London in the last few weeks?"

"I cannot believe that is so uncommon, not in a city of this size, with such a large population of cut-throats and whores."

"Per'aps not, sir. But these killin's are the most brutal I've ever seen. In fact none of us's ever seen the like of 'em, and that's a fact."

The Baron eyes him calmly. "I have seen nothing of the kind reported in the press."

"You ain't likely to. If people knew, we'd 'ave a panic on our 'ands."

"And you come here to tell me this? I assure you, Mr—er—Weller—?"

"Wheeler, sir."

"—Wheeler. I, for one, am not so easily unnerved—"

Sam nods slowly. "I'm glad to 'ear it, sir. But that's not why I'm 'ere. The bodies of these young women were found only a few yards from 'ere."

"I still do not see how this should concern me, any more than any other resident at this address. For you have not called elsewhere in the Albany, I note."

"And 'ow do you know that, sir?"

"I observed your arrival. I happened to be looking out of the window at the time."

"I see."

"And I repeat, why should you call on me, and not on any of the other tenants, some of whom, I am reliably informed, have led less-than-law-abiding lives?"

"That's as may be, sir. The fact is we now 'ave evidence that the man we're lookin' for is a foreigner. Which rather narrows it down. As I'm sure you can appreciate."

There is another pause, a blackly hostile pause.

"Are you accusing me of some involvement in these crimes, Mr Wheeler?"

"Just routine enquiries, sir," says Sam brightly. "Like I said."

But the Baron is no longer deceived by his superficial Cockney chirpiness. If he ever was. He laughs grimly. "London is full of foreigners at present. The police might take their pick of likely suspects."

Sam smiles. "Ah, but there are rarver fewer, sir, as arrived just before these killin's started, and lodge no more'n a mile away. Fifteen of you, to be precise. Accordin' to the 'Ome Office. I've got a list of 'em 'ere."

He takes it from his pocket and holds it out. The Baron pointedly does not touch it.

"There is no reason why anyone should connect *me* with these crimes," he says eventually. "The very idea is ridiculous. I am a member of the Austrian nobility—a scientist, an industrialist—"

"Indeed, sir?" says Sam lightly, folding up the paper again and tucking it in his coat. "All the same, I'm sure you can understand that we 'ave a duty to ascertain whevver any of the persons on this list matches the description we 'ave lately received of the man as might be responsible for these 'einous crimes."

The Baron's eyelids flicker, and he turns away.

"The man in question was tall an' wore a top 'at an' a long dark coat."

The Baron swings round. The policeman—this insolent little runt of a policeman—is staring at his clothes.

"I defy you, *Mr* Wheeler," he says, moving slowly towards him, "not to go out onto Piccadilly and find a dozen men dressed in exactly that manner."

"Funny you should mention that, sir, because that's precisely where he were seen. On Piccadilly. Not four an' twenty hours gone."

He smiles again. "Where were you last night, sir? Between the hours of ten and eleven?"

The challenge is unmistakable now. Sam can hear his own heart—two beats, three, four—

"At dinner, here in my rooms," says the Baron eventually. "As the steward downstairs will no doubt be able to confirm. But frankly, I see no reason why my whereabouts, whether last night or at any other time, should be any concern of yours. And now, as I said, I must ask you to leave."

※ ※

It's gone five in the morning when Charles wakes from a sleep peopled by monsters to the sound of pounding on the street door. It's one of Sam's constables. A young man white-faced and terror-eyed.

"Sergeant Wheeler sent me," he gasps, leaning against the door-post. "He says will you come."

Charles starts to shake his head. "Please don't tell me—"

"There's been a break-in. At the morgue. That girl they found in Shepherd's Market. Someone's broken in and hacked her bloody head off."

CHAPTER EIGHT

Lucy's journal

26 APRIL

We have been here now two days. Though where *here* may be I do not know. We came by night, with the blinds pulled down, and I saw only a courtyard and the man who came forward to take down the luggage, though by the noise nearby of people and carriages I guessed we were not far from some much larger street. We were brought up here, to this door, and this set of rooms that I could see at once have not been lived in for many months, so filthy they are with dust and so empty of any sign of inhabitance. *He* stood there, watching, as my little trunk was brought to me, then nodded without speaking and locked the door behind him. Where he lodges, I do not know, but it cannot be far, for he brings me my meals, but stays only to hand me the tray, and otherwise I am absolutely solitary, kept like a prisoner, in the dark. For he has bolted all the shutters and told me they will remain so. It is for my own good, he says, and the success of my treatment depends upon it, though why the darkness is so necessary, or in what my treatment will consist, he does not say. He allows me a lamp turned low, while I eat, but returns within the hour to remove it, and I must write these pages quickly and then conceal them in my clothes, for I am sure he would take this journal from me if he knew I still possess it. For I no longer trust him, and he has seen in my eyes that it is so. That first night we came, I asked about the housekeeper he said would be here, and he looked me full in the face and said he had made no such promise, and I knew then that he had lied. And sitting here, on this narrow bed, hour after hour, the fear that has been growing upon me all those long silent miles since we departed all but overwhelms me, and I wonder in what else I have been deceived. Did he truly talk to my father, that last day, as he claimed? And if he did not, does my father even know where I have gone? My heart aches when I think of it—it is unbearable to imagine him returning to the house to find that I had vanished, leaving no message, and I curse myself for my own stupidity—for allowing myself to become so bewitched by this man that I sought—no, I *yearned* to have him to myself alone. For I have my wish now, in all its terror. I am truly alone, and utterly in his power. For the door to my bedroom cannot be bolted, and I lie awake at night, listening for his step.

28 APRIL

There were voices this morning. When he brought me my breakfast I heard the noise of heavy footsteps somewhere below, and the muttering of men coming up the stairs. He would have closed the door on me then, but one of the men called up and he was forced to go to the banister to answer him. And so it was that I saw them, one carrying a small mahogany case, the other two bent beneath a long box of cheap unvarnished wood. Weighty, it was, to judge of the way they were bent beneath it, and all three rough men, in aprons and coarse coats—had they not been so, I might have attempted to speak to them, but they kept their eyes averted as they passed, and he directed them to the door next along this landing, where I knew at once that he himself must be lodged. But what those boxes contained or whence they came I do not know, for when I pressed him he said only that he required certain equipment for my treatment, and this would form a part of it. That he had already told me this before, and it would be of no use to explain it to me further because I would not understand. And then he ushered me back inside, and I sank slowly down and placed my cheek against the door and gazed, as the hot tears trickled down, to where the last edge of pale light still seeped through.

30 APRIL

I find myself listening, now, at the wall that separates us. My hearing has become so sharpened I can hear every tiny noise, every minuscule movement. Sometimes I tell myself I can even hear him breathing. For the first days I heard only such sounds as I might have expected— the scrape of a chair, the opening of a door—but last night, after he had taken away my dinner, and my lamp, I heard voices from beyond the wall. His voice, and a woman's voice. My heart began to pound then, and I pressed my ear closer to the wall, but I could not discern their words. But it seemed to me he spoke to her as he used to speak to me, when he would hold my hands and question me and draw me into his eyes. But soon there were no words at all, only the sound of drumming against the floor and low breathless moans that brought the hot blood to my cheeks as my mind made pictures I fought to repulse. And then one long cry. And after that nothing but the silence, and the dark.

I sat there, I do not know how long, wondering if the next sound I would hear would be the key in my own lock, but it never came. And the next I knew was a door opening and closing, and steps descending the stairs.

When he brought me my food just now I said I was not hungry, and I asked him who the young woman was whose voice I had heard.

"You are mistaken," he said after a moment, avoiding my gaze. "There is no young woman here. But we know, do we not, that you have always been vulnerable to the delusions of an enflamed imagination."

"I thought," I stammered, "that you believed me—that I was not mad—"

His eyes narrowed. "And of all the doctors who were brought to see you, *I alone* believed so. You should remember that. I will leave the food. I advise you to eat it."

NO DATE—

I no longer know how long I have been here. Something has happened to me, since the last time I wrote in this book. Whether it is an illness, or the consequence of all these dark and solitary hours, I cannot tell, I know only that I have spent what seems like many days on my bed, unable to move, drifting between half sleep and waking. Sometimes I have roused myself to find he has been here, but I have no recollection of seeing him, and the food he has left me tasted sour in my mouth. I have heard cries in the night, and wondered if it was my own voice echoing in my ears. I have felt the touch of fingers on my skin, and not known if I have dreamed. And I have endured, once more, the nightmare.

It was the light, once, that protected me—it was the sunshine of common day that kept the nightmare confined, and consigned its horrors only to the abyss of slumber. But here there is no light, no day, and the visions of the night hours begin to invade my waking mind. He knows not the torment he is inflicting, for else, surely, he would pity me. For here in the dark I cannot escape them—the looming shapes circling above my head, the hands reaching down towards me, the gaudy lights and the incessant repeating music, and always, always, at the last, that terrible image of my mother's smiling face.

It comes—every night now it comes, and I wake to the sound of my own voice, crying out a name I do not know—

Do not leave me—*do not leave me*—

I was sick today, wretchedly sick, and though my flesh feels scoured and drained, and I tremble to hold my pen, my head is a little clearer. And because my mind is steady now that my body is empty, I am starting to wonder if he has been poisoning me. Whether ever since I was foolish enough to tell him about the young woman I heard, he has secured himself from my inquisitiveness by drugging my food. I know he would not hesitate, for if there is a man capable of such a thing, it is he. And if it is truly so, what hope do I have? He can do with me what he wills, for no-one knows where I am, and no-one comes near, neither maid nor messenger. How I wish now that I had spoken to those men when I had the chance—for I have heard no human voice since, only the muffled drone of the city which rings about us. I listen until the hissing silence thunders in my ears but still no-one comes. I no longer live as others do, by day and night, but by lamplight and darkness. By dark I curl upon my bed, hearing mice scuttling in the skirting, and what must be great birds flapping and scuffling on the rooftop outside. By light I sit here huddled on the floor, enclosed within the pale circle of the lamp, tracing patterns in the bare boards. Following with my fingers where the grain combs into threads, or parts round the whorls in the wood like river water past a stone, but I stop always at those two knots, there, at the edge of the light, which stare back at me even now, sloping and menacing, like the eyes of some great and savage wolf.

When he comes to take the lamp, I beg him, on my knees, for news of my father. I take his hand and caress it, pleading for just a little daylight, but he throws me from him in disdain, saying that my case is a grave one, and the measures he is taking proportionate to my need. Surely, he says, a little patience and perseverance on my part is not so much to ask. And when he has gone, and I am left lying abject on the floor where he left me, I wonder if this is a punishment. The vengeance of a God my father confessed not to believe in, for perverting the powers only a deity dare assume. For surely we offended against Him, in counterfeiting the souls of the dead and conjuring false terror from empty shadows. And perhaps it is for that dire sin that He shows me now what face terror truly wears.

LATER—

I am become a thing of darkness. My eyes are too weak to bear even the dim glow that comes when he opens the door, and I recoil from it in pain, as I recoil from his touch. I can no longer even see his face, as the light streams in behind him and he seems monstrous, like the fiend of some half-forgotten myth. My world has shrunk to these two narrow rooms and I sense it only by sound, and by skin. When he takes the lamp from me, I feel my way along the walls, seeing through my fingers. And once or twice, when my hands have grazed the mirror, or the coal-scuttle, I have seen a dull colour blossom at my touch. Not the icy flames I saw in Vienna, or the beautiful light that rose from Dora's grave, but a meagre glimmer pricking at my nerves. I shrank from this, once, not knowing what it was and terrified that it branded me as mad. And then I gloried in it, because he told me it was a gift—a wondrous talent that drew him to me as to none other before. And then I think of that girl I heard, and those cries so suddenly cut off, and I am afraid.

NO DATE—

It has been three days now, since I have eaten what he has brought me. I have thrown the food into the water-closet, and when he comes I disguise my weakness by cowering in the corner and refusing to go near him. He chides me, then, for childishness and pique and I turn my face to the wall and say nothing. Better far he should think so, than have him guess the truth.

I have made a discovery. The last time he left the lamp I took it into the sitting-room, wondering if despite its dirt and emptiness there might after all be something there that could tell me where I am—some discarded letter perhaps, or tradesman's receipt. And it was then, when I went searching from shelf to bare shelf, that I discovered a door in the corner by the window, concealed in the wooden panelling. My heart rose an instant in a wild hope of escape, only for it to perish cruelly as I realised that there could be no egress this way—that it could be nothing more than a cupboard set into the dividing wall. And yet I persevered, thinking such a hiding-place might still contain something of use. I felt down the jamb with my fingers and found a small metal catch, and the next moment the door swung open towards me. And it was indeed, only a cupboard, barely three feet in depth. Or at least so I thought, until I noticed a tiny circle of light on the far side and saw that it was not a wall at all, but another door, leading to the apartment beyond. I pushed gently but it would not give, so I knelt down as quietly as I could and placed my eye to the keyhole. Because I knew by then what I would see.

I would see *him*.

And perhaps because I am so helpless, so entirely subservient to the power he wields, I have taken to sitting at this door and observing him. It is my tiny vengeance to watch him so, when he has no notion I am there, for it is clear to me he has not perceived that this hidden door separates us. But I have learned nothing from my spying that I did not know, or that might assist me. It is part of his bedroom I can see, a bedroom most luxuriously appointed. There is a large bed, and what I think must be a table, covered with a heavy crimson satin cloth. Sometimes he lies many hours on that bed by day, full-dressed in the clothes he always wears, not sleeping, but not awake, as if sunk in a trance. Sometimes I see him reading from a great quantity of heavy volumes which appear to contain diagrams, or sheets of figures, or obscure mathematical signs, and once I saw a great piece of glass, cut in a diamond shape like the prisms I once studied in my father's books. And when night has fallen and he has brought me my dinner, I hear him, for many hours, writing, the pen scratching scratching scratching across the page.

NO DATE—

It must be more than a month since we left my home, for my bleeds have come. Having endured so much, and so long, this last might seem such a little thing, and yet I am weeping now for the first time in many days, not just for myself and for my father all those long weeks alone and unknowing, but because I am ashamed. I have not brought those requisites with me that a lady needs, and there is no way, here, of obtaining them. Nor will I raise the subject with him, not only because it is unfitting, but because I will never again put myself in his debt. He has taken from me all I had—my home, my father, even the light and air—and now he seeks to take what is left of my dignity.

Perhaps it is because I have been so sick, but I cannot remember so much blood before, not even that first time when I was a girl, or in Vienna before we left, when I was so ill and those doctors diagnosed *chlorosis.* I have conquered my punctilio and my humiliation and torn the bed-linen, winding it into heavy bandages, but still the blood pulses from me as if my last strength were ebbing away, and when I woke last night gasping from the nightmare the bed was drenched with it, and I heard a child's voice crying in the silence. I sat a moment, the wetness thick on my skin, praying I was mistaken or had dreamed it, but then I heard the cry again and knew it was not so.

I crawled to the hidden door and I knelt, trembling, by the keyhole. The curtains were undrawn now, and the white moonlight flooded so into the room that I had to close my eyes for a moment in sudden pain—I had never seen it so bright as this, so powerful as this, and I thought afterwards that he must have employed that prism I had seen in his hands. The light fell full on the table I had seen before, but as my eyes became accustomed to the brightness I saw that its red satin covering was gone and my heart froze as I saw that it was indeed a table, but one such as I had never seen before—a table covered in leather with holes drilled along its edges, and straps threaded through them, and there, there—I shudder even now as I write it—a young woman was lying, half-naked, her ankles pinned by those leather straps. I could not see her face, but I could tell her youth from her slenderness and the little rosebud tattooed near her foot. And then another figure passed close before the door and I saw only black. But I knew who it was. I scarcely dared breathe then, as I watched him move forwards towards the bed, his back toward me, and then he bent low over the girl as he had once bent over me—as he had once bent over my Dora. I knew—I thought I knew—what he would do then, and bit my lip until my teeth pierced flesh. She moaned, just as I had once moaned, but my body had never convulsed as hers did now, thrashing, twisting, thrown again and again hard against the wooden frame. I turned my face away and clasped my hands tight over my ears but I could not shut it out—the drumming of the table against the floor, and above it the sound of a little child crying, *"Mama! Mama!"*

I lay there in the silence that followed, too terrified to move, feeling the blood seep through my thin nightgown, until at last I heard sounds from the room beyond. The sound of something heavy dragging across the floor, then the door opening and steps on the stairs outside. I crept to the keyhole again and saw that the room was as it had always been. The red satin was again in place, and of mother and child there was no sign.

THE NEXT DAY—

I can barely read my writing, so weak are my eyes, so unsteady my hand. Still the blood comes, and now there is pain such as I have

CHAPTER NINE

HER BODY LIES EXPOSED to the air, naked and defiled. There is no sheet to cover her white skin now. Her breast has been pierced, and twists of sinew and muscle and flaccid veins spill from the empty hollow of the ribs to the heart that once beat there. A heart that lies now seeping on her belly. And there on the floor, where her head has rolled, a huge black crow is perched on her forehead, pecking at her eyes.

Sam lurches at the bird which lifts slowly off and makes for the window, its ragged wings beating the stale air.

"Is someone goin' to tell me 'ow the bloody 'ell this man got in?" he barks at the attendant. "You there—Madsen, weren't you supposed to be on duty last night?"

The man blenches. "Yes, sir. I just don't know how it could have happened, sir—I was only gone for five minutes. I got called upstairs when they were bringing in another corpse, and by the time I got back, well, you can see—"

"Yes, Madsen, I *can* bloody well see! And was the window open then?"

"Yes, sir, it being so hot, sir."

Sam looks again at the casement, but for the life of him he can't see how a full-grown man could have got through that aperture. And as for the idea that a child could have done this—

"I suppose it's possible—" begins Madsen tentatively, rather red in the face.

"Go on—I'm all ears."

"There've been a lot of people in and out of the station, sir. Tourists and such, what with the Exhibition being on. Lost children, people wanting directions and so forth. It's possible, I suppose, that someone could have slipped past the sergeant on duty—if there'd been a sudden crowd at the desk. And then if he hid somewhere down here until it was dark, and I was out of the room—"

"That's an 'ell of a lot of 'ifs,' Madsen."

"I know, sir. But I just can't think of any other way he could've done it."

"And 'ow did 'e get out afterwards?"

Madsen flushes. "Well, things did get a bit confused after that—when I saw what had happened I called out to the sergeant and he came down to see—"

"So the desk was unmanned."

"Yes, sir. But only for a few minutes. Sir."

But long enough, as Sam well knows, for someone to make their escape—and especially someone capable of planning such an operation in the first place. He glances at his pocket-watch—he sent young Jenkins for Charles over an hour ago—where the hell is he?

Then the morgue door bangs open and the hefty desk sergeant appears in the doorway.

"Mr Maddox is upstairs."

"About bloody time! Bring 'im down then, what yer waitin' for?"

"He's with Rowlandson. The Inspector asked me to fetch you."

"Tell 'im I'll be there in a minute," says Sam, desperate to buy some time, and well aware that Rowlandson will be asking all the same questions he just did, and Sam doesn't have anything like a satisfactory answer.

"He said *at once*, Wheeler. And judging by the look on his face, he meant it."

Charles is already waiting outside the upstairs office but there is no time to speak before the door is opened and they are ushered into Rowlandson's presence. The Inspector is standing at the window with his back to them. He is a tall man, and his height is further accentuated by his thinness; he has greying hair cut short, and a little beard trimmed in a goatee. It's not yet eight o'clock in the morning but the day is already hot, and the Inspector has his handkerchief in his hand and is wiping the moisture from his neck. When he hears the door he turns to face them, and then comes forwards a few paces and places a newspaper on the table. It's that morning's *Daily News*. Carefully folded so that the story on the front page is facing upwards:

London Daily News

Wednesday, 18 June 1851

DOES A VAMPIRE STALK LONDON?

HORRIBLE MURDERS IN PICCADILLY
FOUR CASES SINCE THE EXHIBITION OPENED
VICTIMS BEHEADED AND DESECRATED

The news we have to report today will, we have no doubt, send a thrill of horror throughout the whole metropolis. We doubt whether any occurrence of the kind has ever created a greater sensation, and it is with the most painful reluctance that we divulge it, but we believe it is our duty to bring to the attention of the public a series of brutal murders that the authorities have sought for some weeks to bury in silence. The police have said nothing of these outrages, fearing an outbreak of general panic such as London has never witnessed, and at a time when the capital is thronged with visitors, but we can now reveal that in the last two months, three women, all of the class known as "unfortunates," have been found slaughtered in the most savage manner in the vicinity of St James's Park, their heads hacked from their bodies and disposed of who knows where. Were that not dreadful enough, we are informed by a most unimpeachable source that the necks showed the unmistakable signs of teeth marks, and the hearts had either been pierced with some unknown weapon, or removed from the corpses entirely.

None of the three women has yet been identified, and yet before an inquest has even been convened, when their desecrated bodies have scarcely even been committed to the ground, another female of the same class has now met with the same gruesome fate.

A NEW OUTRAGE

The latest barbarity occurred only yesterday, when the police station in Vine Street was entered in the early hours of the morning by an unknown intruder, and a fourth corpse butchered in the like horrific manner, within yards of where a sergeant was supposedly on watch. This young woman is believed to have been a resident of Granby Street, and her body was discovered only two days ago. We are assured that it was at that time intact, though showing the same marks of puncture wounds about the throat. There being no other visible injury, and the young woman's skin being unnaturally pale, rumour is rife that both she and the other victims met their deaths by exsanguination.

The obvious similarities in the atrocious mutilations which all four bodies suffered serve only to add the most profound mystery to the horror of these crimes, and forces us to the irresistible conclusion that all were perpetrated by one and the same hand.

As a general rule, the mutilation of bodies is entirely foreign to the English style in crime, and it was with no surprise, therefore, that we learned that the one attested sighting of the perpetrator suggests that he speaks with a foreign accent. Foreigner he may be; fiend he most certainly is. To commit such atrocities in the very heart of London, no more than yards from the lights and crowds of one of its most populous and fashionable thoroughfares, argues for a terrifying and indeed supernatural ability to move among us undetected. For it is impossible, after committing such sanguinary crimes, that he was not literally drenched with the blood of his hapless victims, and yet he was observed in this state by no-one, and certainly not by any member of the police force which is supposedly charged with the protection of the law-abiding citizenry.

POLICE CONFOUNDED

The police have much to answer for in this sorry case. All attempts to discover and apprehend the assailant have met with failure, and we are of the opinion that this unforgiveable dereliction of duty stems in no small measure from a refusal on the part of those charged with the inquiry (*to wit*, Inspector Rowlandson, of Bow Street) to accept a simple fact that will be obvious at once to anyone cognisant with even the barest facts of the case: There is a Vampire at large in London, stalking its most hallowed quarters, preying upon those foolish or unfortunate enough to walk the streets by night.

There are those of our readers, no doubt, who will ridicule such a suggestion, countering that Vampires are nothing but the stuff of children's stories and folk legend, but we believe there is no other rational explanation that can account for the evidence that has been presented to us. Not only do these murders exhibit an unprecedented savagery, they defy all rules of human motive.

There are no known connexions among the victims, and no conceivable benefit that could result from the butchery inflicted upon them, beyond a malignant and bloodthirsty delight in the deed itself. We are bound to conclude, therefore, that these crimes can only be the work of some inhuman monster, raging with a ghoulish lust for blood. For in addition to those facts we have already set out, *viz*, the unnaturally pale condition of the bodies, the removal of the hearts, and the teeth marks upon the necks, there is a further circumstance the police have thus far refused even to consider, and it is this: Each of these foul murders took place at or approximate to full moon; a time, as is well attested, when the grim spectre of the Vampire is at his most powerful, and most menacing.

We have attempted to speak with Inspector Rowlandson on several occasions, most lately last evening, but he has thus far declined to answer any of our questions. It is in the light of this refusal, and in the interests of public safety, that we now feel compelled to break the silence surrounding these heinous crimes. We have no wish to provoke unnecessary alarm, but given the inability of the police to either prevent or resolve these foul murders, we feel our readers must be told the truth, that they might take whatever measures they deem fit to ensure the safety of their own households. For until this fiend has been apprehended, the denizens of Piccadilly and St James will rightly feel the highest degree of apprehension that some new horror might nightly be committed in their very midst, perhaps upon the bodies of their own innocent and respectable womenfolk.

We acknowledge that the current Exhibition has placed an additional strain on a constabulary already struggling to police the vast extent of the greatest capital in the world, but it does not excuse their repeated failure in this extraordinary case. We say only this: If the Detective Branch has neither the intelligence nor the resources it requires to effect an arrest, it might do worse than to call upon the proven capabilities of the private agencies, there being at least one member thereof who has exhibited the true instinct of the detective calling, in both identifying and then apprehending the vicious criminals at the heart of that infamous conspiracy lately set on foot by Sir Julius Cremorne. We have in mind, of course, Mr Charles Maddox, the younger of that illustrious name.

"So would one of you like to tell me what in the devil's name is going on?"

Sam shoots an agonised look in Charles's direction, and Charles takes a deep breath. "It has nothing to do with me, sir. I know it looks like—"

"Too damn right, Maddox, as to what it looks like. The eyes of the Empire are upon this city at present, and in consequence there is an unprecedented attention upon the manner in which London conducts its affairs. The very last thing we need is ill-informed panic-mongering on the part of the press, or the slightest suggestion that the Metropolitan Police is not even capable of catching the killer of a few street whores. When I asked Wheeler to consult with you about this case, I believed I could trust in your judgement and discretion; I did *not* expect you to exploit the fact as a means to advance your own reputation, at the expense of that of your former colleagues."

"And I *did not do so.*" Charles looks at him, full in the face, his blue eyes blazing and his chin high. "I know how it appears, sir, but I swear to you that I have discussed this case with no-one but Sam and my uncle—"

"Are you telling me that you have had no contact—*no contact whatsoever*—with Patrick O'Riordan?"

Charles flushes and his eyes drop.

"I thought as much."

"*He* came to *me*—started spouting this ludicrous story about vampires. I knew it was absurd, but I needed more evidence—I needed to be able to prove it—"

"And it did not occur to you to inform me? That it was *my* decision to make, not yours?"

Sam looks across at Charles. "You never said nuffin' about O'Riordan to me," he mutters. "An' as for this vampire carry-on, well it's the first I've bloody well 'eard of it."

Charles hesitates. "I thought you would laugh." His cheeks are burning now. "Both of you. It was such an outlandish idea—I was embarrassed even to mention it. And as for taking it seriously as a theory of the crime—how could any sane person believe it—"

Rowlandson observes them for a moment. Wheeler, he knows, is loyal to a fault, especially where Charles is concerned, and the reproach in Sam's tone clearly stems more from sorrow than from anger. But that being the case, it's no surprise that Charles is still unable to meet his friend's gaze.

"So," continues Rowlandson, "if O'Riordan did not get this story of his from you, then whom? Who is this *unimpeachable source* he refers to? As far as I have been informed, the details of these cases are scarcely known outside this room."

Sam considers. "The assistants at the morgue, the doctor, one or two constables workin' wiv me. That's it."

"So we have an informer in our midst."

Rowlandson eyes the two of them heavily then turns to look down at the street. About two hundred people are already gathered outside, shouting up at the windows and pressing against the steps, where four of Vine Street's burliest are doing their best to hold them at bay. Their anger is audible even three floors away, and this is the West End bourgeoisie, not an East End rabble. Though there are at least half a dozen prostitutes down there, mingling among the esquires. He can tell by their brazen *décolletage* and tawdry dresses. But there's nothing tawdry about the fear in their eyes.

"As if we did not have enough to contend with," he says grimly. "And how in God's name did this man manage to break into the mortuary? The window is scarcely big enough to admit a man, and the only other access would be through the station-house itself."

"I'm as baffled as you are, sir," says Sam. "The attendant claims 'e must 'ave slipped past the desk, but some of the lads are already startin' to say it's as if 'e walked through the walls."

"That's the last I want to hear of that sort of talk," snaps Rowland-

son. "We cannot afford to give even the slightest credence to this ridiculous theory that a vampire is at large. We need facts, gentlemen,
facts. Not some absurd overheated fantasy. So, what exactly *are* the
facts? Is this malicious piece of trouble-making masquerading as jour-
nalism accurate? What about the dates—do they indeed tally with the
full moon as O'Riordan alleges?"

He strides to his desk and opens his copy of *Old Moore's Almanack*.
"When was the first body found?"

He looks at Charles, but it's Sam who answers.

"May twentief, sir, and the second one on the twenty-first. The fird
one were the twenty-fif, but we've no idea when she actually died."

Rowlandson peels back through the pages. "In May the full
moon was on the eighteenth. Could the third girl have been dead that
long?"

Sam nods. "I reckon it's possible, sir."

"I see. And this last girl, Rose? What's her surname?"

"Danby, sir. We found 'er two days ago."

Rowlandson sighs. "The sixteenth. The day of the full moon. But if
we hadn't worked out this connexion, how in heaven's name did the
Daily News do it?"

Sam shrugs. "Well, as long as you know when the bodies were found,
I suppose it ain't that 'ard to work it out, sir. 'Specially if you're startin'
on the basis that it were a vampire 'as done 'em. It all adds up, then,
don't it. The moon, the be'eadin', the teef—"

"I was coming to that. I had no idea the corpses displayed any such
puncture wounds. The beheadings and the removal of the hearts, yes,
but *teeth marks*? What infernal nonsense is this?"

Sam is shaking his head and opening his mouth to reply when
Charles interrupts him. "There are definitely marks on Rose Danby's
body, sir. And on the third victim. But if O'Riordan is claiming that
those same marks were on the first two bodies as well, he didn't get
that from me, and no-one I've spoken to at the morgue has admitted
noticing anything like that, either. I only found the marks on the third
corpse afterwards, when I went back to examine it again. Only someone actually looking for them would have even noticed they were

there. Frankly, I don't think they're teeth marks at all, and as for the rest of it—"

Rowlandson's eyes narrow. "Go on."

Charles takes a deep breath. "If we accept—just for the sake of argument—that there actually *was* a vampire at work here, then there'd be teeth marks on the bodies, and evidence of considerable if not fatal exsanguination—"

"But I thought that's precisely what we *do* have—"

"Bear with me, sir. It's the rest of it that defies logic—the beheadings, and the cutting out of the hearts. People do that because they think it will prevent the victims of a vampire from becoming vampires themselves. In other words it's the very *last* thing an actual vampire would ever do to a corpse."

Rowlandson frowns. "So what are you suggesting? That these horrible mutilations are purely coincidental—a depraved act of gratuitous violence?"

"Could be," answers Sam slowly. "Or maybe what this killer's really after doin' is spreadin' terror in London, 'specially now the Exhibition's on, an' 'e finks this is the best an' quickest way to do it. An' 'e's right, ain't 'e. I mean, look at them people outside. An' if 'e's after discreditin' the police, then 'e might well 'ave given the story to the *News* 'imself. For if there's one person outside this room who knows the details of these crimes, it's 'im. An' if 'e really does turn out to be a foreigner, like the girls said, then—"

He stops, and flushes, realising what he's done. "That is, sir—"

"*Foreigner?*" snaps Rowlandson quickly. "I thought that was just yet another of O'Riordan's inflammatory fabrications?"

Charles glances at Sam, who stammers, "No, sir. But we only—"

"Good God, man!" barks Rowlandson, crashing his fist down upon the desk, "are you seriously telling me that you had reason to believe this man is a foreigner and you have not thought fit to report that fact to your superior officer? I could have you up on a disciplinary charge for that alone, never mind all the rest of it—"

"It's not Sam's fault, sir," says Charles at once. His own career in the

Met was wrecked on very similar rocks, and he's not going to let that happen to Sam—not if he can help it. "A man was seen running from Shepherd's Market the night Rose Danby's body was found, but it was only yesterday we picked up that the man who killed her might be a foreigner. I'm sure Sam was going to come and speak to you about it first thing this morning."

"Is this right, Wheeler?"

"Yes, sir. It were one of the Granby Street girls as gave us the lead. She seemed to fink the bloke Rose Danby 'ad been seein' 'ad a foreign accent. I've 'ad the 'Ome Office give us the certificates of arrival for the last couple o' months, an' me an' a few lads 'ave started knockin' on doors. Only one so far whose alibi don't quite ring true—strange cove an' no mistake—I'm 'avin' Foster look into it—"

Rowlandson shakes his head. "I'm not sure what's worse—that the public should actually believe a vampire stalks our streets, or having to explain to the Commissioners that this may all be the work of some political *agent provocateur.*"

"I don't think it's either, sir," says Charles.

"Well, if you have some other theory, Maddox," retorts Rowlandson sardonically, "and preferably one that will lead to a swift and decisive arrest, then pray, do enlighten us."

"I think the marks on the corpses might have been made by a scarificator—it's a type of blood-letting instrument. There's a new version that creates a small circular puncture, and can be used not just on the arm but the neck. I think that could be the answer—it would explain the marks, and it would also explain why the corpses were so pale. I've arranged to have one sent here, and I've obtained a list of all the addresses where these instruments have been delivered in the last two months, since the murders started. And if one of those men turns out to be a foreigner—"

A knock then, and the desk sergeant appears once more, this time with a small parcel in his hand.

"Delivery for Mr Maddox, sir. The man who brought it insists it's urgent."

Charles takes the package and rips off the brown paper, and then he opens the box and shows the contents to Rowlandson.

"This is it, sir. The Heurteloup scarificator. If we can prove this instrument made those marks we may be able to quash this insidious vampire story once and for all."

"In that case, Maddox, I suggest we lose no further time."

The three of them descend the two flights of stairs to the morgue. There is an awkward moment when Charles comes face-to-face with the doctor, who cannot be expected to relish this usurpation of his territory, but after a moment he steps back, and they take their places around the corpse. Rowlandson nods to the attendant, and Charles goes to the end of the slab as the man takes the sheet and lifts it away from the severed head. One eye is a mass of pulp now, and the whole of that side of the face is pitted with sharp indentations where pieces of flesh have been ripped away. Charles looks up at Sam.

"There was a bloody great crow in 'ere earlier. Must 'a got in through the window."

Charles takes a deep breath but still his fingers are trembling as he eases the scarificator from its case, all too aware of the doctor's unsmiling stare. He bends over the body and places the circular blade against the punctured skin.

Then he straightens up and replaces the instrument in its box. "It's a perfect fit."

He hears Rowlandson exhale, and the murmurs of the two young constables standing behind him.

"Do you 'ave that list?" says Sam at his shoulder. "The addresses where they sent those instruments to?"

Charles pulls the paper from his pocket and hands it to Sam, and the attendant comes forward to replace the sheet. And as he lifts it up to cover her face, Charles sees for the first time what lies beneath—the heart resting on the belly, the skeins of arteries and muscle oozing slimy grey.

Sam notices nothing of this—he's set Charles's list down beside his own, and is scanning the addresses frantically, looking for a match. But Rowlandson sees; Rowlandson observes.

"What is it, Maddox?"

For Charles is staring now, staring with the horror of a man aghast.

"I've seen this before," he says eventually. "I've *seen this before*—"

"I do not take your meaning," says Rowlandson. "I thought you had examined the body already?"

"No, sir," interjects the doctor. "Not in its present state. I do not admit idle spectators."

Rowlandson turns again to Charles. "Maddox?"

"You don't understand," says Charles, "I've seen *exactly* this before. The heart on the belly, the head removed—only that girl wasn't *real*."

Rowlandson scowls. "We can do without your damn riddles, Maddox."

"You don't understand—it was in Austria, not three months ago, in a collection of waxworks owned by the man I was investigating. A nobleman by the name of—"

"—the Baron Von Reisenberg."

It's Sam's voice, and Charles turns to him, open-mouthed. "How on earth—"

Sam holds out Charles's list, pointing to a name. "The Albany—they sent one of those instruments to the *Albany*. Same bloody address where I went last night. This Baron of yours is the bloke I mentioned before—the one who gave me the creeps—the one with the dodgy alibi. Accordin' to the 'Ome Office 'e arrived at Grimsby on the *Ceres* in the first week of April, and 'e's been at the Albany since the twenty-fird. 'Es been 'ere all this time. For all the killin's. It all adds up, sir," he finishes excitedly to Rowlandson, "it does. It's 'im. *We've got 'im!*"

The Inspector frowns. "Not so fast, Wheeler. I'm not having you two crashing about arresting a member of the Austrian nobility without better cause than that. It may all be some bizarre coincidence. Do you, for example," he says, turning to Charles and gesturing at the corpse, "have any explanation for this—this—*abomination*? Beyond this man's peculiar not to say unsavoury taste in curios?"

"Whatever it is, sir, it's not that. This man is deliberately turning these women into exact simulacra of the models I saw in his collection. Though whether he does so from some macabre and misplaced quest for scientific knowledge, or for his own perverted pleasure, I cannot tell you."

Rowlandson frowns. "What pleasure could there be in such barbarity?"

"There are killers who would find a depraved gratification in the violence of such an act, and others who derive satisfaction of a wholly different kind."

He pauses; Rowlandson is still staring at him and Charles feels his cheeks going red. He can hear the constable behind him shifting uneasily: He for one knows exactly what Charles is talking about.

Charles swallows. "I saw the Baron's waxworks on only one occasion, and by accident, when he left the door unlocked. But from what I did see, it's possible some of them had been used for, well, carnal pleasure. I assumed, at the time, that this explained why he was so careful to keep the collection private."

Rowlandson gapes at him. "This man slakes his lusts on *lifeless dolls*?"

"It's conceivable, sir, yes. But my point is that only *some* of his waxworks resembled living women. There were others that were headless, or mere torsos, and some with the organs exposed. Just like the corpses we found. And one of the waxworks was of a woman with her heart resting on her belly—a woman whose head had been removed. Just like this. This man is systematically re-creating those wax models in living flesh, and I don't think these latest victims are the only ones. A doctor living close to his castle told me that another girl had been found dead there only a few weeks before, and her body was later mutilated in exactly the same way as Rose and the others. I think the Baron came perilously near discovery then—indeed I suspect it was only the superstitious terror of his own peasants that saved him. They believed that an act of such vicious brutality could only be the work of a *nosferatu,* not a real man."

"I am rather inclined to agree with them," says Rowlandson heavily.

"But here, sir, in London, he can move unseen among the crowds and have his pick of desperate and half-starving whores. And if the rumour now runs rife that a vampire is to blame, then so much the better. For the very last person we will then suspect is a man such as he—an industrialist and a scientist, and a member of the nobility."

"That's exactly what 'e said to me," says Sam quickly. "When I questioned him about the murders—"

"Good God, man, you actually *questioned* him?"

"He talked about cut-froats and whores, sir. Only I never told 'im who the victims were. There was no way 'e could 'ave known the girls were tarts. That's when I knew somefing was wrong."

"But anyone might have made the same assumption, Wheeler. The vast majority of the women killed in this city are those who work on its streets."

"With respect, sir," intervenes Charles, "they're also the least likely to be missed. That's why we still don't know who the first three were. That's *why he chose them.* That's *why he came.*"

There is a silence. The young constable standing behind Charles seems scarcely to be breathing.

"And the marks on the necks," says Rowlandson eventually. "The blood-letting—does your theory explain that?"

"I can only guess that he wishes to weaken them, perhaps to render them unable to defend themselves," replies Charles. "Other than that, I do not know."

"And you're suggesting that this Baron Von Reisenberg broke in here last night to mutilate this woman? Despite the enormous risk that he would be seen and caught?"

Charles shrugs. "I cannot think of any other explanation."

Rowlandson looks from one to the other. And then decides. "Take two sturdy men with you, and bring him in for questioning. And *discreetly*. And in the meantime I will deal with our Mr O'Riordan. I want the name of that *'unimpeachable source'* of his, and I fully intend to get it."

⊸❀ ❦

The courtyard at the Albany is thronged with people when the horses pull up, and for one terrible moment Charles thinks that the news has gone before them—that a vengeful mob is gathered here already. But as they step down from the carriage it's obvious that this is a gathering of quite a different social order. There are white-clothed tables bearing pitchers of punch and champagne, and a number of the bachelor residents are accompanied by daintily dressed young women in silk dresses and summer bonnets. The enclaves of the Albany are rarely sullied by the presence of the police, and especially not when *en fête,* and Sam is forced in consequence to leave one of the constables outside to appease the indignation of a red-faced gentleman with mutton-chop whiskers who is clearly the host of these proceedings.

Inside, the corridors and staircases are deserted, and when they come to a halt in front of the Baron's door they hear only silence.

"Police! Open up!" cries Sam, knocking on the door. And then, when there is no reply, he nods to the constable accompanying them. "Go on then, break it down."

The apartment is empty, Charles can see that at once, but he follows Sam and the constable as they search, first the sitting-room and then the bedroom, but all is neat, all is normal. There is nothing amiss, nothing out of place. Apart from one thing. Heaped on the bedspread is a satin cloth of deep red.

"I reckon 'e's definitely 'ad tarts in 'ere," says Sam, eyeing several darker patches on the silk. "But if 'e did kill 'em, it don't look like this was where 'e did it."

Charles goes to the desk on the far side of the bedroom, but the surface is clear and clean, apart from a deep scratch where something heavy has been clumsily moved. The drawers are empty, too, at least at first sight. Though when he pulls one out he feels it catch, and bends to find a sheet of paper caught in the back. But when he eases it out it proves to be nothing but scientific annotations, covered with sketchy diagrams and tiny hand-scribbled notes of letters and numbers, but none of it in any pattern Charles can recognise.

"What's that?" asks Sam.

"I'm not sure—it's all in German. Looks like some sort of optical diagram—this here is a prism with the lines showing light refracting through it." He turns the paper. "And this might be a concave mirror, with some sort of wiring attached to it—"

For a moment, as he says it, there is a half memory of a half thought, but as quickly as it comes it is gone, and he cannot grasp it again. A moment later he shakes his head and turns again to look slowly round the room. And that's when he notices it. Where the slanting sunlight from the window zigzags across the panelling there is a slight misalignment. It's only the tiniest imperfection of line, but it's enough. He moves quickly to the wall and slides his hand along the edge of the wood. Sam comes up behind him, and then the two of them hear a soft click as a door swings open. But the cupboard—for it's hardly more than that—is bare. Sam sighs and turns away, but Charles is suddenly on his knees, pressing his finger against a dank stain on the floor. A dank stain that comes away red.

"Blood?" says Sam, leaning over his shoulder.

Charles nods. He gets to his feet and starts feeling along the back of the cupboard.

"It's another door," he says quickly. "But I can't get it open—we'll have to go round the other way."

Less than a minute later they're standing in the vestibule of the adjoining apartment. The stench of shit and rotting food in the shuttered, airless space has the young constable gagging in his handkerchief, and as Charles recognises what else it is he can smell, he feels the bile rise in his own throat and he throws open one of the doors and rushes to the nearest window and opens it wide. He takes huge gulping breaths, feeling the breeze on his face and hearing the sound of girls laughing in the courtyard below. Laughing in the sunshine. And then he turns back slowly to face the room, knowing what it is he will see.

There is blood everywhere.

Pools of it spilt across the wooden boards in trails of footprints and dark smears. Hand marks of it running along the walls, and next door, in the bedroom, a bare mattress so drenched with it that the floor below is saturated. And when they open the water-closet even Sam has to cover his mouth. The bare bed explains itself now. The closet is heaped with blood-stained bed-linen, torn into strips and wrapped into wads, the cloth sodden black-red and stinking.

"Jesus Christ, Chas," says Sam behind him, coughing, "what the bloody 'ell 'appened 'ere?"

Charles stares at the spewing water-closet. "I think someone's been kept in these rooms. Locked here like a prisoner. And for a long time."

"So this is where 'e does it? 'E keeps 'em caged up in 'ere for God knows 'ow long, an' then 'e kills 'em and cuts the bodies up? No wonder it looks like a bloody abattoir."

Charles looks round. "This blood is new—some of it isn't even dry. Whatever happened in here, it was only a few days ago."

Sam stares at him, his face white. "Jesus, not Rose's little girl—"

Charles turns and goes back into the sitting-room and stands there looking at the pattern of the blood-stains. The faint trail leading to the hidden door, the deeper, darker trail from the front door to the bedroom and from there to the water-closet, the footprints smeared here and there, and the marks of fingers along the walls, as if feeling their way in the dark.

"No," he says at last, "it was a woman who was kept here, not a child. The marks on the wall are too high to be a child's. I think the bleeding started on the bed and carried on for several days, during which time she moved about these rooms, sometimes on her hands and knees. And she ended up there, in the water-closet. The blood is heaviest and newest there."

"So what exactly are you sayin'?"

Charles hesitates, realising for the first time that whoever this woman was, she must have been in this very room, terrified and bleeding and only yards away, when Sam stood face-to-face with the Baron not twelve hours before. And he wonders then if the same thought has crossed Sam's mind, too.

"I think she had a miscarriage, Sam. I think she lost her child."

The constable turns and stumbles out of the room, and they hear him being horribly sick in the corridor outside.

Sam shakes his head sadly. "Poor bastard! His wife just lost a baby. It were the third time, too." There's a pause, then, "Could she still be alive, this woman? I mean if we're sayin' none of this blood were from Rose—"

"I don't think so—it's too new. And in any case the doctor at the morgue would have seen at once if she'd recently been pregnant."

"In that case where is she—the woman who was 'ere? Is she dead, too?"

Charles sighs. "I don't know, Sam. I just don't know."

Sam watches as his friend starts to pace around the room. Charles thinks best when he's walking, even in such a small place as this; even in such a scene of horror as this. Was only one girl kept here, he wonders, or were they all imprisoned before they died? How did Rose come to be discovered dead in Shepherd's Market, but without any of the tell-tale disfigurements inflicted on the other girls? Did she manage to escape the Baron, only to be hunted down on the street and killed there? Was that why her body was intact when they found her? And if another girl was indeed kept in this place all these weeks, why was she allowed to remain alive so long? And then Charles remembers those other waxworks in the Baron's castle—those girls with their legs spread and their unborn babies unpeeled to the air, and it's his turn to stumble outside with his hand over his mouth.

He's still wiping his face when the other constable comes labouring up the stairs, sweating and out of breath. He looks at Charles and then at Sam, standing in the doorway.

"I was just speaking to the steward, sir, a Mr Nicolas Williams his name is. He says the tenant of these rooms left suddenly this morning, just before dawn. He says there was a long wooden box strapped to the carriage roof. Like a coffin, he thought. Only then he remembered there'd been a delivery a few weeks back from a maker of medical apparatus. Apparently one of the delivery men said it was one of those tables surgeons use. For dissection, sir."

Sam shoots a glance at Charles. "Does this Williams know where the man was goin'?"

"No, sir, but something the man let drop made Williams think he was heading for the Channel—he asked about steamers from Folkestone."

"And was there anyone wiv 'im? A woman? A kid?"

"He thought there might have been a woman in the carriage—the man did come here with a woman, apparently. A young woman. Williams was a bit reluctant to admit it, seeing as women aren't supposed to be on the premises. Not in the apartments at any rate. I got the impression this man had paid Williams well over the odds to keep it quiet."

"What did she look like?"

"It was dark when they arrived and she had a veil over her face. And no-one's seen her since."

"And there was no sign of the kid? A little girl?"

The constable shakes his head. "Sorry, sir. But I did find this in the refuse receptacles around the back," he says, holding out his hand. "This being a bachelor establishment, I thought it might be significant."

Sam takes one look at what he's clutching and swears under his breath.

It's a child's rag doll.

⟞ ⟝

Back at Vine Street the temperature is soaring and tempers are fraying. One of the officers at the door has the beginnings of a black eye, and some of the crowd have cobbled together makeshift banners and placards. It's clear to Charles at once that the mob is much more angry and much less middle-class than it had been even an hour before. There are rough-shod men shouting, and the police are being jostled and abused. It has all the makings of a riot.

According to the desk sergeant, Rowlandson is still upstairs, "and absolutely not to be disturbed, not even by you, and certainly not by any of this lot."

He cocks his head in the direction of the people crowded in the corner. It's the area that normally does makeshift service as a waiting room, but the two or three worn and spindle-less chairs are hopelessly inadequate for the numbers now herded there. Some huddle together and others press against the constable deputed to keep a clear path through from the door, but if the mood outside is irate, the atmosphere inside is anxious, and afraid.

"Who are all these people?" asks Sam in an under-tone. "What the 'ell are they doin' 'ere?"

"Getting in the bloody way, that's what they're doing. Thanks to the confounded *Daily News*, every Tom, Dick, and Harry in London thinks their missing wife or daughter's been abducted by a bleeding vampire. That one there," he continues, gesturing in the direction of a man at the edge of the group, with a leather case wedged between his feet, "claims his daughter disappeared two months ago in Whitby. Bloody *Whitby*, I ask you—must be nigh on three hundred miles!"

Charles looks across at the man. He must normally be handsome, but his face is pale and hollowed by anxiety. There is grey about his temples, and threads of silver in his beard. He looks up every few moments—every time a door opens, or there's another burst of noise from the street.

"I told him to hook it," continues the sergeant, "but he refuses to budge. Insists on seeing whoever's in charge. He'll have a bloody long wait, that's all I can say."

The sergeant is shaking his head, but Sam and Charles have both remembered where the Baron first came ashore, and are already moving towards the man, who starts up at once saying, "Is it Lucy? Have you found her?"

"Might be best if you came wiv us, sir," answers Sam in a low voice. "There's a room out the back 'ere."

The man is paler now, if that were possible, but he picks up his bag and follows them into the room behind the desk. It's where they keep the lost property, and the lanterns and flasks used by constables on night patrols. The shelves are stacked with umbrellas and briefcases and solitary gloves, and there's a strong smell of stewed tea. Charles points the man to the only seat, and he sits down slowly, still clutching his bag.

Sam gets out his notebook. "The sergeant told us you reported your daughter missin', sir."

The man swallows. "I last saw her in Whitby. On the morning of April twentieth."

"And you are?"

The man flushes a little now. "Alexander Causton. But I am not usually known by that name."

THE PIERCED HEART ✢ 177

Sam and Charles exchange a glance; no policeman likes an alias, and the man senses their disapproval. "It's not what you assume," he says quickly. "I have a stage *persona*, that is all. I am the theatrical illusionist Professor de Caus."

Charles notes that definite article—not *an* illusionist, but *the* illusionist; this man clearly has some reputation, or at the very least pretensions to it, but Charles, for one, has never heard of him.

"And you live in Whitby?" continues Sam.

"I was born there, but I have not lived in this country for many years. I have worked on the Continent. First in Paris, and latterly in Vienna."

And hence the slight stiffness in his speech, thinks Charles. The stiffness of a man who has not routinely spoken his mother tongue for a very long time.

"So you came back for an 'oliday? Visit the family?"

Causton hesitates. "My daughter has been unwell for some time. I consulted many doctors in Austria, but none was able to help—none could even say what ailed her. I thought a change of air and scenery might be of some benefit."

He pauses, but his face has darkened now; this is clearly not the whole story, not by a long way.

"There was another reason, wasn't there, Mr Causton?" presses Charles.

The illusionist looks up at him, and then away. "I had also arranged to meet an eminent scientist, who I discovered would be in England at this time. He assured me he could treat my daughter's condition, and I was naïve enough—stupid enough—to believe him."

The bitterness is savagely apparent now.

"And it's this man you believe abducted your daughter?"

"I was away barely an hour, but when I returned the house was empty and she had gone. He left me a message saying he had taken her to Edinburgh for further treatment. He insisted that we had discussed it, that I had consented to it, but it was a wicked falsehood! I had agreed to nothing of the kind. He sought only to throw me off the scent."

The man gets up and starts to pace the room. "I was such a fool—such a blind, gullible *fool*! He claimed the therapy he had pioneered required complete darkness—complete silence. That my presence would serve only to threaten its accomplishment—"

Charles's heart sinks. "You allowed him to be alone with your daughter?"

Causton nods. "You must remember that he was a man of science—a man of *medicine*. And a member of the aristocracy in the country I now consider my home."

Charles shakes his head. "I fear noble blood is no guarantee of rectitude, or not, at least, in the case of the Baron Von Reisenberg. I have proved that to my own cost."

Causton stares at him. "I have not uttered his name—how did you—" He stops, and when he speaks again his voice trembles between fear and hope. "So you *know* about him? But in that case you must know where he is—you must know what he's done with my Lucy—"

Sam holds up a hand. "It's early days, sir. Let's just say we do know this man 'as been in London for some weeks, and we 'ave reason to believe your daughter might still be wiv 'im. And if she is, there's a chance we can find 'er and bring 'er 'ome."

"I will do anything—God knows what that villain has done to her—"

Charles and Sam are silent; neither is about to reveal what they found in that apartment, or what Charles deduced had happened there.

"One question, Mr Causton," says Charles. "It is more than seven weeks since your daughter disappeared—what have you been doing in that time?"

"I went first to Edinburgh—I left Whitby that very afternoon, not staying even to pack. I scoured the city looking for them, but there was no trace."

Charles nods slowly; that would have taken, what—a week, two? Causton looks at him, evidently divining his thought. "After that I returned to Whitby. I consulted the police, but as soon as they heard that my daughter was of age and the Baron unmarried they claimed they were unable to assist me. But it is unthinkable that she would have left with him of her own accord—*unthinkable.*"

There's something in his voice that suggests to Charles that Causton is trying to convince himself as much as them. And something in all of this that still doesn't quite add up.

"So why did you come to London? Why did you think he might have brought your daughter here?"

"I could think of nowhere else—no other plausible alternative. I knew he might easily conceal her in a city of this size, and so I bought a ticket and boarded a train. That was three weeks ago. Ever since then I have been walking the streets for hours every day, looking for any trace of her—starting at every fair-haired girl I glimpse. I have enquired at hotels, I have been to the Home Office, but everywhere I have met with refusal—no-one has been prepared to give me any information whatsoever. And then, this morning, I saw that newspaper."

Sam glances up from his notebook, and Causton bridles. "I am well aware that that uncivil fellow at the desk thinks me insane, but as soon as I saw that report, I knew—there was no possibility of coincidence. And that is why I refused to leave here. That is why I insisted on seeing someone in authority. Someone like *you.*"

Charles frowns. What "coincidence" can the man mean? All the victims were young women, and one of them, at least, was fair-haired, but surely the resemblance ends there? This Lucy, whatever else she might have been, was no whore.

Causton looks from one to the other. "You do not know of what I speak?"

"No, sir," says Sam, nonplussed. "Afraid we don't."

"No-one has informed you about what happened in Whitby? I should have thought, in the circumstances—"

"Mr Causton," says Charles, glancing at his pocket-watch, "we have no time to waste. This man already has several hours' start on us. If you have anything to say that might help us, then say so, and quickly."

"Very well. Soon after our arrival in England, Lucy was befriended by the daughter of a lawyer in the town. This girl—Miss Holman—suffered from some kind of wasting sickness that left her pale of skin and weak in limb. I think it was one reason why they were so drawn to each other. But within a few weeks Miss Holman sickened suddenly and died, leaving Lucy inconsolable. I did not discover what took place thereafter until I returned from Edinburgh, but it seems the very morning Lucy disappeared Miss Holman's father received word that his poor daughter's grave had been desecrated—her body had been exhumed and the most appalling defacements inflicted on her helpless remains."

"Jesus Christ," mutters Sam, under his breath. "Not a bloody novver one."

Causton nods. "I am afraid so. The heart had been cut from the chest cavity, and the head removed. Days later, they had still not been able to discover it. And so you see, now, why I had to come."

Sam snaps his notebook shut. "Wait 'ere, would you, Mr Causton?" he says, beckoning to Charles.

Out in the front office the two of them almost collide with a man with heavy eyebrows and strongly chiselled cheekbones, wearing a coat thickly encrusted with braid. Charles recognises him at once: Richard Mayne, one of the two Joint Commissioners of the Metropolitan Police and the man personally responsible for the policing of the Exhibition. No wonder Rowlandson was not to be disturbed. And no wonder, when they are admitted, that the Inspector is in a less-than-affable mood. But as he listens to what they found in the Albany, and what they have since found out, his anger subsides and the policeman in him quickly subvenes.

"We have to go after 'im, sir," concludes Sam. "This Von Reisenberg—'e already 'as nearly 'alf a day's start on us."

"Well, in that case, Wheeler, he'll have been on the boat-train hours ago, and bound for the Continent long before we can apprehend him."

"Not necessarily, sir," says Charles. "The steward at the Albany said he asked about the steamers, but *not* about the trains. If he has a young woman with him, he may not want to run the risk of going by railway. He'll want privacy—"

"Which means 'e could be going by road," interrupts Sam. "We could still catch 'im at Folkestone, if we take the boat-train. There's one that goes on the hour. That gives us forty minutes—we could still catch it."

Rowlandson sighs. "Very well. What you found in those apartments is enough cause for an arrest. But you wire me from Folkestone before proceeding to the Continent, Wheeler—do I make myself clear? I do *not* want to run the risk of a diplomatic incident, and certainly not with the damn French."

"Understood, sir."

"In the meantime I will have a search made of the area about the Albany. We may yet be able to find that child; let us hope what we do *not* find is the headless corpse of the unfortunate Miss Causton. I will also wire to Whitby. But I will be most surprised if the local constabulary can assist us in any meaningful respect. They no doubt dismissed the whole episode as a malicious prank."

"And O'Riordan, sir?" asks Charles. "What did he have to say?"

Rowlandson's brow sets. "That scoundrel? He claimed he never spoke to that 'source' of his. Says an envelope was left for him at the *Daily News*. No name, no address."

"And did he show the letter to you?" asks Charles. "Do you have it?"

"No, Maddox, I do not. He *claims* he burned it. Needless to say I have no intention of leaving the matter there, but you will have to leave that aspect of the investigation to me, for I need you to accompany Wheeler here. You have met this Von Reisenberg—you know what he looks like, and how he is likely to behave. Your expenses will be reimbursed, you need have no fear of that."

Downstairs, Sam sends a constable out onto the street to hail a hansom, and then they return to Causton, who rises from his chair at once at the sight of them.

"We have very little time, Mr Causton," says Charles, "we will be setting off in a few moments—"

"You go in pursuit of him? Let me come with you—please—"

"I'm afraid that won't be possible, sir," says Sam quickly. "But you can rest assured—"

But before he can even finish Causton is upon him, clutching him by the arms, his fingers digging into his flesh. "You don't understand— you must let me come with you—she is *my daughter*—"

"There's no need for that, sir," intervenes Charles, pushing himself between them in some alarm. "You can trust us to do our duty—"

"But don't you see?" cries Causton, his eyes wild. "Finding her is *my* duty—I must go with you—how else will I—how else—"

And then just as suddenly as his anger flared he has turned away, and they watch as his body is racked with sobs.

Charles goes towards him and places a hand on his shoulder. "Mr Causton, I am not, as you perhaps believe, a police officer. I was once, but now I function in a personal capacity, offering my services as what you might call a 'private' detective. If you wish, I can do the same in this case—pursue this man on your behalf and attempt to retrieve your daughter and bring her home. My duty, in that case, would be first and foremost to *you*."

Causton turns, wiping his eyes. "I would pay anything—sacrifice anything—"

Charles takes his notebook from his pocket, scribbles a few words, and then tears away the sheet. "There is no time now, but if you go to this address my uncle will tell you anything more you require to know. And if you need to communicate with me, you may do so through him. I will send a message to him now to tell him about your case, and I will ensure that he is kept apprised of my whereabouts."

Causton takes the paper like a rope thrown to a drowning man. He tries to speak but his emotion wells over and he turns away. Charles touches him lightly once more on the shoulder, and then he and Sam are gone.

Within half an hour their hansom is pulling up at London Bridge station; Sam goes for the tickets and Charles makes his way to a platform billowing with gritty smoke and thronged with passengers for the Folkestone train. Businessmen, families, farmers, labourers, clerks; but no-one even remotely resembling the Baron Von Reisenberg.

"Looks like you might be right," says Sam, coming up to him and tucking their tickets into his top pocket. "There was only one ovver train this mornin', and the inspector claims 'e didn't see anyone resemblin' this Baron of yours. So looks like 'e could well 'ave gone by road, like you said. Vine Street are wirin' to the 'arbour office, asking 'em to detain anyone answerin' 'is description. Wiv a bit o' luck we'll get there before 'e does."

"I hope you're right, Sam," replies Charles grimly. "I hope you're right."

CHAPTER TEN

Lucy's journal

I WAS TOO weak to walk and so he carried me. Down the stairs and out into the air. The air! Even the dirty atmosphere of the city was scented nectar to me after all those days confined. But the gas-lamps by the door struck my weak eyes like suns and I had to cover my face and look away. The real sun was only barely lightening the sky, and yet the world had the freshness of early morning, so I adjudged it to be the glow of sunrise, not of twilight. The courtyard was empty of all but the carriage, and I saw at once it was the same one we had travelled in on our way here, the same hooded and silent driver, the same trunks piled by the horses. The man was lifting in small wooden chests that clinked as if containing glass, and when I lifted my gaze I saw that strapped to the roof was that long box I had seen delivered so many weeks before, but I knew now what it contained. I looked around wildly, hoping to see a servant, a tradesman, a passer-by, but all was deserted. He felt my body stiffen in his arms, and his grip tightened as he nodded to the coachman to open the carriage, and I heard him laugh as I struggled, putting out my hands to grip the door, but too feeble to do anything but vex him. He stowed me on the seat, wrapping blankets about me, but less for warmth than to hamper my movements and render me immobile. Then he pulled down the blind and locked the door, and his footsteps retreated across the paving-stones. I strained my ears, thinking I discerned voices, but I cannot be sure if my hearing deceived me. A few moments later I felt the carriage dip and sway as the driver climbed up onto the box, and then the door opened once more and he entered, tapping the ceiling with his cane to signal for departure.

I sat with my face against the window, feeling the jarring of every cobblestone, listening for some sound that might tell me where we were, or where we might be going, but I heard little beyond the sounds of a city waking. The trundling of carts, the scrape of the crossing-sweepers' brooms, and here and there the sound of voices. Common people, such as would be heading to work at such an early hour. And soon even those sounds faded and the carriage picked up speed. If it was London I had been sequestered in, we were leaving it now. All this while he had spoken not a word, and though I would not look at him I was aware, every moment, of his presence, and could not rid my nostrils of his smell. I think I must have slept then, lulled by the motion of the carriage, for I became suddenly conscious that the motion had ceased. I heard voices again outside and turned to see his eyes upon me, staring into mine, warning me against any movement, any sound. As my senses sharpened I could hear about us the noise of an inn yard—horses' hooves, the shouts of ostlers, the roll of wheels. Then the carriage door opened and the coachman passed in a plate of food and a flask. *He* refused to partake of them, handing the provisions instead to me. I hesitated a moment, remembering how I had been convinced he was drugging me, but I could not see how he could have doctored this food, and I took up the bread and butter like a creature half-starved. As indeed I truly was—no food had ever tasted so flavoursome to me, no milk so sweet. He watched me as I ate, an expression of revulsion on his cold features, as a man might look who was compelled to watch others feasting on human flesh. I felt stronger at once, and so far emboldened that I asked if I might use the privy. His eyes narrowed, but after a moment he nodded. He got out of the carriage and I heard him speaking to someone in the yard, and then he returned to the door and handed me a pair of spectacles such as I had never seen before. They were mounted on thin wire but the lenses within them were dark, almost to blackness, and a piece of glass extended round to the side of the eye, so that scarcely any light could enter. He told me to put them on, and let down my veil, and then he handed me down.

He kept my arm tight through his as we walked, and I thought every eye must be upon us, but though I glimpsed hazily through the glass three stable-lads in aprons, smoking by the water-pump, and two serving girls emptying slops, none of them seemed to remark our presence as he led me quickly to a lean-to behind the inn. He stood outside as I went in. I bled still, but less heavily, and I was able eventually to clean and neaten myself, though my hands and legs trembled. I must have taken longer than he wished, for soon he pounded upon the door, telling me we must depart. I rose to my feet, feeling at once a rushing in my ears and that strange taste of metal in my mouth that has always, before, been a herald of affliction. I stumbled to keep up with him as we returned to the carriage and he closed the door upon us once more. And now I slept indeed, pitching almost at once into a plunge of darkness. I saw my father weeping, only it was not the countenance I knew and loved but some terrifying aged visage, his features withered by grief. And then the picture shifted like one seen underwater and *he* it was I saw, *he* it was who stared back at me, unblinking, unmoving. And then the dream dissolved once more and I was swept, desperate and terrified, into the nightmare, ringed about by the glare of dancing lights, my face pawed by hands reaching down, and always the music, the music, the incessant repetitive music—

Do not leave me—

"I have no intention of doing so. Of that you may be sure."

———

I thought for an icy moment that I dreamed yet, for the music still remained, but when I opened my eyes I realized that it was *his* voice I had heard, and that I must have spoken aloud in my dream. But the music had not ceased, jangling tinnily on and on, and I looked around in panic, only to find him looking at me with a contemptuous disdain. "It is nothing but a barrel-organ. Rather incompetently played. Please try to control yourself."

"Where are we?" I asked, struggling up in my seat. How long had we been travelling?

He chose not to answer me, but as the music passed by and faded I heard the squall of gulls and knew we were nearing the sea.

"Are we at Whitby?" I cried, with a surge of absurd joy. "Are you taking me home?"

But he did not reply, and then I sensed that the carriage was descending a slope and I heard the sound of a train's whistle and the rattle of railway lines, and knew it could not be the place I longed to see. Suddenly the carriage gathered pace and we seemed to career along at a gallop until we came finally to a halt. The driver leapt down and opened the door. We were on a quayside, and I could see a steamer moored a few yards ahead, with black smoke issuing from its metal chimney. The horn blew and I saw men on the dockside shouting and running towards us.

"Your veil and glasses if you please," he said quickly, making haste to step down. "There is no time to lose."

CHAPTER ELEVEN

Britain does not boast a faster form of transport than the train Charles is now travelling on, but it is, all the same, not nearly fast enough. As the downs and fields and market towns roll away past the window, Sam watches as his friend checks his pocket-watch every fifteen minutes, willing the miles to pass.

"We'll be there not long after two," he offers once, "there's no way 'e can get there quicker 'an that," but Charles scarcely seems to hear, and they lapse into an uncomfortable, fretful silence that lasts until the train leaves the last junction and begins the short descent into Folkestone, over the viaduct and the swing bridge to the station hard by the sea wall. News of their arrival has gone before them, and an anxious official of the South-Eastern Railway Company is awaiting them on the platform, clutching the message telegraphed from Vine Street.

"Clarence Watkins, station manager, at your service," he says, shaking their hands as the passengers push past them. He has an almost unpleasantly jovial manner, his face pulled into a rictus of grinning insincerity. "I am here to assist you, gentlemen. You may rely upon my diligence, and my discretion. I hope I may trust to the same."

He shoots a glance around him at this, and Charles can understand why. The station is thronged with people, waiting for trains, meeting trains, disembarking from trains. The last thing this man—or his employer—wants is any public unpleasantness.

Sam has clearly divined his apprehension. "We're not out for makin' a scene, Mr Watkins. Just doin' our job. Jus' like you."

Watkins nods and leads them towards the harbourside. The sea glitters in the sun, and the gulls dip and lift, calling and circling; Charles can see families promenading farther along the beach, children running on the sand, and parasols a-flutter in the breeze off the water.

"The steamers depart from here," Watkins tells them. "The next one is at three, the one thereafter at five o' clock. If the man you seek travelled by road from London this morning he will be lucky to make the next crossing. You may wait in the office here, if you wish—it will ensure that he is not forewarned of your presence, and you run no risk of missing him thereby, as all passengers have to present their passports here before they are permitted to board."

Moreover—as Watkins has quite clearly already concluded—such an expedient will also serve to keep them discreetly unseen by the steam-packet's clientele.

"Very well," says Sam. "And if one o' your lads could rustle us up some lunch then we'd be most appreciative."

Watkins opens the office door. "I will see what can be obtained," he says, without any great enthusiasm, and then the two of them are left alone. A pimply young man arrives soon after with two pies and a pitcher of beer, swiftly followed by the Foreign Office agent, who raises the blind at the window with a snap and declares the office open for business. Sam wipes his mouth on his sleeve and takes up a position immediately behind the man's chair, and Charles watches as the customers for the three o'clock passage begin to assemble.

And it is as fine a cross section of British society as you could hope to find—pompous *paterfamilias,* sailor-suited children dragged by small dogs, parties of pupils shepherded by schoolmasters, nervous new travellers clutching packets of dry biscuits to ward off *mal de mer,* a gaggle—or giggle—of chic young women bedecked for the boulevards, and an exotic creature dressed in bright moth-like silks who can only be destined for the *Comédie-Française*. But of the Baron, there is no sign. They wait, all the same, and just as smoke begins to belch blackly from the chimney, one of the sailors on the quayside gives a cry and points up towards the bridge. A carriage appears on the viaduct, racing at full speed, and Charles throws open the office door, heedless now of being seen, concerned only to catch him—catch him and save her, if she yet lives. He races onto the quay, where sailors are calling to those in the coach, shouting that they have only a few moments to spare, and then a man in a tall hat is stepping quickly down from the carriage to the quay and Charles is running—hearing Sam's voice behind him but taking no heed—running towards that carriage and throwing open the door—

CHAPTER TWELVE

FIFTEEN MINUTES PAST THREE. It is quiet in Buckingham Street. In the drawing-room, the French clock ticks, and Maddox sits in his accustomed chair. There is a large leather-bound book on his knee, which he is affecting to read, but more than half of his attention is being lured away by Betsy, Nancy's little daughter, who sits cross-legged on the sill at the open window, one small arm about the cat, pointing out people in the street to him as they pass by. Thunder is, as Maddox well knows, more than able to fend for himself, but the little girl lacks his sense of self-preservation—or at the very least his perfect sense of balance—and more than once the old man has had to issue a stern warning about leaning out too far. It sounds stern, at any rate, but there is a special quality in his voice that renders his watchful love perceptible even to the child. The little girl's voice chatters on, more voluble with the cat than she ever is with the human inmates of this house—*"that's Mrs Shoap, she's nice but she has two big dogs so you won't like them, and that's the muffin man, I call him Joey but I don't know if that's his real name"*—until it is broken, suddenly and unexpectedly, by the peal of the doorbell downstairs. Betsy must be becoming bored with her monologue, because she immediately jumps up and races off downstairs. The cat, suitably unfazed, stretches unhurriedly, scratches behind one ear, then leaps lightly down and disappears through the door.

Maddox returns to his book, hearing, on the edge of his mind, the sounds of voices downstairs. One is Abel Stornaway's—slow, Scottish, wary—but the other he does not recognise. What he can discern, however, is the agitation in the man's words. And so it does not surprise him that the door soon opens, and Abel appears around it.

"A Mr Causton to see 'ee, guv. Says young Mr Charles told 'ee what it's about?"

Maddox looks up from his book. "He did. By all means, show him in."

The man, when he enters, is not quite as Maddox had envisaged him. He is smaller, slighter—there is no stage charisma here, no presence to command the eye. For unlike Charles, Maddox has indeed heard of this man, even if he has never seen the marvels he manufactures.

"You are known as Professor de Caus, I believe. In your professional capacity?"

The man flushes; and Maddox senses that he may have become uneasy both with his part and his past, and he wonders whether it is his return to England that has occasioned this, or what has happened to his daughter.

"The name is not merely a play on your own, I take it, but a reference to Salomon de Caus?"

The man starts. "There are few who know that name, these days. But yes. It was a deliberate choice."

Maddox turns a page of his book. "Hydraulic engineer, theorist of perspective, eminent mathematician, contriver of mechanical miracles and speaking statues, optical illusionist, and even, some say, occult magician. Yes, I should say it was indeed a suitable choice."

The man comes closer. "That book—"

Maddox turns to the title page; the paper is mottled with age, the leather dry: *New and rare inventions of water-works shewing the easiest waies to raise water higher than the spring by which invention the perpetual motion is proposed. A work both usefull, profitable and delightfull.*

"That's the John Leak translation of 1603," says Causton, in wonder. "That book is extraordinarily rare. And extraordinarily expensive."

"I collect books," says Maddox simply, closing the volume and placing it carefully on the table beside him. "And in any case, the subject is of interest to me. Do, sit down."

Whatever Causton might have expected in this house, it was clearly not this. He takes a seat, but sits on the edge of it, like a nervous pupil. And Maddox notices now that he, too, has a book in his hands.

"What brings you here, Mr Causton? I would be happy to explain my great-nephew's scheme of charges, if that is what concerns you."

"I feel so foolish—I could have given this to him before, but I was distressed—I was not thinking coherently—"

He is still clutching the book, and Maddox sees that there are various loose sheets interleaved between the pages.

"It is a scrapbook," he explains, seeing Maddox's eyes upon it, and flushing again. "Lucy—my daughter—began it as a child. It is a record of my work—of *our* work."

Intrigued now, Maddox holds out his hand and Causton gets up and brings it to him. "But the chief reason I have brought it here is because it contains portraits of Lucy—I thought you might be able to send one to your nephew, so that he is familiar with her appearance."

He opens the book on Maddox's lap, and leafs quickly through a handful of playbills and newspaper cuttings. "These at the back are the most recent. Here—this is very like."

And there she is. Softly shadowed and sepia-toned. Curls of bright hair hang about her face, but how dark her eyes might be Maddox cannot guess, for her eyelids are closed and her chin lifted, trance-like.

"Is it the effect of the daguerreotype that she looks thus?" he asks, for the girl's skin seems agonisingly pale.

Causton shakes his head. "I wish it were, but no. It is the consequence of her condition. She has suffered from night spasms and sleepwalking since she was very young, and most especially since her mother's death. Some of the doctors who examined her diagnosed a chronic and pernicious *chlorosis*—"

"A form of anaemia?"

"Indeed. But in recent months there have been other symptoms, other phenomena, which none of them could explain. Or could explain only as the proof of madness, or hysteria."

"I do not take your meaning."

"For some years Lucy has assisted me in the *phantasmagoria,* indeed she exhibited an uncommon facility for it, even as a child—"

"She must take that talent from you."

The man flushes. "Lucy is not, in fact, my daughter, though I have long since regarded her as my own and loved her as such. I married her mother when Lucy was five years old—we met when I worked for a short time with a travelling fair where Margaret, also, was employed. She was a widow, and had been supporting both herself and Lucy for several years. That, of course, was before I met Monsieur Étienne-Gaspard Robertson. Before"—this with a lift of the chin—"I had my own establishment."

Maddox nods. "My apologies—I should not have interrupted you. You were saying—your daughter has been your amanuensis."

"It was more than that—Lucy has been the prime mover in many of our most successful representations—she would play the armonica, operate the lantern—"

He stops, and a cloud crosses his face.

"But then something changed," says Maddox. It is an assertion, not a question.

Causton sighs. "I have wished, so many times since, that I had acted differently. Lucy was averse to the idea from the start, but I persuaded her—I said it would make our fame, secure our future. And our need for money was very great. The popularity of the *phantasmagoria* was waning, and our expenses were considerable. But of this, of course, she knew nothing. I did not consider it a subject fit for a young woman."

Maddox waits, having learned, many years before, the value and use of silence.

Causton takes a deep breath. "I created a new spectacle. A new purpose for the magic lantern. One in which Lucy played the most vital and central part."

"And what was it that you had her do?"

"She spoke to the souls of the departed. She summoned the spirits of the dead."

"I see."

There is silence awhile. The ticking of the clock, the shouts of children on the street, and a sudden furious yowling as Thunder defends his territory in the yard behind the house.

"Clearly," says Maddox eventually, "your daughter did not communicate, in truth, with the dead. So in what did this performance consist? You had, I take it, some kind of mechanism—some stage apparatus?"

"I employed an Influence Machine. A glass ball, which would spin and glow when Lucy laid hands upon it. My intent was to produce a suitably spectral appearance, while suggesting that the apparitions were conjured by the miracle of science, not the deceptions of sorcery."

"It was a deception, all the same."

"That was Lucy's view. But I said it would do no harm. How wrong I was, how wretchedly wrong. And yet how could I have known that the harm it would do would be not to those who witnessed it, as she feared, but to Lucy herself?"

"She was injured in some way?"

He nods. "She said she found the touch of the machine—distressing. That it produced a sensation of heat and pain in her nerves. But as it made no such impression on me, I was disinclined to take her words seriously."

Maddox eyes him, wondering whether he, too, had eventually come to see his daughter as either mad or hysterical. Is that what kindles his guilt now? Because it is guilt that drives him, there is no question of that. Love, yes, but guilt more.

Causton looks up and sees Maddox's face. "You must understand—the things she described—there was no physical cause—no discernible illness that could possibly have occasioned them. And then later, when she started to talk of seeing things in the glow of the machine—of brightly coloured flames of cold light—no sane person sees such things, Mr Maddox. The doctors I consulted insisted that an asylum was the only remedy—"

Maddox frowns. "But you did not, I deduce, take that course."

"No, I did not. Because it was then that I remembered something I had come upon when I was preparing the new spectacle. In the course of my research I had read mention of the work of an Austrian nobleman—of studies he had conducted which led him to conclude that certain sensitive persons may perceive the touch of crystals upon the skin as heat or, conversely, cold. I could not recollect where I had read this, but I did recall that he had carried out an experiment with a young woman in which he gave her a magnet to hold which had been exposed to the light of the moon, and water to drink which he had steeped for many hours in the same light. The water induced violent vomiting, while contact with the magnet produced a sensation of the most distressing uneasiness, and the feeling of an inward struggle in her breast and head. Apparently the effect was even more pronounced if she remained in a darkened room for some hours before the experiment took place. The symptoms—the very language used—was exactly what my Lucy had described. It came to me at once that *this* might be the explanation—that it might be the magnetic current generated by *my own machine* that had caused her new affliction, and the many hours we spent in the dark, in the *phantasmagoria*, had only served to accentuate it. I ceased our performances at once and wrote that very day to this Baron Von Reisenberg. I received a reply from him by return of post. He informed me that he had conducted several such experiments on individuals he termed 'sick sensitives,' and that young females were particularly susceptible to the phenomena he described.

He said he would be in England for the Exhibition, but he was willing to travel earlier, if that would assist me, and see Lucy at our house in Whitby."

Causton gets up and walks to the window. "I wonder now if any of it was true—whether all his so-called experiments were merely a blind—a means to obtain unhindered access to innocent and vulnerable young women."

Maddox nods slowly. "But he did, indeed, treat your daughter?"

"If you may call it that. He claimed she was a most interesting case." His voice is bitter now. "That she had enabled him to draw a vital new conclusion which he was confident would lead to a momentous step forward in his work."

"Did he say what that was?"

"Not specifically. But I remember that he became most animated when he discovered that Lucy had been diagnosed with *chlorosis*. And that her cycle of menstruation coincided always with the time of full moon. He was so confident, I was foolish enough to hope for a cure— that he might be able to restore her to health. And now—"

Maddox leans over, rather laboriously, and fumbles for the bell-rope. "If you will forgive me a moment," he says, reaching now for paper and pen, "I must wire at once to my nephew. With luck, I may be able to get a message to Folkestone before he arrives there."

A few moments later Billy puts his head round the door, and is dispatched to the Post Office on the Strand, with an injunction to go at once and no loitering. Billy stares with undisguised curiosity at Maddox's visitor, and then at the paper he has been given, but as he cannot read, he's unlikely to find much enlightenment there.

Causton, meanwhile, has been watching, clearly torn between relief that something is happening, and bafflement as to what that might actually be. When the door closes, Maddox turns again to him.

"If you can leave me an address where I might find you, I will ensure that you are kept informed of my nephew's progress."

"You wish to keep the scrapbook?"

"If I may. Should my nephew fail to apprehend this man before he leaves the country, I will ensure that a picture of your daughter is sent on to him."

When Causton is gone Maddox sits for a while, pensive, but the day is warm and some time later he starts awake to a knock at the door. It's Billy, who hands him a telegram and then hovers, shifting from foot to foot while Maddox reads it.

"Very well, Billy," he says eventually. "That will be all. You may bring tea, if you would."

"Right you are, Mr Maddox."

The old man lifts himself a little in his chair, stiff after his sleep, and it's only then that he realises that little Betsy is sat on the floor at his feet, with the scrapbook on her knees and the pictures strewn haphazardly on all sides. Maddox smiles. "You like looking at the people, Betsy?"

She looks up at him and nods, in that over-strenuous way little children have.

"Dis one," she says, pointing a slightly sticky finger. Maddox edges forwards in his seat and looks down. It is another daguerreotype, but this time the girl pictured can't be much more than eight. She is sitting on the lap of an older woman, clearly her mother, and both are in their Sunday best, the little girl with her hair ringletted and ribboned, and the woman in a heavy gown of some sombre unreflecting colour. She is heavy-set and dark-haired, the woman, and neither is smiling, though given the immense period of time they would have been required to sit, unmoving, for the portraitist, that is not, perhaps, so very surprising.

"Could you pass it to me, Betsy?"

The child crawls across to the picture on her hands and knees and presents it in a charmingly formal fashion, to the old man. He touches her golden hair a moment then whispers, "I think I can hear your mother calling."

You might wonder how he knows this, since Nancy is at this very moment two floors below them, behind the closed kitchen door, and the little girl (whose hearing must, surely, be more acute than his) has showed no signs of noticing anything, but Betsy does not seem perturbed by such considerations, and merely smiles, retrieves her doll from the sopha, and skips off happily downstairs.

As for Maddox, he sits staring at the picture in the silence, his left hand fluttering a little as it does when he is tired, or distressed. And then he turns again to the *escritoire* at his side, takes a sheet of paper and his pen, and begins, slowly, to write.

CHAPTER THIRTEEN

"LUCY!" CRIES CHARLES, HIS voice hoarse with anxiety, seizing the handle of the carriage door. *"Lucy!"*

But when he throws it open all he finds is an elderly lady in a black silk mourning gown with a fat pug dog on her knee, frowning at him over her *pince-nez*. And then Sam is at his side, and the man in the tall hat is striding round the coach towards them, his face irate. "What in heaven's name do you think you're doing? Who are you? How dare you approach my mother in this insolent manner?"

"Metropolitan Police, sir," says Sam quickly, as the pug starts up yapping and growling. "Case o' mistaken identity. Our apologies."

Then he's pulling Charles away, and hauling him back towards the railway station, hissing, "What do yer think yer doing? You'll get us both in 'ot water at this rate. We'll just 'ave to wait, Chas. We knew 'e probably wouldn't be 'ere this early. We've jus' gotta be patient."

"No," insists Charles, frowning. "Something's wrong, I know it."

He looks back to where the man in the tall hat is now presenting his documents at the foot of the gangway, and the elderly lady is being wheeled up onto the ship. "I'm going to board. I think Von Reisenberg's given us the slip—gone another way. I think he asked about

Folkestone deliberately, knowing full well that we would question Williams. If I take this crossing I could be in Paris by the early hours—I can get a train to Vienna from there."

"But Rowlandson said we weren't to go any furver—"

"Yes, I know he did, but that only applies to you, not me—*Causton* is my client now. I have every right to pursue his interests, in whatever way I see fit."

"So what am I supposed to do in the bleedin' meantime?"

"Wait to see if he comes for the five o'clock boat and then send a message by it to the telegraph office in Boulogne. They can wire me at the Gare du Nord. If you have him, I will return at once. If not, I will change trains and go on at once to Austria."

Sam starts to object but Charles is not listening. "And wire my uncle as well, will you—he'll worry, else."

And with that he's striding towards the foot of the gangway and fumbling in his pockets for money and his passport, not noticing that Watkins is toiling up from the office, waving a piece of paper in his hand.

"A wire for you," he calls, half out of breath, "from a Mr Maddox, in London."

But the steamer is blowing its horn now, and Charles can do nothing but seize the paper and stuff it into his pocket, before racing up the swaying plank to the ship, and the sea.

CHAPTER FOURTEEN

Lucy's journal

I HAVE BEEN here now, two days. This room high in his castle, and low under the sky.

The crossing from Dover to Ostende took more than twelve hours, and as the day drew on the weather worsened, and we were soon pitching in heavy seas. He locked me in my cabin, telling me to sleep and be still, and I lay there, as the waves rolled beneath us, and the tears rolled down my cheeks onto the rough cotton pillow.

When we reached port, it was some time before he came to summon me, telling me, once more, to shield my eyes before he led me up through the empty decks. And despite the shadows I walked in I could tell, as I stepped gingerly down the walkway to the dockside, that the sky was darkening and the rain falling. The quay-side was almost deserted by then, with but one cab waiting, which took us through the wet and dreary town to the railway station, where a man in livery was awaiting us. His own servant, then, I thought, my heart sinking, as I realised at last—as I should have done hours before—where it was he planned to take me. In my present state of weakness my mind quailed at the thought of so many miles alone with him, so many, many miles in the closeness of a railway compartment, but in this, at least, my fears proved groundless, for he handed me into a compartment alone, then drew the blinds down and closed the door, and a few moments later the train jolted heavily into motion.

And so it was that the journey was conducted. We changed trains at Cologne, and again at Leipzig, but there was no stop, no stay, and it was scarcely more than a day since we left Ostende that I awoke before dawn and lifted the corner of the blind to see the outskirts of Vienna. It was weeks since I had seen full sun, and my eyes were weak as a newborn's, smarting at even the thin grey light then streaking the eastern sky. At Vienna, we were met by a carriage emblazoned with a coat of arms, and for one long last day I sat opposite him in the carriage, drifting in an uneasy slumber in which the sounds outside mingled with words half-heard and faces half-seen. And then suddenly I was awake, and the wind was whipping the coachman's cloak against the carriage, and the rain pattering on the roof, as we started up what I could tell at once was a long steep slope, the horses straining and the wheels slipping on the wet cobblestones. Then the carriage came to a halt and when the door opened it was to darkness, and the glow of moonlight on ancient lichened walls, and I knew that I had entered the Baron's domain.

And all at once he was changed. It was as if the passing of his own threshold possessed some supernatural power, for his demeanour became at once gentle and gracious, even conciliatory. He sat me by the fire in his great dim echoing hall, and had servants bring me tea and hot *apfelstrudel*. My throat tightened then, not just at this kindness unlooked-for, but at these reminders of my childhood, for my mother used to make *apfelstrudel*, even though she was an Englishwoman, and I remember my father's assistants saying that no-one made such light sweet pastry as she did, not even their own grandmamas. He watched me as I ate, then rose and took a seat closer to mine.

"I know that these last weeks have been a trial to you. That you have thought my conduct harsh, even cruel, and condemned me for heartlessness. But there has been a reason behind every action I have taken. The hours you have spent in darkness, the food and drink you thought was poisoning you"—I started at this, but he continued as if he had not perceived it—"all these things are come now to readiness, for tomorrow, tomorrow we will at last begin our great work."

There was a flush in his hollow cheeks as he said this, such as I had never seen before, and a light of fervour in his pale eyes, but before I could ask him what he meant he had risen from his chair and was gone.

A man then appeared who introduced himself as a Herr Bremmer, and gestured me to follow him. He was a small man with small eyes made yet smaller by the thick glass of his spectacles. We went up a flight of stone steps, and then another and another, until I was breathless, clutching my side. He halted and waited respectfully until I was able to continue, and we made the final slow climb to the room he said was to be my own—a room shaped as an octagon, and lined with books, with no windows, and the lamp turned low. There was another chamber leading from it, with a carved four-poster bed, and heavy iron shutters closed and bolted. The man bowed and retired, and I dragged myself in relief to the bed, where I fell at once into undreaming sleep, without staying even to remove my clothes.

When I woke I saw that a meal had been laid in the little sitting-room, and the air was filled with the smell of new bread. I ate hungrily, wondering if it was breakfast or supper I was consuming, since I had no way of knowing what time it was. I was just finishing the last of the hot sweet coffee when there was a knock at the door and I received my summons. Herr Bremmer conducted me down to the gallery, and thence to a small door, set centrally on one side. This he opened and gestured that I should go up the steps. I looked at him, suddenly apprehensive, but he did nothing but repeat the same gesture, and so, my heart beating hard, I complied.

The stairs circled up and up and I found myself at last in a vast space, wide and tall. But I sensed that, rather than saw it, for the room was entirely dark—so dark not the slightest glimmer reached the eye. If there were doors they were curtained close, and indeed the air felt close and smothered, as if all the walls and windows were muffled. But such places were no longer strange to me. It was just as it had been in the apartment in England, and as my senses sharpened I perceived I was not alone. There was no movement—no step—but I knew he was there. I could smell his body; I could hear his breathing.

"There is nothing to fear."

I turned back, towards the voice, and then I felt him come up behind me and take each of my wrists in his hands. Perhaps he felt the hard throb of the pulse, for he said again, "There is nothing to fear. This is where our work begins. Our great and marvellous work."

And then he led me forwards, three steps, four, five, before lowering me slowly into a chair. I found there was a table before me now, covered in some heavy, deadening cloth that had the soft touch of baize. I heard a movement, as of a long curtain drawing to, and then the table began to rotate beneath my hands. I started back, and I heard him say, "Do not be alarmed. All I require you to do is place your hands on the objects that will appear before you. Place your hands upon each one and tell me what you feel—what you see."

"But—"

"Trust me, Lucy. Do as I say."

There was the sound of a little silver bell then, and the table came to a halt. I put out my hands, and felt the touch of metal. Smoothly polished and cool, no doubt, to the skin, though not to mine, for a prickling warmth spread at once from my fingertips and I saw my hands reflected in a sudden flaring glow.

"I've seen it before—this colour—"

"What colour?" he replied quickly.

"Red, a dull red."

"And how does it appear?"

"There are flames—slow, coiling flames. As I saw before, at the *phantasmagoria*."

And as I saw, though I did not say so, at my poor Dora's grave.

"I do not understand—I have told you all this already, when we were at Whitby—"

But then the little bell rang once again and the table turned. Some type of boulder, this time, heavy and rounded but not of stone. It was almost oily to the touch, and the cold flames that rose from it were a pale milky white. And so it went on, the sharp points of a raw crystal, glowing cool blue, then the pitted surface of some raw ore that burned hot and greenish and yellow, and then a rock of the same rough texture but which flickered with the most beautiful soft violet I had ever seen. Each time it was the same—the ringing of the bell and the turning of the table, and each time the same questions, as he catechised me to and fro on what I saw, and what I felt. I do not know how many there were or how long it went on—I only knew that at the end of it I was so drained and depleted that he summoned one of the servants to carry me back to my room, where I lay on the bed, staring blindly at the ceiling, and wondering where, in all of this, was the Lucy I had once been.

And the day that followed it was the same. Only when the bell rang for the first time what came to my fingers was a square block of some dense, gritty metal. A magnet, I knew that at once, and I gasped as I placed my fingers upon it and saw the bar blossom at once in a rush of fire radiance, the flames circling and spiralling in brilliant rainbow colours, from crimson-gold and orange at one end to a deep bluish indigo at the other.

"It pains you?" he said quickly.

"No, no!" I said, feeling my body flood as if with cool dawn air. "It is so beautiful—so *beautiful*!"

"Turn the bar about, and place your hands upon it again."

I hesitated, loath to lose the loveliness of it, even for a moment, but I did as he asked, and my fingers had barely skimmed the iron when I felt them close involuntarily in a spasm of pain and the same rush of heat, the same agonizing agitation of mind, that had afflicted me in Vienna, when first I touched the Influence Machine. I cried out in pain and tore my hands away, and I heard the curtain slide back and a moment later he was standing by me.

"I am sorry," he said. That was all, "I am sorry."

It was the first time he had ever apologised to me—after all these weeks, after so much pain, so much loneliness and fear, it was his kindness, now, that brought me to weeping.

"We have made a great advance, today," he said at last, when I had composed myself. "I said once, in Whitby, that you had a wondrous talent, and you do, Lucy, you do. Together, we will astonish the world."

"But I don't understand—"

"You are not required to understand. You are required only to obey."

He placed his hand under my chin then, and lifted my face, moving one finger against my skin like a caress, touching me as he had not touched me since that night he spoke of, when I saw the ghost lights at Dora's grave, and he talked to me in soft words of my rare and precious gift. And then he bent his head to my neck and put his mouth to my skin.

I lie here now, thinking again of that caress, and abhorring my own body that it should respond to him still. Even now, after all that has passed between us. Even now, after—

✦ ✦

I walked again last night—walked or dreamed—but night it was, for the moon was full and heavy, lifting slowly into the sky from red to bronze to pewter milk. I stood in the chill air, high above the castle, looking down where the river ran, and the black trees rustled in the darkness. I could see the stone causeway leading to the gate, and a little chapel where a tiny light burned, and the ancient gravestones woven about with mist. But there was one that was not ancient, where there were flowers not yet wilted, and as I gazed there came the same slow flicker of light I had seen rising at my Dora's grave, and I saw that there was a figure standing before it, a man in a long dark coat, and I thought it was him and I did not know whether to cry out or cower away. And then he was gone and I turned, and saw that all about me suddenly there was light—mirrors of polished silver about my feet like so many shining basins, each one looking towards the sky and curved to cup the glory of the moon into spheres of dazzling radiance. There was a dark smell of sulphur, or of phosphorus, and the humming I could hear was not, this time, in my own mind, but in hundreds of little golden wires that circled each mirror globe in a thick braid of serpent coils that led away towards the tower and out of my sight. And then a bank of dense black cloud closed over the moon and I could see no more.

⤙❦ ❦⤚

When I awoke, there was a dimness in the room as of dawn, and I found there was breakfast set out for me in the little octagonal room. I sat there, as I ate, looking about me, and wondering for the first time, at all the books on the shelves about me and whether, if he would not speak to me of his work, there might be some answer I could find here. There were so many volumes, though, that I scarce knew where to begin, until my eye alighted on one that had not been pushed fully back, and when I pulled it out towards me I saw that it was in English, and that a page was marked with a slip of paper— a paper but recently left, with notes upon it also in English, written crossways in a large and confident hand. I touched the paper then, following the words with the tip of my finger. I do not know what drew me to it, but I was curious suddenly, and I turned to the page that the writer had marked, and I began to read. And thus it was that when I was summoned, again, to that darkened room above, I went with a heart that was full of foreboding, because I understood at last what he wanted with me, and what the true nature of his great purpose had always been.

The moment I stood on the threshold I knew that something had changed. What had been empty, was now occupied. In the centre of the floor there was a bed—the same one that I had seen through the keyhole in his apartment, with the holes in the leather, and the tightening straps. I was afraid then, afraid of that bed and what I could see now hung suspended from the roof-beams high above it. And then I remembered my dream and I knew what it was, and where it had come from, but some force yet drew me to it—something irresistible, overwhelming, but I did not know if that compulsion was pleasure, or fear.

"Come closer, Lucy. Lie down upon the bed."

He was somewhere beyond, in the shadows on the far side of the room. I hesitated, then moved forwards a little, my breathing coming fast and shallow, as I advanced towards the bed and laid myself down upon it, my limbs trembling, looking up into the dark. And then I heard the clank of some metal mechanism and what was hanging above my head began slowly to descend, and as it drew nearer I saw a faint phosphorescent glow and it began to throb with its own pale light, but I could not move, could not do anything but watch it approach, and as it came down towards me I felt that radiance grow in my own flesh, that energy surge in my own veins. I heard the machinery cranking still, but I had eyes only for that light, a desire only to be inside that light, to touch that light, and as the coil of wires came at last within reach and I yearned out towards it, I saw an explosion of brilliant white fire burst at once upwards and outwards from my hands, and as my body convulsed in a cold glare of shivering ecstasy I heard his voice cry out, somewhere far away,

"My God, I see it! The light—the light!"

CHAPTER FIFTEEN

AND WHAT OF CHARLES, all this time? He arrived as expected, tired, hungry, and dirty, at the Gare du Nord soon after midnight, to find there was no message for him at the telegraph office. So far, so predictable perhaps, but then he found, to his fury, that the best and quickest way to Vienna was to retrace the journey he had just taken all the way back to Amiens and travel thence via Dusseldorf, Leipzig, and Dresden. If losing so much time were not frustrating enough, the bureaucrat at the ticket office seemed to be doing his level best to thwart him, and it was a good long time before Charles was finally convinced that there was no faster way, and that there was, moreover, no train to Amiens until eleven o'clock in the morning. It gave him a few hours' sleep, though, and (more important) time for a brief visit to one of the city's most venerable institutions. Whatever that was, and whatever he found there, the consequences are writ across his face as he walks back through the damp Parisian streets to the Gare du Nord, and it may likewise account for the fact that he stops at a small and low-ceilinged shop on the Rue de Ponthieu, where he makes the purchase of a flint-lock pistol.

It's almost impossible for Charles to contemplate his journey with any degree of patience now, but even the weather appears to be against him, as one delay compounds another, culminating in a sudden landslip between Gotha and Weimar that leaves the train standing for nine hours in the teeming rain. And so it is that when he arrives at last at Vienna to find the *poste restante* office closed he decides he cannot linger—if there are letters there from his uncle they will have to wait—and by the time his hired carriage is approaching the outskirts of the Von Reisenberg estates, he calculates dourly that the owner of those estates could easily have been returned here as much as three full days.

He has the driver let him down at the edge of the forest, some half a mile from the foot of the causeway, and watches as it disappears from sight into the trees. It is twilight, and the moon is rising, waning gibbous. And again there is that strange sense of doubling—of light reflecting up from the castle roof as if the moon were twinned between the earth and sky. But Charles knows now that this is no anomaly of nature, and his face sets grimmer and darker as he climbs the last yards to the castle door.

He has had many hours to contemplate what he will do now, hours of sleeplessness on cold rattling trains, in narrow uncomfortable seats, but even so, when he comes to a halt before the Baron's tall stone archway and hauls on the bell-chain, he has no idea at all what he is going to say. And when the door opens to reveal the bespectacled man he saw here once before, he realises that all this time he has assumed that it would be the Baron himself who would confront him, and having readied himself for that confrontation he is forced instead to an impotent patience, as a message is taken indoors, and the minutes pass, and then finally the man reappears and permits him inside. The two ascend the steps to the Baron's gallery of specimens, where the man shows him in, bows, and closes the door quietly behind him.

Charles stands there, his eyes adjusting. There is only one candle burning in an iron sconce at the far end of the room.

"Mr Maddox, you take me somewhat by surprise. I was not aware that the Curators believed it necessary for you to make another visit. Indeed I have already received a most courteous letter from them, accepting my gift."

Von Reisenberg comes towards him out of the shadows, a large book open in his hands and what passes for a smile on his long bony face. But Charles is not smiling.

"You know very well why I'm here."

The Baron snaps the book shut. "I am afraid I do not. But what I *do* know is that you were not invited. And are not welcome."

"I have come for Miss Causton. Her father sent me to bring her home. To ensure that she is safe."

"In that case you may consider your duty discharged. Miss Causton is perfectly safe. She is my guest, and while she is under my roof she is under my protection. I can assure you—and her father—that she came here, and stays here, most willingly."

"You actually expect me to believe that?" Charles's eyes are blue ice.

The Baron smiles. "But of course. I am what you English delight in terming a *gentleman,* and you—" He hesitates a moment, "—no doubt consider yourself the same. You are honour-bound to believe me, are you not?"

"An *English* gentleman would bring her here, and let me speak to her myself."

"That is not possible. She is resting, and cannot be disturbed."

"I have her father's authority, and I am therefore in a position to insist."

"You are in no such position. You are in my house, on *my* private property. I have any number of servants at my call. And you should know by now, that I am not a man who makes idle threats."

There is a pause. A pause of lengthening and deepening hostility.

Then suddenly Charles turns and begins to walk up the room, slowly, deliberately, between the glass cases and the scientific instruments, noticing as he did before, but with new knowledge this time, that one brass microscope still bears a slide of some thick red residue. And noticing, also, that a number of the mineralogical samples are missing from their allotted places. On an impulse he reaches into one of the cases and seizes a chunk of some dark uncut ore which is gravelly and scratchy to the touch. He is aware of the Baron behind him, unmoving, watching, and he lets the moment prolong almost to impossibility before turning to face him, tossing the piece of rock from one hand to the other, one hand to the other, one hand to the other.

"Before I left London," he begins, "I was convinced that you were some sort of fiend. A monster who took a depraved pleasure in murder and mutilation—"

"That is an outrageous and slanderous accusation."

"—but when I received a wire from my uncle, at Folkestone, I was forced to think again. To admit that I might have been wrong about you, all along."

He pauses, but the Baron will not take his bait.

"Very well, I will continue, whether you wish to hear it or not. My uncle wrote to inform me that he had received a visit from Alexander Causton, during which he had spoken at length about his daughter's state of health. And then I recalled what you told me, not ten yards from this very spot, of the years you spent studying the afflictions of the mind. Of somnambulism, and night terrors, and hysteria, and neurasthenia—all those disorders that have terrified mankind for so long, and given rise to so many barbaric superstitions, condemning the sufferers to incarceration as dangerous lunatics. And I wondered sud-

denly if that very word—*lunatic*—might be the key to it all. Because I
remembered then a slip of paper I found in your apartment in the
Albany, and a chart of obscure letters and numbers I could make no
sense of, at the time. But now I began to speculate whether those
numbers might refer to the phases of the moon—and whether *that*
might be the answer. The answer I was seeking, and that you had already found."

He stops, but still the Baron is not to be drawn.

"All the way across on the steamer, hour after hour, as I followed
your trail, I followed your *mind*. And it came to me eventually, what
must have happened. I think all those years of study led you to conclude that those age-old superstitions had at their heart a vital grain of
truth. And it was then—at that very moment—that you first heard
about Lucy Causton, and when you travelled to England to meet her,
what you discovered came upon you with the force of a revelation. Not
only were the symptoms of her mental condition particularly marked
at the moment of full moon, but she suffered also from a severe form
of *chlorosis*, moreover her *menses* coincided exactly with the lunar cycle,
such that her blood ran unnaturally thin at the very moment when her
affliction was most manifest. And as your theory took shape, you began
to posit a direct relationship between thinness of the blood, and lunacy, and the influence of the moon. And you believed you had, at last,
found the answer to all your years of searching. Why the symptoms of
mental distress are always most pronounced when the moon is at the
full; why those symptoms abate so noticeably if the sufferer is kept
indoors, secluded from all exposure to its rays; and why—above all—
those who are most prey to these conditions are young *women*, whose
bodies ebb and flow to the same monthly cycle as the moon and the
tides. Am I correct, thus far?"

The Baron's eyes narrow, but he says nothing. And if Charles's tone
has been coolly objective thus far, there is a treacherous silkiness to his
voice now. "And then, of course, it all began to make sense to me. Why

you purchased the scarificator only *after* you had met Lucy Causton. Why you sought out those girls in London, and bled them so brutally. Why they died, all of them, at full moon. And why you dismembered their bodies when you had finished with them. I never could understand why we found no trace of what you removed—rats and dogs might have accounted for the missing hearts, but the *heads*? Surely some vagrant or scavenger would have come upon those by now. But they were never there to be found, were they? You kept them—kept them and brought them back with you in those boxes the steward at the Albany saw loaded onto your carriage. Carefully preserved in ether so that you could dissect them here, at your leisure, and prepare your proof. Because that's what you wanted with those girls, wasn't it. *Proof.* Incontrovertible physical evidence to substantiate your theory. To force the establishment whose approval you so desperately crave, to take you seriously. To acknowledge you as a *true scientist.*"

The Baron laughs sardonically. "This ludicrous diatribe proves one thing and one thing only, and that is the lamentable depths of your own ignorance. For all your claims to scientific understanding you are nothing but a *dilettante*—a rank amateur—"

Charles comes closer now, step by slow menacing step. "I may be a mere amateur but I know that no scientific enquiry, however high-minded, however well intentioned, gives the man who undertakes it the right to use other human beings as you do—to behave as if they were some baser form of life without rights or lives of their own—to cut them open like animals on the vivisection table *while the blood is still warm in their veins*—"

And now, finally, his fury fires fury in return.

"I paid those damn whores and paid them well, and all of them—*all of them,* I tell you—left my apartment alive. They are still on the streets plying their squalid trade, for all that I, or you, or that uncouth policeman Wheeler know of the matter. Yes, I bled them, but it was in the interests of medicine—in the interests of *science.* But as to the rest of what you allege, Maddox, I deny absolutely doing any such thing— it would be the act of a madman—"

He stops, for Charles is smiling now, in the coolly triumphant manner of a chess player who has just manoeuvred his opponent into a trap of his own making.

"So you admit it. Those girls *were* in your apartment in the Albany. At last, we are making some progress. Let us assume, then, for a moment, that you are telling the truth. That when you were done with them, you let them go, even if in so weakened a state they could scarcely walk. Perhaps you could explain to me—as a mere *amateur*—what use such an experiment could possibly be. I can only assume you wished to see if it was possible to induce a hysterical episode—whether a thinness of the blood, artificially engendered, could make an otherwise healthy young woman susceptible to the influence of the moon. Leaving aside whether such a procedure is in any way justifiable, its scientific method is surely utterly flawed—you would have to observe them over weeks, months even, and with no knowledge of their previous state of health—what valid conclusions could you possibly draw in but a few hours—"

"You know nothing about it," snaps the Baron. "Nothing at all."

Charles smiles again. "That may indeed be true. But there are other things I *do* know. I spoke of my uncle's message, but I did not tell you all it contained. He told me—and I am sure you will correct me if I am wrong—that Causton first came upon your name in the pages of a journal. A journal which gave an account of other experiments you had undertaken; experiments of quite a different order, and quite a different purpose."

"That is entirely irrelevant," says the Baron, but he has turned away now and will not meet Charles's eye.

"On the contrary, it could not be *more* relevant. Because it explains something that has puzzled me ever since that night you had me attacked—"

The Baron turns on him. "Attacked? What kind of a man do you take me for?"

But Charles will not be distracted. "I have only fitful memories of that night. And for a long time I distrusted even those, fearing my own mind had deceived me, but there was one thing I could trust, and that was my own handwriting. I wrote something in my notebook before it happened—three initials, and a number, that was all. It could have meant anything, or nothing. But as soon as I saw the word *journal* in that wire from my uncle, it all came back to me. It was something I'd seen here, something I *read* here. In that room upstairs. In the *Blackwood's Edinburgh Magazine* for 1847."

He turns to replace the piece of ore carefully in its case and then faces the Baron once more. "I cursed the delay at Paris, but it gave me time— time to go to the Bibliothèque Nationale and find that article again. You think you've found it, don't you? The secret that eluded the alche- mists. The occult energy that animates the universe. The Holy Grail of all science for over a thousand years. And it is *your* work that will reveal it, *your* name that future generations will revere. Yours is the one great unifying theory that explains *everything*—not just the madness of lu- nacy, but all those other things you talked of—the *aurora borealis,* the ancient temples of standing stone, the ghostly apparitions seen at graves. That's why you were so interested in the Forman papers in the Ashmole bequest, and that's why you experimented on those girls. Be- cause you want to know why Lucy Causton can perceive that energy— make that darkness *visible*—while others can see nothing but the night. You wanted to find out what it is that makes her so special— whether it's the thinness of her blood that so sharpens her perceptions, or some other quality that only 'sensitives' like her possess. She isn't the only one, is she? There have been others with her precious gift. That young Dutch woman whose mangled body was found under your walls, that girl I heard with you here in the castle—the girl *you* denied was ever here. This science you practice is as much a Moloch as the vilest superstition, and I will *not* allow Miss Causton to be the fodder for it."

They stare at each other, all pretence at an end. Charles can see the blood pulsing under the Baron's eyes, and the clench of the thin cadav- erous fists.

"You are not the first," the older man spits, a line of saliva hanging from his sallow teeth, "to come here flinging wild and unfounded al-legations in my face. Others have stood where you are now and ac-cused me of even more evil crimes. But whatever you *or others* believe, I am not a fiend. My work strives for the good of mankind, and no such advance has ever come without a price."

"Whether that is true or not, you have no right to force others to pay that price—others who do not even know what you are asking of them. That last young woman—the one you mutilated in the Vine Street morgue—she had a *child*. A child no-one has since been able to find."

The Baron makes a dismissive gesture. "That brat, if she lives, will become nothing better than the trash her mother was. And I say again, I have mutilated no-one, and as for contemplating such an act in the precincts of a police-station—" He smiles a thin smile. "I may be many things, Mr Maddox, but I am *not* a fool."

There must be something in Charles's face, for the balance between them seems suddenly to shift.

And it is the Baron's turn, now, to advance in menace. "You will leave my house, Mr Maddox, and you will not return. My work, and those who assist me in it, are none of your concern. You will not be warned again. *You*, of all people, know of what I am capable, if I believe myself threatened."

"I will go to the authorities—I will tell them what you are doing here—"

The Baron laughs. "And you think they would believe you? They would think it the ravings of a lunatic. And then they would consult their records and see that you have only recently been released from the Melk asylum. Indeed, they might consider it their duty to have you returned there—that the madhouse is the only fit place for one so prey to dangerous delusions. Are you prepared to take such an enormous risk?"

"I will not leave without Miss Causton. *I will not leave her here to die.*"

"I have more of a care for that young woman than you can ever know." The Baron is so close now that Charles can smell his breath.

THE PIERCED HEART   ✝   219

"She has a rare gift—an extraordinary talent. I will see no harm comes to her, you may be sure of that. And you may tell her father so. Not that he merits such consideration—he is nothing but a jumped-up charlatan who uses her for his own ends."

"You can stand there and say that, when you are doing the same, and worse—when you have used her in the foulest possible way—"

And then there is a knock at the door and the tension that has been winding tighter and tighter between them snaps like a severed spring.

"Freiherr—"

It is the man in spectacles, and he is insistent. The Baron throws Charles a venomous look and strides to the door. After he and the servant have conferred in lowered voices, he gestures back towards Charles as he leaves, saying, loudly and in English, "See that he is escorted off the premises. And then release the dog."

The man holds the door open, and Charles hesitates, but then follows him out of the room. As he descends the stairs he sees that the Baron is leading a young man into the library, a young man in a long coat and carrying a leather bag. Charles cannot see his face. But there is something—some vague memory that snags at him.

Out on the causeway the air is fresh and clean after the suffocating atmosphere inside, and he stands a moment taking deep breaths down into his lungs, and wondering what the hell he is going to do next.

And he may not be the only one. I imagine you might very well be wondering why Charles seems to have capitulated so easily. Why he did not stand his ground, just then, and refuse to leave until he had seen the girl he has travelled so far to find. After all, he would have been more than a match for the Baron's nervous assistant, had he chosen to take him on. No, there is some other reason for his wavering. Something, perhaps, in what the Baron said to him, that gave him pause. About that break-in at the Vine Street morgue and how only a fool would do such a thing. And that is, in truth, the strangest, most inexplicable part of the whole affair, the one element of the case that Charles cannot fit into his new theory. Because if he's right, and it's science that is at the heart of this—if it was a thirst for knowledge that killed those girls, and not a thirst for blood—then Charles has to accept that the Baron's logic holds. However insane Von Reisenberg's theories, however callous his exploitation of those girls, he would never have imperilled his great discovery by taking so great a risk.

The moon is bleaching the world black and white, and the only colour in the landscape is the yellow glow of the lamp burning in the window of the little chapel at the foot of the causeway. The light casts long shadows across the gravestones, across the ancient memorials crumbling into decay, and that one tomb that is so much newer than all the rest, watched over by its exquisite carved angels and wreathed about with fresh flowers. Charles frowns. *Fresh* flowers? Then he starts down the causeway, slowly at first and then with quickening pace. He pushes open the wooden gate and wades through the damp and springy grass to the grave. The flowers are luminous in the light, spiked and star-like, their heavy odour pungent in the air. Pungent, and unmistakeable. For Charles knows suddenly what these flowers are, and why they've been placed here. But it's only when he reads the epitaph on the stone that the final piece falls into place at last. For this is not the first time he has read this surname. It is the same one that is printed on that little slip of white card two inches by three that he still has, even now, in the pocket of his coat:

WILHELMINA VAN HELSING
Filia et dilecta soror
1834–1851
Requiescat in pacem

And now he knows. Knows who that young man is who has just entered the castle behind him; knows why those girls were found mutilated in the way they were, and why Rose's dead body had to be mutilated in its turn, even in the police morgue, and even at such a terrible chance of discovery; knows why Dora Holman's corpse was dug up and dismembered, and why the young woman buried in this very grave was taken from her coffin and beheaded, barely a week after she died. It was an act not of butchery but mercy, not cruelty but love. Because the young man who did it was her own brother.

What was it he said to Charles that day, in the serene and sunlit surroundings of the King's Library? *"Those who resort to such methods act only in pity and compassion. To permit the souls of those they love to rest as true dead, and take their place among the angels. Or so such simple people believe."* Charles can still see the smile that accompanied those last words, the smile of the educated, the enlightened, the man of science. But that was all a façade. It is not just the simple peasants on the Von Reisenberg estate who believe the Baron to be *nosferatu;* Abraham Van Helsing believes it, too. Believes it so wholly and so zealously that he is prepared to desecrate the body of the sister he adored to save her immortal soul.

For all his lies, and all his cruelties, the Baron was telling the truth when he insisted the girls left his presence alive. And yet he condemned them to death as surely as if he had killed them with his own hands. For the scars he left on their bodies marked them, in Van Helsing's eyes, as Undead, as those who cannot die, and who can only be prevented from preying on the flesh of the living by the severing of the head and the piercing of the heart. Charles's mind is racing now, as all becomes finally clear. Van Helsing must have been following the Baron for months, ever since his sister died and he found on her neck the marks he saw as vampire's teeth. First to Whitby and then to London, and now, again, to Castle Reisenberg, tireless in his pursuit of the young women he believes the Baron has despoiled, unflinching in his determination to free them from the curse of a deadly eternity. And how bitter the irony that this mission of mercy has made him a murderer—a more monstrous predator than even the Baron Von Reisenberg has been.

Was Van Helsing still in Austria, when Charles first journeyed to the castle, and did he make it his business to find out who Charles was, and what business had brought him here? And did he follow him in London and contrive that meeting in the King's Library, in the hope that Charles would put the evidence together and warn the police that a vampire was abroad in the very heart of the metropolis? And when that warning miscarried, did Van Helsing turn in desperation to the *Daily News,* knowing no newspaper could resist such an extraordinary story? And now Charles's blood runs cold at the thought of the bag he just saw in the young man's hand. A bag large enough to conceal all the tools he needs for his butcher work. And it will not be the Baron alone he has come for, but all those he believes he has corrupted—

Lucy, dear God, *Lucy*—

And now he is running, scrambling up the causeway wet with dew and coming to a slithering stop at the castle gate, his heart pounding, not just from exertion but fear. It is not the demon of his memory, not the hell-hound red in eye and maw, but it is a brute all the same. A vast mastiff with a spiked collar, steaming and stinking in the night air. It starts towards him, snarling, but Charles is prepared this time; he takes his gun from his coat and as the shot rings out the dog falls dead, the hot blood streaming down towards Charles's feet. By the time he gets to the castle door the sound has brought a rush of servants out into the courtyard—as many as Charles has ever seen in this preternaturally quiet and people-less place. But it's Bremmer he lights on—Bremmer who *speaks English.*

"You have to let me in," he cries, as two of the stable-hands lay fists upon him. "That man who just came here—he's the brother of the girl who died, isn't he—the girl from Delft—"

Bremmer hesitates, then nods.

"He means the Baron harm—he's been planning this for a long time—"

And then the air is split with an ear-rending scream and Charles breaks from his captors' grasp and pushes past Bremmer into the hall, throwing open the door of the library with a crash. There are books all over the floor, priceless volumes strewn broken-backed, stands up-ended, glass cases smashed. But the room is empty. He strides back out and races up the stairs, feeling his old injury ache, as if reawakened by the beast that gave it, to the door beneath the tower he has found un-locked only once before.

Until now.

He pushes the door open gently, hearing voices. Not the low hoarse tones of the Baron, but another—younger, stronger, angrier. Charles's breathing is so loud he can scarcely make out the words, and he begins hesitantly up the steps, unsure whether surprise will be his ally or his downfall. It is dark in the space he emerges into, lit only by a single lamp, and stifling in a way he cannot understand until he reaches out a hand and finds the walls have been lined with some sort of dense cloth. In the centre of the room, there is something hanging from the ceiling, looming in the shadows, and creaking as it turns back and forth in some unseen current. For one heart-faltering moment he thinks it is a body, but then his eyes adjust and he can make out heavy loops of coiled wire. And directly beneath them Abraham Van Hels-ing, his back to the door, bent over something out of Charles's line of sight. And as for the Baron Von Reisenberg, he is lying on the floor unmoving, his mouth forced open and gaping with star-like flowers, his eyes rolled back white in the glassiness of death.

And then Van Helsing moves and Charles realises with horror that what he is standing over is a dissection table—the same one, surely, that the Baron had with him in London, the same one those girls must have lain on, half insensible, as the Baron bled them. But now it is Lucy Causton who is lying there, dressed only in a thin nightgown high at the neck, her wrists tied to the sides of the bed. Van Helsing moves again and Charles watches him attach a leather strap about her left ankle, adjusting the tightness with the precision of a surgeon. And beside him, on the floor, is the leather bag, open now to reveal knives, a hammer, and a thick wooden stake. The girl's hearing must be extraordinarily acute, for though Charles has made no sound she lifts her head slightly and their eyes meet. She is white with terror, but she makes no movement as he gestures her to silence and he begins to move towards her. But then a board creaks and Van Helsing turns. Turns, and sees, and knows.

"Ah, Mr Maddox. I wondered if you would be joining us. You are rather earlier than I expected."

"Don't do this, Van Helsing. Stop now before you spill more innocent blood. I know what you think—what you believe—but the Baron was not a vampire. A monster, yes. But it was science that made him so, not necromancy. The girl is blameless—as much his victim as your own sister."

Van Helsing laughs. "Your ignorance is matched only by your arrogance. I saw that at once, when we met that day in the Library. That English condescension, that haughty disdain. You think yourself so superior, do you not, so modern and so wise? And yet you are as blind as a child, duller of wits even than the uneducated people hereabouts whom you treat with such scorn. They know better than you of the truth of the *stregoica*. They know there are such beings as vampires— that there are mysteries which we can only guess at, and which even your so-called science cannot explain. Even had I not the corroboration of my own unhappy experience, the records of the past give proof enough. And you have even less excuse, for have you not seen the evidence with your own eyes? For all your pride in your capacity for observation, have you never asked yourself why Von Reisenberg should shun the light of day? Why no-one has ever seen him eat the food of man? Why his teeth are so elongated and so sharp? Why all mirrors have been removed from his domain?"

Charles shakes his head. "I know that would seem to prove what you say, but there are medical conditions that we still do not understand—illnesses that render the sufferers sensitive to light, and cause their gums to bleach and recede—"

Van Helsing laughs hollowly. "A ludicrous hypothesis, and yet because you deem it 'scientific' you are prepared to give it credence. Oh I admit that at the first I, too, was a sceptic—my education had taught me to scoff at such things, just as *you* scoff. But you have not lost a sister—you have not loved her since she was a little child, and seen her prey to sleepwalking and the terrors of the night, and heard the doctors say there was no hope. You have not taken her under your protection, and travelled with her half a thousand miles in the hope that a change of air might effect a cure. You have not seen her sicken thereafter day by day, growing pale and paler still, until her breathing was painful to see. You have not found her lifeless body, and seen the marks of teeth about her throat. I *saw them,* I tell you, and there was no mistaking what they were—those little round holes edged with white that do not heal—"

"No," interrupts Charles, starting forwards, "you are wrong—those marks—they were made by a scarificator—a medical instrument. He used it to bleed them, for the sake of his experiments. He had some great theory about the energy of the universe—"

Van Helsing is laughing now. "And you dare consider *me* deranged!"

"I know it sounds insane, but he genuinely believed he had made a momentous advance—that the sufferings of young women like your sister were due to their special sensitivity to moonlight, a sensitivity stemming from a dilution of the blood. That's why those girls in London looked so pale—that's why they had those wounds—"

Van Helsing shakes his head. "It is not I who err, Maddox, but you. This instrument you claim he used, where did he obtain it?"

Charles opens his mouth to speak, but then falters. Van Helsing smiles thinly. "It was in London, was it not, when he visited your so-called Great Exhibition?"

Charles swallows, then nods.

Van Helsing's contempt is glacial. "You set such store by your capacity for logic, and yet your reasoning will not withstand even the most basic examination. For if he purchased that instrument in London, how do you account for the marks I saw on the neck of my own Mina more than three months before? How do you account for what I saw on the throat of that young woman in Whitby?"

Charles sees the girl start. "I knew I had seen you before," Lucy says, looking up at Van Helsing in the pitiful eagerness of doomed hope. "You were at the abbey that day—you raised your hat to me—I thought you so gentle, so *gallant*—"

Van Helsing smiles down at her, a smile to turn the heart to ice. "And indeed I am," he says softly, putting a finger to her cheek, "for I will do you the greatest service any man may perform. I will rescue you from an eternity of working wickedness by night and growing ever more debased by it by day. I will save you from murdering innocent babes in their cradles, and feasting upon the flesh of those you most love—"

"It was you," she whispers, the tears running down her face. "It was you I saw that night, in the cemetery, with my Dora. I thought it was him—I *blamed him*—but it was you, all along—"

"She had crossed to the Undead long before that night—the marks on her neck left no room for doubt."

"I was with her every day, and I saw nothing."

Van Helsing's eyes narrow. "She hid them—in the cunning manner of her kind. However fervent you are to excuse her, Miss Causton, you cannot deny the truth. Your friend had taken to wearing a black band about her throat, had she not?"

"That was for the brooch—so she could wear the brooch—the one *I gave her*—"

Van Helsing shakes his head. "How naïve you are, how very trusting. And she would have preyed upon that—upon *you*—had I not acted when I did. That black band was most efficacious, by way of concealment. But it could not deceive me. They were still there, those marks, when I broke open the grave and tore that band away. Her body was as perfect and intact as my sister's had been, when I found her corpse lips black with the blood of a little child—a child that had been found with its throat torn open, as if by some wild and rabid beast."

"What do you mean?" cries the girl, before Charles can prevent her. Because he knows what was done to Dora Holman's body, and he wants to save this girl the pain of it—the impossibility of forgetting it. "Why would anyone do so terrible a thing as disturb the peace of the dead?"

"It was *I* who gave her that peace," replies Van Helsing, stroking her face. "When I lifted the lid of the coffin I saw her lying there radiant with the bloom of the Undead, her lips full and red and moist, and then she opened her eyes and looked at me—"

"No, *no!*" cries the girl, struggling against her constraints, and Charles can see now, that there is a knife in Van Helsing's hand, a knife with a long hooked blade, and dark stains along the edge. Old blood, long dried. The blood of those girls in London, murdered and mutilated, and of young Rose Danby, who died in the dirt, in terror and exhaustion, begging for her life.

Van Helsing's voice is softer now, almost tender, as he caresses Lucy's golden hair. "Believe me, it pains me to tell you this, but it is the full and terrible truth. Your friend's eyes that once had been so gentle were then as hard as stone, the pupils so dilated they seemed as black as fathomless wells. And then her bosom began to heave and she smoothed her hands voluptuously over her own breasts until the nipples were hard and she whispered to me like a street whore, 'I have been waiting for you—kiss me—make love to me!' And I saw that there was blood on those swollen lips, and I knew what I must do. I took the stake in my hands and plunged it, without mercy, into her heart. She writhed, and twisted, and her beautiful face was curdled into a vile thing of fury and of vice, and as I drove the stake deeper and deeper still, she screamed like a demoness and the blood spilled over her lips and ran over her white death-robe but I never faltered, never shrank from the gruesome necessity until she lay finally still and my high task was done. And then I took this knife and cut off her head in one sweep, and filled her sagging mouth with garlic flowers. And as the scent rose all about me I saw that she was changed, and the face that had been so foul was sweet and pure once more. She was at peace. Just as you will be at peace—"

The knife is at the girl's throat, and Charles's gun is to his hand, but the angle is all wrong, he cannot do it—cannot risk a shot that might kill the girl.

"I believe you," he says, starting forwards. *"I believe you."*

Van Helsing stops and stares at him.

"I had a beloved sister, too," stumbles Charles. "A sister who was lost through my own fault—my own carelessness. I know how unbearable such a loss can be."

Van Helsing frowns, but his grip on the knife is looser.

"I will help you," insists Charles, hoping that the despair—the lie— is not as flagrant as it sounds in his own ears. He sees the girl's mouth open, but he cannot afford to look at her. "I will help you put an end to the menace of Von Reisenberg forever, and rid the earth of his hideous kind." He strides now to the bag and lifts the stake from it. "Tell me what I must do."

Van Helsing's eyes narrow. "Why should I trust you? How do I know you are sincere?"

"Because I will help you with the girl."

Charles's heart is beating hard now, and his legs shaking, but he walks as composedly as he can to the head of the table. The girl's fear is palpable; he can smell it on her.

"No," she whispers. "Please."

He hesitates; what he's about to do is a tremendous risk, but there is nothing else, no other way. In her weakened condition, after what happened in the Albany, surely Von Reisenberg would not have used the scarificator on her—surely he would not have endangered his most precious possession, or harmed the one person who could vindicate a lifetime's ambition.

"Should we not," he says, his throat tight, "ascertain first, and conclusively, that the girl has indeed fallen victim to his foul predations?"

Van Helsing is sardonic. "She has been alone with him for the better

part of two months. And you have only to look at her—her breathless-
ness, her pallor—"

Charles shakes his head. "That might derive from another cause. I
saw evidence, in London, that Miss Causton has recently miscarried a
child—miscarried badly. She lost a great deal of blood—"

He had wondered if she knew; if a girl so innocent would have even
known she was pregnant, and he sees from her face now that he was
right. Her eyes widen and her lips part, but no words come as she
shakes her head slowly from side to side.

"Very well," says Van Helsing, reaching a hand to the collar of the
nightgown. "There is one piece of evidence she cannot dissemble."

But as he pulls the silk aside there is a rending crash and one of the
windows shatters open in a rain of glass and splinters and the lamp
gutters and goes out. The moon must be clouded for the room is utterly black, and filled with the sound of wings beating. The huge leathery wings of an enormous bat, shrieking and clattering against the
walls, swooping over Charles's head and into his face. He beats the
thing away but there are fingers now at his throat, gripping him from
behind, wrenching his head back and down and there is something
cold and thin at his throat and the breath is squeezing from his lungs
and he can hear his own voice crying out as the world explodes in a
crescendo of light.

The moments that follow etch his retina like photographic stills. Van
Helsing, blinded, raising his hands to his face and falling backwards.
The girl standing in a blaze of white flame, her hands raised high above
her head like an angel in ecstasy. And then the light going out and the
dark closing back and the two men are on the floor, rolling over and
over, kicking and clawing, and there's the sound of furniture toppling,
and specimens are falling about them and rolling on the polished floor
and the knife is spinning away, and he is thrusting Van Helsing back

and down and closing his hands about his neck, closing his hands about the neck of a man he knows to be a murderer—

"Don't you understand," gasps Van Helsing. "He has taken her—*he has taken her*—"

Van Helsing starts to cough and retch and Charles can hear suddenly the sound of wheels. He leaps to the open window and out onto the parapet. Far below, in the courtyard, a carriage has come to a halt by the door and a man is lifting Lucy Causton into it. A man who stops, for one tiny moment, and looks up to where Charles is standing, before stepping quickly inside and shouting to the coachman to make all speed.

The Baron Von Reisenberg.

It's too late to follow them—too late to prevent them—and Charles can do nothing but watch as the carriage gathers speed at the gate and begins down towards the causeway.

"Shoot," croaks Van Helsing behind him. "You have a gun. Use it. Use it to stop him!"

It's too far away and the gun only a pistol and there is no hope of the bullet finding its mark, but like a man in thrall Charles raises his aim and fires. And then time slows to a heartbeat and he can hear his own pulse thundering in his ears as the horses rear at the noise, and their hooves slither on the wet stones, and the coachman cries out, and the carriage lurches from side to side, gathering pace and careering faster and faster until it plunges headlong over the side of the causeway and rolls, splintering, in an agony of screaming horses and breaking wood, to a shudder, and a stop.

By the time Charles gets to the gate the servants are already crowded about the coachman where he was thrown clear but not safe, his body broken. Far below, the carriage lies shattered, half submerged in the river, one door hanging open and the wheels spinning. Charles barks at Bremmer to send for the doctor, then races down the causeway and onto the shingle, slipping and stumbling, out of breath, half out of his mind, up to his knees in water, until he reaches the overturned coach where the Baron Von Reisenberg is lying, his face turned up to the moon, his mouth running with blood, and the metal spike of the carriage axle pierced through his heart.

"Lucy!" cries Charles in panic, wading round to the opposite side. "Lucy!"

The carriage is slowly sinking now, the sand sucking at its weight, and he wrenches desperately at the door. He can see her inside, but she is not moving, not answering. The carriage lurches, dips sickeningly, but all at once he has the handle open and she is in his arms and he is carrying her out and up the slope, and laying her gently on the ground. There is a graze on her cheek, and a deep cut on her neck, but she is breathing, she is alive. And as he cradles her head and takes her hand in his own it is as if some energy passes between them, and she opens her eyes and looks at him. Looks at him in pain and bewilderment, and a distant anguished recognition.

"Don't leave me," she whispers, at last. "Don't leave me, Charles."

EPILOGUE

My dear Charles,

I send this letter to the *poste restante* in Vienna, in the desperate hope that it may reach you in time. I parted, earlier, with Alexander Causton. He brought here a picture he wished me to send to you, that you might know his daughter if you are able to find her. I say "his daughter," and I know he called her so, to you, but I must tell you now that the girl you seek is neither his daughter, nor as old in years as Causton has always believed. I have enclosed the picture that he so wishes you to have, but I have also enclosed another—an image of this girl when she was very young, and seated on her mother's knee.

It is an image that has stopped my very heart, for I have seen this woman's face before, though only once, and many years ago. She was part of the travelling fair that was visiting Windsor in July of the year '35. A fair I know you will remember, for you talked afterwards of the lights, and the crowds, and the music of the barrel-organ. This woman was among many whom I interviewed in those first few frantic days, when I was so desperate for any clue, any trace. I remember her solemn features, her wary replies, her insistence that she had seen nothing, heard nothing, knew nothing. But I do not remember a daughter. For whatever she may have said to Causton, whatever lies she later told to hide her crime, the child she claimed was *not her own*.

I know the courage and the resolve you bring to every task, but you do not know the terrible import of the one you undertake now. You must find this lost girl, Charles, find her and bring her safely home to those who love her and thought her forever lost. Not for Causton's sake, though he employs you, but for your own sake, and for mine, and for your poor mother, abandoned all these years to a grief so deep it had no possibility of cure. One look will suffice— take but one look at the picture I send you and you will know at last who Lucy Causton is.

She is your sister.
She is *Elizabeth*.

AUTHOR'S NOTE

THE BARON VON REISENBERG is based in large part on a real man. Baron Karl von Reichenbach was born in Stuttgart in 1788 where his father was Court Librarian. He was not a nobleman by birth, but was given that honour in recognition of his contributions to both science and industry. He was responsible for the same discoveries I give to my fictional Baron, including creosote, paraffin, pittacal, and various other chemical formulations. In 1839 he withdrew from his chemical studies and devoted himself to the investigation of magnetism and other related forces such as electricity, heat, and light. As a result he became convinced that there was another invisible energy force in the universe, a force that was present in both moonlight and sunlight, and was akin to both electricity and magnetism. It was an "occult energy," in fact, that suffused the entire cosmos, and he named it the Odic force, or simply the Od. He believed it was, in effect, the "blood" of the universe, and explained everything from the *aurora borealis,* to ectoplasm, ghost lights, the "table-turning" seen at séances, and the siting of ancient standing stones. The Baron came to his conclusions after working with dozens of people he called "sensitives," a number of whom were suffering from nervous conditions. These people claimed to be able to see luminous flames emanating from the poles of magnets.

Von Reichenbach devised special apparatus to further test his theories, including the construction of metal plates on the roof of his castle, which were positioned to capture sunlight and moonlight and connected by wires to a special dark room below. His sensitives would be kept in this room for many hours, and then asked to hold the ends of these wires, and describe what they could see. Von Reichenbach also began to experiment with specimens of minerals and metals from his geological collections, presenting them to his sensitives on a rotating table, one by one, in a room completely insulated from all other sources of light. He found that some sensitives could see flames of different colours, ranging from green (from copper) to red (from zinc). Steeping water in moonlight could make the sensitives physically sick, and some disliked being close to mirrors; young women were found to be particularly sensitive during menstruation. While he was conducting his experiments, the Baron himself kept to a strict diet and would not touch metals.

Von Reichenbach gradually became convinced that "lunacy" was the result of a greater-than-normal sensitivity to the Od. He interviewed hundreds of people suffering from sleepwalking, night terrors, hysteria, and other mental afflictions, and concluded that ancient superstitions relating to the influence of the moon might actually stem from the effects of Od force in moonlight. He discovered that when those who suffered from "lunatic" conditions were exposed to the light of the moon, it produced physical symptoms such as muscle cramps and a feeling of heat on the skin, as well as the sensations of mental distress and unease.

Many of those living in the neighbourhood of Von Reichenbach's estate became fearful of this tall and mysterious man dressed in black, who frequented newly dug graves, walked alone on paths hidden from view, and confined young women in his castle. He even became known by some as the "Sorcerer of Cobenzl" (the castle had previously been owned by a man of that name).

Von Reichenbach's theories were first published in Germany in 1849, and translated into English the following year. He divided contemporary scientific opinion, with some academics hailing his discoveries, while others questioned his methods, and asked for more objective proof than the eyewitness accounts of subjects who were often both disturbed and vulnerable, and therefore highly suggestible.

Though Von Reichenbach came to believe he could see the Odic light himself, he was never able to provide scientifically robust proof of his theories, despite apparently capturing "Odic emanations" on daguerreotypes, the first of which was published in 1861. In her poem *Aurora Leigh* (1856), Elizabeth Barrett Browning referred to *"That od-force of German Reichenbach / Which still from female finger-tips burns blue."*

There was indeed an article in the *Blackwood's Edinburgh Magazine* in 1847 entitled "On the Truths Contained in Popular Superstitions." This contains a brief account of an experiment Von Reichenbach conducted with a Fraulein Maix, which describes how she felt "an inward struggle in her arms, chest, and head" when asked to hold a bar magnet. The rest I have invented.

Von Reichenbach's theories have since fallen into disrepute, at least among the mainstream scientific community, and the fact that Hitler apparently responded enthusiastically to the idea of an Odic force has doubtless done nothing to help his subsequent reputation.

I am indebted to *Lost Science* by Gerry Vassilatos for my first encounter with the Baron and much of the detail on the real Baron's experiments. I later read Von Reichenbach's own *Researches on Magnetism, Electricity, Heat, Light, Crystallization, and Chemical Attraction in Their Relation to the Vital Force.* Other aspects of my fictional character are my own invention, such as the fact that he may be suffering from either *lupus* or porphyria (as yet undiagnosed in 1851), as well as my character's particular obsession with conditions of the blood, and the experiments he conducts in London to investigate them. The real Baron died in 1869, in a hotel bed.

My inspiration for the Baron's waxwork collection came from

Marina Warner's wonderful book *Phantasmagoria,* which includes a photograph of an animated wax "Sleeping Beauty" modelled by Philippe Curtius in 1765. Warner's book is a fascinating account of the phenomena of illusion and the imagination, from smoke and mirrors, to light, shadow, cloud, and ghosts. It was also an invaluable source for material on eighteenth- and nineteenth-century *phantasmagorias,* and the illusions they employed, including the famous Paris stage show of Étienne-Gaspard Robertson.

"Influence Machines" did indeed exist; the one I describe is based on the device invented in 1706 by Francis Hauksbee, a student of Isaac Newton.

The account of the Fox sisters in chapter 4 is taken from an actual press report in the *New-York Tribune* of August 10, 1850. See Herbert G. Jackson, *The Spirit Rappers,* chapter 8.

It was Charlotte Brontë who called the Great Exhibition "vast, strange, new and impossible to describe." Readers who are interested in learning more about it will find many websites devoted to the subject, and an excellent and extremely informative edition of the BBC Radio 4 programme *In Our Time* can be found at www.bbc.co.uk /programmes/p003c19x. The extract from the catalogue in chapter 7 is a real example.

I confess to taking a small liberty with dates in relation to the Ashmole Bequest, which was actually housed in the Ashmolean Museum until 1860, when it was transferred to the Bodleian Library.

I would like to thank my husband, Simon, and my friend Professor Stephen Gill for reading this novel in its early stages. I also owe a great deal of gratitude to my agent, Ben Mason, and my editor at Random House, Kate Miciak.

ABOUT THE AUTHOR

LYNN SHEPHERD is the author of the award-winning
Murder at Mansfield Park, and the critically acclaimed
The Solitary House and *A Fatal Likeness.* She studied English at Oxford and has been a professional copywriter
for more than a decade.

www.lynn-shepherd.com

ABOUT THE TYPE

This book was set in Caslon, a typeface first designed in 1722 by William Caslon (1692–1766). Its widespread use by most English printers in the early eighteenth century soon supplanted the Dutch typefaces that had formerly prevailed. The roman is considered a "workhorse" typeface due to its pleasant, open appearance, while the italic is exceedingly decorative.